Praise for K.A. Mitchell's *Chasing Smoke*

"K.A. Mitchell writes seriously hot, seriously smart man-on-man romance. If I could recommend only one writer in this genre, it would be Mitchell. She's the writer to watch."

~ *Josh Lanyon, author of Man, Oh, Man! Writing M/M Fiction for Kinks and Ca$h*

"K.A. Mitchell has an uncanny ability to make us feel the emotions of her characters."

~ *Rainbow Reviews*

"[K.A. Mitchell has] a gift for writing sex...because every single [sex scene] advanced the emotional plot, every single one pulled me in and was damn hot, and every single one was different and fun."

~ *Joan, Dear Author*

Look for these titles by K.A. Mitchell

Now Available:

Temperature's Rising
Custom Ride

Serving Love
Hot Ticket

Diving in Deep
Regularly Scheduled Life
Collision Course
Chasing Smoke
An Improper Holiday

Chasing Smoke

K.A. Mitchell

A SAMHAIN PUBLISHING, LTD. publication.

Samhain Publishing, Ltd.
577 Mulberry Street, Suite 1520
Macon, GA 31201
www.samhainpublishing.com

Chasing Smoke
Copyright © 2010 by K.A. Mitchell
Print ISBN: 978-1-60504-598-6
Digital ISBN: 978-1-60504-578-8

Editing by Sasha Knight
Cover by Anne Cain

First Samhain Publishing, Ltd. electronic publication: June 2009
First Samhain Publishing, Ltd. print publication: April 2010

Dedication

For Chris, there from the beginning to the end.

Thank you Erin, Kathy and B.F.S for services above and beyond.

Thanks for the title, Casey.

Chapter One

Something was wrong.

Daniel tuned out his mother's ever-helpful advice. "With the garage full of moving boxes you'll have to park in the driveway, dear."

Since Daniel had put at least thirty of those boxes in the garage himself, he was already aware of that. But it wasn't what was wrong.

He studied the front of his mother's soon-to-be former house. The Navigator's headlights cut across the snow-covered lawn, creating a storybook gleam on the thin layer of ice. He missed the small white lights—calculated precisely to the most tasteful ratio of bulbs per bough—sparkling in the bushes, but they were already packed. The sole exterior concession to the Christmas season was a fresh balsam wreath with a small red ribbon on the door.

The open door. Porch light off.

Alarm jarred him from satiated and nostalgic to hyper-alert. "Wait a second, Mother. Stay in the car."

"Danny, it's freezing out here. If it's some kind of a Christmas surprise—" She opened the passenger door.

"Someone's been in the house. The door's open."

His mother climbed out, ignoring the bad combination of high heels and winter-slick driveway. "Honestly, honey, your job makes you so suspicious. Maybe your sister and Peter came home after all. We have an alarm system."

"I know we do. I set it when we left." He'd also left the porch light on and the one in the hall. The house was completely dark. "Get back in the car and call the police. Use my phone." He tossed it onto the seat.

"Where are you going?"

"To look around."

"Why don't you wait for the police?"

"I am the police, Mother."

"You work for the government."

"As a policeman." He'd been on a desk for six years, analyzing data for Homeland Security, but he was still a cop. He'd transferred from the FBI as soon as the department was created.

"Why don't you wait for your brother?"

Daniel summoned as much patience as he could muster. "Rob is an orthodontist. Unless the criminals need their braces tightened, I think I'm better able to handle it." He wanted to show his mother the hip holster under his jacket, but she would only complain about why he'd worn it to the restaurant.

With an arch to her brows that said she was only humoring him, his mother climbed back into the car. The lights from Rob's minivan cut across his face. Daniel held up his hand and signaled his brother to roll down his window. He spoke as low as he could, trying to keep the information from his nieces. Though he probably could have bellowed and their eyes wouldn't have strayed from the DVD screens dangling in front of their faces.

As his sister-in-law reached for her purse, he said, "Mother's calling." Rob and Shannon both looked at him as if he'd said something completely ridiculous. He nodded as Shannon pulled out her phone.

Daniel turned back toward the house.

"I'll come with you." Rob reached for the door handle.

"No. You keep Mother from getting out of the car. And keep

the cops from shooting me." He pulled the Glock from its holster.

"Why don't you just wait for the police?"

And people wondered why he hated coming home to the Valley. "I'm trained. I'm just going to look."

If they'd cut the power, that would have taken care of the alarm. But the alarm company should have checked.

The reason why Sure Safe Alarm didn't look into the service interruption made Daniel's foot slide as he hit the walk. Ice. Last night's storm had caused spotty power outages—enough for the alarm company to not bother checking.

He waited outside the door, listening and letting his eyes adjust. His senses and his reason told him the house was empty. Even if a burglar had been surprised in the act of looting Christmas gifts, he'd have disappeared while Daniel tried to halt the inexorable press of Mrs. Julia Gardner-Holcomb.

He drew the pistol and went through the drill anyway, checking corners, high and low, back to the wall. By the time the police car pulled up in front of the driveway, he'd cleared the downstairs. He holstered the Glock and went back outside.

The cops looked at his badge, but still asked him to wait outside while they checked over the house. In the interest of law enforcement cooperation, Daniel stayed outside, but leaned into the Navigator to push the remote on the garage door opener. As the door rolled up, he kept a hand on the Glock.

Nothing. Dark and empty.

The cops were standing in the garage when he walked up. Daniel ignored the officers' disapproving looks and stared at the mess of overturned boxes illuminated by the crossing beams of the police Maglites. He winced as one of the officer's shoes ground a piece of his mother's beloved Spode china to a powder.

Rob and his mother came up to flank him.

A single, short gasp slipped from his mother as she took in the scattered pieces of her life, and then she regained her usual aplomb. "Well, this should save me some money on storage."

✧

Daniel sat with his mother while Rob and Shannon put the girls to bed. Once Ashley and Samantha heard Christmas wouldn't be affected, they were uninterested in anything but whining about how they'd get to sleep without a bedtime video. The power surged back on just before the female officer came into the den.

"The detective wants to talk to you."

His mother rose.

"Um, no, ma'am. Agent Gardner."

Daniel followed Officer Acevedo into the garage.

No preamble, no warning. Trey Eriksson was just there, leaning against the whitewashed wall, looking even better than he had fifteen years ago when he'd shipped off to basic training. Better than he had when for a polite, silent instant they'd shaken hands in the receiving line at Daniel's stepfather's wake.

The shoulders were broader, the hair darker and shorter than the long wheat-blond strands that used to flop in his eyes, but the face hadn't changed much, except for the neat beard around his lips and chin, the same square chin that had frustrated a teenaged Trey with its smoothness. When Trey stared straight at him, the challenge in those ethereally light eyes made Daniel's heart punch against his ribs, sent the pulse jumping in his temples, his throat, his dick.

"Agent Gardner?" Trey's voice held no clue to what he was thinking. Of course, he'd had time to prepare.

Trey knew exactly who the fuck he was. Knew who he'd be interviewing. Hell, he'd had time to pull Daniel's service record up in the squad car. Trey probably knew the last six guys Daniel'd fucked, down to their boxer-or-brief preference. Trey knew he'd be seeing Daniel when he had gotten a call to 312 Paxinosa Ave on December 23.

Daniel was the one with the breath knocked out of him.

Not that Trey had an obligation to keep in touch with the Gardners. Mother had told him Trey was with the police. Though when Daniel had first heard it, he'd wondered for a second if she meant Trey had been arrested. Daniel knew how close Trey's anger was to the surface, even if he hid it well enough to pass for civilized.

Mother's next news report about Trey came almost a decade later. "I saw Trey Eriksson at the Food Lion. He's a detective now. Remarkable what with his father." It wasn't that remarkable. Nothing could stop Trey when he made up his mind. Nothing.

Daniel had filled out, wasn't the skinny kid he'd been at seventeen, but Trey still made him feel like the geek he'd been. Trying to regain some control over the situation, Daniel folded his arms across his chest and didn't wait for questions.

"We left the house at seventeen thirty." The shift to military time was second nature. "The front door was locked. I set the alarm myself. We had dinner reservations at Dunham's. We got to the restaurant at seventeen fifty. We left at nineteen fifteen and drove directly back here. I saw the door open, told my mother to call the police. I didn't notice any other cars on the road." When Trey tipped his head, Daniel said, "I am familiar with procedure, *Detective*."

"So I heard. Homeland Security?"

"Want to see my badge?"

"It checks out. So when you entered the house—is that standard procedure for federal officers? Entering a potential crime scene alone?"

A turf war? Fifteen years later and they were in a fed-versus-local turf war?

"I was interested in protecting my family, Detective."

"Did you notice anything?"

"I didn't see anything. Or anyone."

"Is anything missing?"

"Not that we've been able to determine." Daniel nodded at the debris in the garage. "Of course, we've been sitting in the dark until a few minutes ago."

"None of the electronics touched?"

"No. And my nieces reported none of the Christmas presents were missing."

Trey's jaw moved. Maybe that twitch was all that was left of his heartbreaking smile.

Mother hadn't mentioned a wife. Daniel couldn't ask it, but he wanted to know. *Do you have any kids? Did you finally stop faking it with cheerleaders or was that thing in my room an isolated incident or six? Not that I counted.*

"Mrs. Holcomb, ma'am. The detective will call you when—" When Officer Acevedo's pleading voice broke through, Daniel felt the shift of Trey's attention like a physical loss. The tension between them snapped free like a pine bough under the weight of last night's ice.

"Trey, dear." Officer Acevedo was no match for the former Mrs. Mayor. "I'm glad to see you, even under these circumstances."

"Thank you, Julia." As if Trey ever came to the Gardners under anything but unpleasant circumstances. But that wasn't fair. It was just some crash-and-burn karma. On both sides.

"Why don't you and the officers come in and I'll make you all some coffee. I don't even want to look at this disaster until tomorrow."

The patrol officers looked over at Trey through frosty breaths.

"That would be great, Julia. Thank you."

Daniel waited, making sure Trey would have to pass by him to get into the house. He didn't know about Trey, but the familiar electric charge prickled across Daniel's skin. Trey paused, eyes dropping to Daniel's mouth, a glance so quick no one else could have seen it, and then he was following the patrol officers into the house.

Rob was in the kitchen now, and they all went through how glad everyone was to see each other again. Rob—who'd shared the house with Trey for only six weeks before departing for Cornell—got a hearty handshake and a first-name greeting, questions about his wife and kids.

Daniel got "Agent Gardner."

Once the greetings were out of the way, Rob confirmed everything Daniel had already said. Rob didn't notice anything. He couldn't say if anything was missing.

Shannon made her appearance, still in the dark green dress she had worn to dinner. Daniel's sister-in-law was a beautiful woman, and he waited to see how Trey reacted to blonde and stacked.

If Trey's eyes were dropping to the folds arranged to draw attention to Shannon's cleavage, Daniel couldn't tell.

"Trey lived with us for awhile, right before I left for school." Rob came to stand by his wife, but he wasn't displaying any jealous mannerisms.

"Oh, yes. I remember you mentioning it."

And no one mentioned why. Daniel wondered if Trey resented the tacit knowledge. Everyone knew, but no one talked. As if by that silence they could erase the Erikssons' existence, remain clear of the taint of violence, instability. Of course, Trey might have found the silence better than the constant whispered chorus of neighbors and coworkers from that interminable summer all those years ago, a chorus which persisted until Ron Eriksson was safely locked away. Daniel had heard them. At the grocery store, the mall, repeated endlessly on the news. *But they seemed so happy.*

Trey had talked to Daniel about what it had been like that day. Once. Under the rumble of almost constant thunder, like the noise would make the words less powerful. If Daniel hadn't already been in hopeless love with Trey before that moment—a

15

schoolboy crush, Daniel reminded himself from the distance of fifteen years—but if he hadn't spent every Sunday in church praying Trey would love him back before that night, he would have after. But Daniel's crush had started a long time before. When the Erikssons first moved to Easton, Pennsylvania.

Daniel didn't know who Trey was then. He was just the boy with the light blond hair and grey eyes who had gotten between Daniel and those assholes Steve Drake and Jason Matthews when they'd jumped him again after middle school. Even though Trey had walked off with Steve and Jason, Daniel had run home to find out everything he could about the Oakland Raiders football team so he could have something to talk about with the boy who'd been wearing the silver and black jersey.

The boy in the Raiders jersey had become the man in jeans and the U.S. Army sweatshirt stretched across his broad chest. The boy who'd spent most of his time here hiding out in their finished basement was now exchanging small talk with the family in the kitchen while drinking coffee out of one of the Christmas mugs that had eluded Mother's packing.

The patrol officers left first with effusive thanks for the coffee. With the familiarity of an almost-son of the house, Trey put his mug in the sink.

"We'll follow up on this, Julia. I promise. If I were you, I'd have someone from the alarm company come over tomorrow to check things out. Don't let them give you a story about the holidays. This is what you're paying for. In the meantime, I'm sure Agent Danny can handle things."

Agent Danny? He briefed people at the White House, for God's sake. Fuck Trey's condescension and fuck himself for letting this house, these people turn him into that stupid confused teenager again.

Daniel wanted to yell and shove Trey like he had the night before Trey left. Demand Trey see him, Daniel, for a second before that sharp focus turned inward again, shutting Daniel out.

"I'll walk you out." Daniel's voice was steady and even.

An almost imperceptible shrug from broad shoulders before Trey led the way out of the kitchen, through the laundry room, out into the garage. Daniel followed immediately, but Trey wasn't leaving room for conversation, crossing the driveway so fast he might have been on skates—or simply smart enough to wear the heavy, thick-soled boots Daniel could see beneath his jeans.

Daniel skidded down the driveway in his dress shoes, certain Trey would just get into his black Charger and drive away, but Trey waited for him, leaning back against the driver's door, arms folded across his chest.

It didn't take a course in body language to read the warning signs.

"What?" was all Trey said.

What had Daniel expected? He hadn't. Hadn't ever thought he'd see Trey Eriksson again. Read about him in the paper when he killed someone, but not see him.

"You have some kind of problem with federal agents?" Daniel asked.

"No. I don't have a problem, Danny."

"Daniel." Like it made a difference. Like insisting on the name he'd worn since he left home could keep that frustrated, horny, lovesick teenager from erupting to the surface like a bad case of acne.

A curving driveway's length away from the garage lights, Trey's expressions were hard to read, but Daniel thought he blinked an acknowledgement. He wished he could see Trey's eyes.

It was the wrong thing to bring up, but Daniel had to say it. "I'm sorry about your dad."

Trey only turned and opened the car door. "We done here, Agent Gardner?"

No. Things were just as unfinished as they'd been fifteen

years ago. And even though Daniel was good at expressing himself in six languages, always able to find an answer for the emergency question of the hour, and had a name-your-salary offer with one of the top private security firms in the country, standing here facing Trey, he couldn't think of one thing to say that would get him the information he wanted.

"Did you ever find out anything about that night?"

Trey jerked the car door open so hard he knocked Daniel back a step. "Give the department a call when your mother figures out what's missing."

Chapter Two

Nothing in his old bedroom said: Here Daniel Gardner spent a pathetic adolescence. Sometime between his graduation from John Jay and making it through Quantico, the room had been made over to a generic guestroom in shades of blue. Even though the bed now faced the closet instead of the window, the bedframe was familiar, and when he stretched out on it, the dips and sounds told him it was the same double mattress.

Oddly, it hadn't been until Trey moved into Rob's room across the hall that anything had happened. Daniel thought he'd die that first month, when Trey slept on the hastily purchased single bed stuffed in Daniel's room. He'd suffered agony as he tried not to stare when Trey dressed in their room, tried to ignore the smell of him fresh and soapy or full of summer sweat or the sounds he made as he lay awake every night. Nights of knowing all Daniel had to do was roll over to see Trey's eyes glitter in the dark, to reach into the space between their beds to touch him.

Daniel could jerk off every hour for a year and not make up for spending that summer with an almost constant hard-on.

He ignored the way the Ghosts of Erections Past had his cock twitching and pressed a stored number on his phone. He was about to cancel the unanswered call when Scott picked up.

"Hey, Dan. 'S late. Everythin' okay?" Scott's voice was husky with sleep, his accent almost as thick as when they had sex.

"It is now." And then Daniel realized how that sounded, hoped Scott wouldn't read anything into the words.

"I'm flattered."

"I just wanted to let you know someone broke into my mother's house."

Scott was instantly alert. "Is everyone okay? What did they take?"

"We don't know yet. So much stuff was already packed. Mostly they made a mess." *Oh and Trey was here.*

"But everyone's okay? Did you get to use your sexy special agent mojo?"

"I swept the house."

"Gun drawn?"

"Yeah."

"Mmmm. You're making me hard." Scott's laugh warmed Daniel's ear, even two hundred miles away.

"Shut up." But he could feel the smile on his own lips, and as much as Daniel had been glad for the time away, to have a break from Scott asking where Daniel thought things were going between them, he missed Scott enough to say, "Sure you don't want to change your mind and drive up, just for Christmas? Mother won't even make us sleep in separate beds."

"No thanks. I'm trying to stay sane for the holidays. That means no families. Yours or mine. Speaking of minds, have you made yours up yet?"

"Scott—"

"I know. You'll think about it. The house. The job. Me. Just...keep me in the loop, okay?"

It wasn't exactly a hang up, but Scott's rough good-night was full of frustration. Daniel was sliding the phone back in its case when it vibrated against his palm. He smiled. Scott was like that. Quick to anger, quick to apologize.

Daniel answered with his best phone-sex voice, "Hey, baby."

There was a sound like a strangled laugh. Not Scott's. *Oh fuck.* He checked the number on the display. *Number unavailable.*

"Guess you're still...up."

Daniel had gone fifteen years without hearing that voice, but it only took one night to relearn it. Trey. He must be making use of all the paperwork they'd filled out. Or interagency cooperation made Daniel's unlisted number available.

He decided to ignore the innuendo. "Why? Make an arrest yet?"

"No." A pause then, "Danny."

He could accept the name when Trey said it like that. Soft and full of want. The way he had when their bodies were hard against each other, skin to skin, cock to cock. When Trey pulled Daniel down tighter, hands splayed on his ass, murmuring *Danny* like it held the answers to everything Trey needed.

"You cut your hair," Trey said at last.

"Yeah." Daniel's fingers ran through the close cut, gelled into submission. "It got in the way." Long curls sticking to his face, to Trey's neck, getting in their eyes. "The Bureau has a standard look, and so does the DHS."

"Makes you look older."

"I am." *But you don't look it. Bet you still get carded for beer.*

Trey had a reason for calling. He had a reason for everything. And it wasn't only to talk about hair. "I didn't know your mother was moving so soon. If you find anything of mine— or my dad's—hang onto it for me."

There was no sentimentality involved. Even after fifteen years, Daniel recognized that tone. It was the case. Trey's parents' case.

"Sure."

Everything else, the *Danny,* talking about his hair, all Trey's way of softening him up, opening him to the real purpose. Verbal foreplay. Trey was good at everything. And he wasn't quite done. Daniel could hear that too. He waited.

"So...*baby?*"

"I thought you were my boyfriend." If that wasn't a loaded statement.

A quick cough. "Right. Okay. Good night, Danny."

Trey stuffed the phone in his pocket and watched the last light in the Gardner house go out before starting his car. He told himself he'd take one slow tour around the neighborhood to see if anything was out of place amid the perfectly maintained houses on the hill, residences of doctors, lawyers and politicians. Even the current Vice President-elect had once lived up on College Hill.

It was only a few blocks but a world away from the middle-class neighborhood where Trey's family had lived. When he'd had a family. They'd been sandwiched on the steep part of the hill, in with all the other cops and firemen and teachers. Social stratification measured by feet above sea level.

The lawn of the house backing up to the Gardners was lit by a mind-blowing array of blinding Christmas lights. Probably a big hit with Pennsylvania Power and Light, not so much with the neighbors. Trey checked it for any sign the burglar had fled through the yards on foot. The icy coating on the lawn was undisturbed. The driveway was so clean Trey would lay money on it having the wires to heat it and keep it snow free.

He'd check everything again when the sun came up.

If nothing else because he owed Julia Gardner-Holcomb. She'd taken him in when her own family was falling apart. Taken in the kid with a murderer for a dad. He owed Julia, and he'd have caught the case anyway even if he hadn't been listening to the radio. Everybody at the station from the janitor to the Chief of Police knew his history. And for all that brothers-in-blue shit, they still kept their distance. Like disaster was contagious.

Maybe it was. Maybe it had spread to the Gardners. Why would someone break into their house just to knock over some packing boxes? Trey'd taken a look around the first-floor rooms, and though they were stripped to minimal furnishings for Julia's move, he'd counted three laptops, a digital camera, an iPod, two plasma TVs and a pile of Christmas presents. All of them liftable. Not to mention the couple hundred cash in the kitchen drawer he'd seen while looking for a spoon.

People were freaks, but people who did crime and were smart enough to not get caught immediately usually had an end game in mind. Even if it was only to get their next fix.

The break-in didn't track. And maybe he was trying to force the pieces to fit, but why, exactly when Julia Gardner-Holcomb started packing up the house, was there something worth taking?

He cruised down Paxinosa Avenue again, eyeing the lawn and driveway of three hundred twelve. Someone had cut it a little close at the end, laying a few inches of tire tracks over the icy snow. He could have someone take a print, if he could get anyone to come up on Christmas Eve for a B and E with no significant property loss.

He paused at the corner again and the radio crackled.

"We have reports of a suspicious car at the site of that B and E on Paxinosa. You want it, Eriksson?"

"I got it."

He swung a U-turn in the intersection and drove back, cutting the engine as he stopped at the curb on the opposite side of the Gardners' Tudor. He fished out his phone and hit redial.

As soon as Danny picked up, Trey said, "It's me."

"What?"

"The car driving on your street. It's me."

The house was still dark, but Trey thought he saw a shift in the patterns of darkness in the front window.

"Why?" Danny asked.

"Same as you. Looking around."

"You still don't sleep?"

Since his mom died, he usually stayed up until he was exhausted enough to drop where he stood. But he didn't want Danny's sympathy. "It's called working a case, Agent Gardner."

The front door opened. *Fuck.* Danny Gardner was a complication he did not need right now. It had been bad enough seeing him, seeing the way the sharp fine features and long bones had matured into a tall sexy man who wore his eight hundred dollar suit as comfortably as Trey wore jeans and a T-shirt, but then Daniel had to go and stand right next to him, close enough for Trey to make his skin tingle when he looked in those dark changeable eyes. He thought it wouldn't be as hard to talk to Daniel on the phone, but his voice, all sex and heat in that *hey, baby* hadn't made it any easier for Trey to keep his focus.

I thought you were my boyfriend. So grown-up Danny fucked guys. Information Trey wished he didn't get, even while he'd been trying to find a way to ask for it.

Now in jeans and a thick sweater that looked every bit as expensive as the suit had earlier, Danny was rapping on his window.

Trey popped the locks.

Danny slid inside. Trey didn't remember him taking up so much room before. His legs dropped open in answer to the challenge.

With the car off, it was too cold not to be direct. Danny shifted to face him. "Find anything?"

"No."

"Has this been happening a lot? I mean in the neighborhood, in town?"

"No."

"So it is weird. To break in and leave all those electronics. Like they were looking for something else."

Danny hadn't said anything Trey wasn't thinking. Maybe he was a good cop. Or maybe he could still read Trey's mind.

Danny went on, "I wonder if they found whatever they were looking for."

"Did Julia have any ideas?"

"Mother thinks my work makes me paranoid."

Mother. And that hadn't even been the strangest affectation in the Gardner house. Nothing but meticulous attention to the social rules. Every emotion pressed flat under an icy veneer. No wonder Danny had been so anxious to cut loose.

"I get why I'm trying to figure things out at dark o'clock on Christmas Eve, but what are you still doing here?" Danny tapped Trey's knee.

"I owe it to your mother to—"

"Bullshit. You think it could link back to your parents' case."

"How the fuck—"

"Every single thing you do is because of that case. Who'd know that better than me?" Danny made a one-note angry laugh.

"If you knew the answer, why'd you ask the question?"

"Masochistic streak."

Trey's anger faded as Danny quirked a sardonic smile.

"Kinky." But what Trey meant was bitter. When the hell did Danny get so bitter? He was going to change the world. Trey tried to keep from wondering how else Danny had changed, how his tall frame and lean muscles would feel against Trey's body. "What would your boyfriend say if he knew you were parking with another man?"

"I guess I'll have to remember not to mention it. The stuff you wanted me to keep an eye out for—you want to poke around looking for it yourself?"

Danny had always believed in Ron Eriksson's innocence, even when his own son lost faith. He wondered if now, with his Quantico and Homeland Security training, Danny would see the case for the slam dunk it had been on the law's side. Ron had killed his wife and turned the gun on himself, but the bullet had only ripped away a part of his brain, part of his humanity, leaving him with jumbled words and memories, including the one about men in ski masks gripping his hand, forcing the gun to his chin.

"It's Christmas Eve. I don't want to bother your family."

Danny looked out through the windshield. "I'll be in the garage all day tomorrow sorting stuff under Mother's watchful eye. With a 'real' policeman there, the possibility exists that she will consider me properly supervised."

Trey realized Danny had phrased it so that letting Trey dig around seemed like a favor. He laughed. It sounded good. When was the last time he'd laughed? "You've become a sneaky shit."

"I always was. I've just gotten better at it."

"I should have noticed when you snuck into my car."

"I opened the front door, walked down the driveway and across the street. Hardly a stealth attack. Or are we talking about something else?"

Maybe Trey was. Which was exactly why he shouldn't say, "So, what time tomorrow?"

It was a quick smile, gone almost before Trey could read the triumph in it. "Ten?" Danny slid out of the car before Trey could answer.

Trey called in a favor and managed to get a photographer up the hill about an hour after dawn to take a couple shots of the tire tread he'd noticed last night. He took himself out for coffee and then came back at ten to knock on the garage door, at first hoping Danny would be the one to open it, and then hoping it would be anyone else. He didn't know whether he'd be relieved or disappointed if Danny had been called back to the capital by some emergency. But there he was, white, professionally straightened teeth bared in a grin.

Trey remembered the day Danny'd gotten those braces off. A Friday. One of the nights his parents and Danny's got together for cards. They were an unlikely set, the Gardners and the Erikssons. But the bond forged between Ron Eriksson and William Gardner in Vietnam wasn't affected by social status. Even Julia relaxed when she was in the Erikssons' house. It was just that kind of place.

On that Friday Danny had followed Trey up to his room, grin firmly fixed, and for the first few minutes, Trey couldn't figure out what was so different. Then he blinked and he knew. "No more metal-mouth."

Danny shook his head, the smile lighting up his face, crinkling the corners of his surprisingly green eyes. Trey didn't think he'd ever seen Danny smile before, and now it hit him, silky warmth spreading out from his belly—and into his fifteen-year-old dick. His dick had a mind of its own—especially in his dreams. Boys and girls at first, but now mostly boys—men. Chests and hands and dicks, everything hard and rough against him, no matter how many times he tried to think about soft and pretty girls.

But Trey'd never really noticed Danny before. Not that smile. Not the way his eyes were dark and brown and green all at the same time. And definitely not his mouth. Definitely not how soft those wide lips looked.

His mom's voice made him jump. "Do you boys want to bring some food up here or are you coming back down?"

They weren't doing anything wrong, but his mother couldn't come in here. Trey had to get out. "We're coming down." He yanked open the door and pushed past her.

Seventeen years later, Danny smacked Trey's arm to drag him to the cold garage in the present. "Coming in?"

"Yeah." The Danny in his head had nothing on the Danny in front of him.

Danny's black sweater hugged his body so close Trey didn't have to imagine the hard muscles underneath, but he did. His fingers twitched as he thought of touching the warm solid flesh under the silky fabric—cashmere, he'd bet. He could have done a hug for old time's sake, if the Gardners were the hugging type. In the year he'd lived with them he hadn't seen much human touch. No wonder Danny'd been so desperate for it.

"Sorry," Danny said as Trey stepped through the side door to the garage. "Mother was going to start on the boxes at oh-eight-hundred, and the only way I could slow her down was to tell her you were coming."

"So why are you sorry?"

"Because then breakfast became brunch. Held for you."

"Ahh." Instead of affection, the Gardners got food. Elegantly served food. Sublimation, the psych books he'd read called it. "I'm really not dressed for—"

"Trey." Julia's head popped out through the doorway into the garage. "Don't worry about that, dear. We're happy to see you. You don't have any plans for the holiday, do you? You'll come to dinner tonight? And tomorrow, of course."

Why hadn't he realized this would happen? He cut a quick look to Danny to see if this had been his plan, but Danny's face betrayed nothing. Either he hadn't engineered it or he had learned to hide his feelings.

In the year he'd lived there, Trey had learned everything was easier if you let Julia have her way. "Thank you, Julia. That would be great. But I might be called into work."

"Certainly, dear. I understand. Don't worry about bringing anything."

But Trey would have to. He'd have to make sure he left in time to get to a liquor store before they closed. Even though Dr.

Gardner had long since departed for greener—younger—pastures, the rest of the family still knew their way around a fifth. Julia could drink gin like a sailor on shore leave and not slur a word or take a false step.

Brunch was a testament to the miracle of the Food Network. Cupcake-shaped eggs baked in ham-slice wrappers, strips of cinnamon-sugar-encrusted French toast all accented by kiwi and star fruit and pomegranate seeds. The only surprise was to find it served on hard plastic banquet plates.

Julia watched him pick up the plate and the plastic silverware. "I hope you don't mind. The Christmas Spode china is—was—packed."

From the slight hitch in Julia's voice he knew the china was part of the debris in the garage. He didn't know what Spode was—had a vague memory of plates with an anemic-looking Christmas tree on them—but despite her reserved manner, Julia had always been kind to him. He hated to think that just by having lived here more than a decade ago, he'd cost her something she treasured.

The topic at brunch—served from the kitchen island and eaten standing—was Julia's move. She already had an offer on this house, it was simply a matter of finding a condo close to Rob and his family in Harrisburg.

"When did you get the offer, Julia?"

"The realtor called me the day after we officially listed the house. And it was exactly our asking price, which as you know in this market..."

"Is lucky," Rob agreed.

And not particularly odd, but still, it was another weird circumstance. "Exactly when did you list it, Julia?"

"The first of the month. Of course, I told them I couldn't possibly be ready before the new year. Fortunately, Danny's going to take care of the closing for me."

Danny met Trey's gaze. "I took a few weeks' vacation."

Unwanted, the thought came to Trey's mind, *What does*

your boyfriend think of that? He forced his attention back to what mattered. From what he knew of real estate, the housing market was dead in December. Again, a quick offer wasn't exactly suspicious, but added to the break-in, things were hinky enough to get Trey thinking.

He stepped around the island, intending to put his plastic dish in the trash, when he saw Shannon and Julia's plates in the sink. There were reasons the rich were rich, his dad had always told him. Starting with, they don't spend money.

His mom had served Christmas dinner off whatever they had to his aunt and uncle and cousins. The house was loud and busy, kids tearing through every room, wired on toys and sugar.

Trey turned to Shannon. "Where are your girls?" He realized it had come out in his interrogation voice and he smiled ruefully.

She returned his smile. "If they aren't fighting over the remote, they're watching some marathon on one of the kids' channels."

Danny followed Trey's lead and scraped his plate into the garbage. Either he'd taken too much food or he didn't eat much. Judging from the fit of that sweater and the khaki pants—even though he'd tried not to notice the way they fit over Danny's ass—Danny didn't carry any spare weight.

"Thank you," Danny said as they stepped down into the garage.

"What for?"

"Giving me a reason to be out here instead of trapped in there with them."

Trey didn't have an answer for that. Even if Julia was washing the plastic dinnerware and usually seemed cold enough to chill a side of beef, Danny still had a family to bitch about.

"Shit. Sorry, Trey."

Fucking mind reader. He shrugged. "So why'd you agree to

stay here to close up the house?"

"I had a lot of vacation time coming."

Trey knew all about that. He only took a day if the chief insisted.

Danny stopped glancing around at all the boxes and held Trey's gaze. "I wanted to be somewhere else for awhile." The seriousness disappeared in Danny's familiar grin. "Besides, Mother will be going to Harrisburg with Rob tomorrow. As soon as I have an address, I just have to supervise the movers and finish packing."

Trey didn't really hear much after Danny's "be somewhere else". So things with the boyfriend must not be all Hey-baby good. Why the hell did he care?

"Where do we start?" Danny asked. "Do you know what you're looking for?"

"Don't you have a search pattern already mapped out, Mr. Homeland Security?" As soon as the words left him on a frosty breath, he wished them back. But despite what happened in Warner Brothers cartoons, visible breath couldn't be taken back. Danny should have punched him. Trey couldn't figure out why he kept needling him.

Danny just stood there, broken picture frame in his hands. "What the hell is your problem?"

"I don't have a problem, Danny." Trey's denial was automatic. Did he? Was he pissed at Danny for doing exactly what he'd promised? He'd left this—in Danny's words—shithole of a town and become important, rich and successful. Someone else. Trey had left too, but he'd come back. He'd never asked Danny to stay. But Trey hadn't thought about what it would be like to never see Danny again.

And even though Danny had begged Trey to come with him, Trey hadn't given him an answer, just taken off. Trey dragged a hand over the top of his head and looked back down at the overturned boxes. "I'll start over here."

Half an hour later he'd heaved countless broken dishes and

glasses into the trash bin and had a foot-high pile of artwork from the Gardner children's elementary period. So far other than destruction, they hadn't figured out what the burglar had wanted.

"Hey." Danny held up an intact picture, unframed. "Isn't this your dad with the governor?"

"Mr. Vice President-Elect, you mean?" Trey stepped over a pile of art books that had resided on Julia's coffee table at one time or another.

Standing at Danny's shoulder, Trey looked down at the image of three men in police dress uniform. The former Chief of Police, now Vice President-Elect Mike Kearney, stood with Lieutenant Mastroanni and the newly promoted Sergeant Ron Eriksson at the dedication of the Southside Police Substation.

Trey stared at his father's picture. Trey had gotten so used to the shrunken man in prison orange, much of his left side paralyzed from the aborted "suicide" attempt. Trey still put quotes around the word, even in his head, though sometimes, when he was staring at the bright green glow of the numbers on the clock as they spun through another night, he wondered if belief in his father was nothing more than force of habit. All these years Trey had been looking and he'd never turned up a thing to back up his father's story.

The man in the picture was big, healthy and happy. His parents had fought—everyone did—but he'd always hear them laughing later, teasing and joking about whatever had them angry an hour before.

It was nothing like the cold furious silences—often preceded by the sound of breaking glass—he remembered from the months before Danny's dad had moved out.

Danny pulled out another picture from the pile of folders. "Here's one of you and me and my stepfather when we took that camping trip up to the Delaware Water Gap."

"What a fucking disaster that was." Trey took the picture.

Mayor Sandy Holcomb clutched one end of a tarp while

Danny and Trey struggled to tie it to a tree.

"I don't remember that it stopped raining long enough to take a picture."

"When the tent washed into the ditch, that's when Julia and your sister went to the hotel."

"Yeah. He was a little gung-ho about the outdoorsman stuff, but he was good to Mother."

Trey had wished Mayor Holcomb had headed for the hotel too that night. He didn't realize how hard it would be to be as close to Danny as the optimistically named three-man tent put them and not touch him. Even soaking wet and miserable. "Ever hear from your dad?"

"Every December 15 I get a card and a check and a picture of him with trophy wife number two. He's a freaking cliché."

"Sorry."

"Why? You didn't have anything to do with it."

"Felt different about it then."

"I was sixteen. Things change." Danny was looking at him carefully.

Trey was tired of going around the issue. He stepped closer, hands on Danny's shoulders, driving him into the cinder-block wall as the picture went spinning to the floor. "Something you wanna ask me, Danny?"

Danny pushed away from the wall, hands gripping the sides of Trey's face, long fingers dragging Trey forward until their lips met. Cold skin and then the wet warmth of Danny's mouth. Heat rolled through Trey's belly, washed along his nerves. Better than the first time, their first kiss, but worse, so much worse. Because back then, the only thing that pulled him away from that kiss was his own fear. Now, there were so many other reasons to step away. But Danny's tongue in his mouth tugged at something deep inside Trey until his grip shifted to pull Danny in tight.

Danny's hands moved off his face and he shoved Trey

away. "Planning to make me your dirty little secret again?"

Trey's boot caught on the pile of art books, sending him back a few extra steps. "Christ. Still so fucking dramatic."

"Like running off to join the Army wasn't?"

"You know why I had to."

"Why you thought you had to."

"Not again, Danny." He knelt to straighten the spilled pile of books. "Here's another picture." He stopped when he turned it over. The Polaroid was yellowed with age and cracked from a fold a third from the top running through one of the men's faces. Six soldiers perched on or around sandbags, behind them, also cut by the same crack, a hand-painted sign reading Can Tho, the airbase where Trey's dad had been stationed in Vietnam. Flipping it over, Trey scanned the handwriting. Faded, blurry names, but he picked out Ron and Bill. "Our dads." He handed it up to Danny.

"You keep it. I don't think Mother will care." Danny squinted at the faces. "It was probably your dad's to begin with."

"Stuffed in one of these art books? Why?"

"Beats me." Danny squatted down, tone suddenly eager. "Which one?"

They looked through the pile. *The Lure of the Local. The Spiritual in Abstract Art. Frank Lloyd Wright. Hieronymus Bosch.*

Danny slapped a hand over the cover on that last one. "Jesus. That stuff gives me nightmares."

Trey lifted Danny's hand to look at a picture from the book. It was a little freaky, in a demons-fresh-out-of-circus-hell way.

Danny turned the book over before handing it to him. "Do you think what book it came out of means something?"

Trey spread his hands in question. "Probably not."

"Take 'em anyway."

Trey didn't need the help, but Danny grabbed eight of the heavy books and led the way out to Trey's car.

"We'll be back from church by six. Dinner's at seven."

"What about midnight mass?"

"Bite your tongue. We're Episcopalians."

Chapter Three

For the first time Daniel thought he could emotionally appreciate ritual. The familiar rhythm of his mother's traditional Christmas Eve dinner kept him from thinking of the man sitting next to him. Of how Trey standing close had somehow meant Daniel had to kiss him and get the answer to the question he couldn't figure out how to ask. He still didn't know if Trey had accepted being gay, but Trey hadn't lost the ability to fuck with Daniel's head with just a kiss.

The doorbell rang in time with the French silk pie hitting the table. Daniel knew his mother was hoping it was his sister Melissa. The idea that anyone could consider living across the country reason enough to miss the last family Christmas in the Gardner home had yet to sink in, but with the break-in last night, he wished she'd be less eager to run and open the door. He was barely in the hall, Rob and Trey immediately behind him, when she flung the door wide.

"Mrs. Holcomb?" asked the familiar voice.

His stomach gave dinner a sickening flip. Damn. He'd been looking forward to that chocolate dessert. "Scott. Come on in."

The first round of introductions took place in the foyer. Mother barely missed a stride. With a "Call me Julia," she placed both hands over Scott's in a brief welcome. "I'm so glad you changed your mind and accepted the invitation."

Daniel wasn't.

After dinner, the girls were hurried to bed in their new

Christmas pajamas so Rob and Shannon could finish wrapping and arranging gifts. Mother, ever conscious of her duty to her guests, enlisted Daniel to play pinochle with Trey and Scott. Daniel must not have given Scott an accurate picture of the force that was Julia Holcomb, since he tried to demur. Daniel gave him a look of pity as Scott found himself not only playing but setting up the table and finding the cards.

Trey and Mother were a hundred points ahead after the first hand, and Daniel felt his competitive nature kick in with force. With a better second hand, he managed to get the lead back to Scott, and they were able to set up a cross-cut until Mother changed tactics.

"I saw Ginny the other day, Danny. She's opened a bookstore on Cattell Street. She asked about you."

Scott shot Daniel a horrified is-your-mother-trying-to-fix-you-up? look. Before Daniel could assure him his mother was not that deluded, Scott led hearts instead of diamonds, allowing Trey to steal back the lead.

"That's nice," Daniel said.

"You should call her. I believe she opened it with a *friend*." Mother burdened the word with all the power of euphemism in her command. "Perhaps you and Scott could celebrate the new year with them."

Scott caught on with an almost inaudible "Oh," but since Daniel couldn't make any of his lower trump good now it didn't matter.

"I haven't seen Ginny since we graduated," Daniel told his mother who apparently labored under the delusion that gay men and lesbians were a perfect social pairing.

"She asks about you all the time," Mother persisted.

At last Trey came to the rescue. "Ginny Banyon? Redhead?"

"Yes, lovely girl," Mother said with a trace of regret. "Still is."

Daniel felt compelled to come to Ginny's defense. "It's hardly a shame, Mother."

"What isn't a shame, dear?" His mother scooped in a four-point trick.

"That Ginny is lovely."

"Of course not. Why would you say that?"

Scott sipped his decaf coffee and eyed Daniel over the rim. Right about now, Daniel would bet Scott was regretting his impulsive four-hour drive.

With the next hand, Daniel finally had something worthwhile and moved the bidding up high and fast. They were already down one hundred and fifty points. Trey matched each bid, challenge in his eyes. There was no way he could be outbid on this hand. Trey's lips twitched as the bid climbed over a hundred. At a hundred and twenty, Daniel read the look in Trey's eyes.

"Fu—For crying out loud. You've got a double run."

"Thousand aces?" Trey nodded at Daniel's hand. The shorthand communication, the looks, made an unwanted warmth prickle under Daniel's skin.

"That's a tough one, Danny," his brother said on his way through the dining room.

Scott leaned back in his chair. "Do you all take cards so seriously?"

Mother looked at him over her hand and then to Daniel as if he were responsible for the odd question.

"If it's worth playing, it's worth winning," Daniel explained.

"You should see them at Scrabble," Trey said.

"Quixotic," Rob and Daniel said at the same time.

"A perfectly acceptable word." Mother was still smug about it.

"Worth 248 points on a triple word score," Rob said through gritted teeth. He'd almost beat Mother that time.

Mother smiled. "I believe it's your bid, Trey, dear."

✧

It was only sensible for someone to check the doors, windows and alarm system. The fact that Daniel was also hoping his meticulous inspection would give Scott enough time to fall asleep was pure cowardice. And so was his overly conscientious brushing and flossing, but his parents had put a lot of money into his smile.

As it turned out, he could have saved himself the twenty minutes with guilt and shame gnawing at his guts, and gone right to full dread. Scott was awake. Propped up against a pillow reading. Waiting.

"Hey," Daniel tried. The knots in his intestines weren't Scott's fault. Just a by-product of his presence.

"Hey." Scott put his book down and waited until Daniel had stripped to shorts and climbed in bed before shutting off the lamp.

As Daniel pulled the sheet and blanket up to his chest, Scott moved the pillow away from the headboard, saying, "Your mom's really nice."

"Mother is always on her best behavior."

"Hmm." Scott's hot legs tangled with Daniel's cold ones, brush of hair, hard weight of muscles. Comfortably familiar. For the past six months they'd slept at each other's apartments, Daniel usually at Scott's—except when things got hectic at work.

Daniel knew it should have been more than just familiar. Something inside should react to the light press of that warm thigh on his balls, the way Scott's breath tickled through Daniel's hair.

Scott wrapped an arm around Daniel's shoulders, pulled them face-to-face on their sides.

"How old were you when your dad left?"

"Almost seventeen."

"Did you like your stepdad?"

"He was fine." Daniel shifted, pulling back enough to look into Scott's face. "What is this?"

"It's called conversation." Scott jerked his arm away from Daniel's back and put it on the pillow over his head. "I just met your family, Dan. I wanted to know a little more about them. And you. Besides. Isn't that the way you like things, when they're all about you?"

You could go to school too. We'll get an apartment. Why don't you want to come with me?

This isn't about you, Danny.

Daniel rolled away onto his back. Scott sighed and followed, landing on Daniel's chest. Long lashes dropped over Scott's dark, sexy eyes. "I'm sorry. I'm just..." Scott let it trail off with a shrug.

"What?"

"I don't know."

Daniel thought Scott did. They both did.

"Dan. I'm sorry."

"It's all right."

"I'll make it up to you." Scott kissed the hollow of Daniel's neck, mouth sliding lower, warm and wet tongue gliding down Daniel's breastbone. His dick knew what that slick kiss was leading to and it wanted to rise up and greet Scott's mouth. The conscience-free head didn't care that Daniel felt guilty for not wanting Scott here at all; it just wanted wet-hot pressure. Jaw clenched against a groan, Daniel grabbed Scott's silky auburn hair and pulled him off.

"What the fuck?" Scott's voice held hurt and shock.

"Not now."

"Jesus, Daniel. It's been over two weeks."

"I told you I had to clear a lot of work so I could help my mother close the house." Guilt was now making more bowties in Daniel's intestines than you could find at a thousand-dollars-a-plate fundraiser. He tried to soften the rejection by playing with Scott's hair.

Scott sighed, and when he spoke again, some of the intensity had gone from his whisper. "Since when do you turn down getting your dick sucked?"

"Since my mother is right down the hall."

Scott made a choking sound. "Bet you never said that when *he* was living here."

Daniel's pulse jumped, a loud thump echoing in his ears. "Trey?"

Scott turned, gaze hard on Daniel's face, even in the dark. Daniel swallowed. "I don't even know if he's still gay."

It was true. Not pushing Daniel away from the kiss this morning didn't mean anything. Like their first kiss hadn't meant a damned thing at school the next day, hadn't kept Trey from ignoring him. And the first time they'd gotten each other off hadn't stopped Trey from making sure every loudmouth in school knew he'd nailed one of the basketball cheerleaders three days later.

"Oh, but he was gay enough back then?" Scott asked.

Daniel shrugged.

"Trust me, he's still gay. Or at least gay for you. Boy was looking at you like a two-year-old at a birthday cake."

No drawl in Scott's voice, but the rhythm of those last words exposed his Georgia roots and Daniel was suddenly trying to breathe around a hot gluey lump in his throat. Because right then, he knew he wasn't ever again going to be hearing Scott's accent get thick as syrup when he rode Daniel's cock. Wasn't going to have that silky auburn hair to play with while Scott sucked him off, tight lips and the perfect hint of teeth to get Daniel begging. Wasn't going to see that smile as they passed each other sections of the *Post* over toast and coffee, hear Scott's soft, contented sigh when Daniel came to bed late and wrapped them tightly together.

"And don't pretend you didn't notice," Scott added.

41

"I'm sorry." That was all Daniel had to offer at the moment. And Scott could apply it to as much or as little as he wanted.

Daniel jerked awake to a sudden noise. It couldn't have been too loud, though. As light a sleeper as Scott was, it hadn't woken him. He was still curled up on his side—as far away from Daniel as the double bed would allow.

Another soft creak downstairs. If Daniel had been sleeping instead of dozing, he'd never have heard it. The noise could be Rob or Shannon doing something with the girls' toys, but Daniel knew it wasn't. He rolled out of bed, pulling on jeans and a sweater. As he fastened his jeans, he switched on the light and tapped Scott's arm.

He blinked rapidly and then focused on Daniel.

"Someone's in the house. Go wake up my brother and get everyone in Mother's room, then call the police."

"Sure it's not Santa?" Scott said around a yawn.

Daniel turned from checking the clip on his Glock. "Scott."

"Jesus. You're serious. Okay. But then I'm coming downstairs."

"Don't."

"You shouldn't be alone."

"You're a CPA. Stay upstairs."

The adrenaline pumping through Daniel's body made every sound sharp and clear. Even on the landing he could hear the rustle of Scott dressing. Below him he heard someone waiting. The absence of sound. Breath held. Muscles kept rigid. His eyes were adjusting to the dark, shapes and shadows resolving into familiar objects.

Daniel reached the last stair, kept his back to the wall and paused. Doing this alone, he'd get one chance to grab the guy before he bolted. On a hunch, he decided to look in the den first. Quick check on points and he spun left. Another turn and he was in the doorway to the den. A figure crouched on the other side of the desk. No light. A black outline in the darkness.

Daniel thumbed off the safety and the figure jerked. "Don't get up."

Trigger finger ready to squeeze off a shot at the first sign of movement, Daniel studied the man—it was definitely a man. Shoulders broad, hips narrow. "Federal agent. On your knees. Hands on your head. Slowly."

The dark figure complied with a deliberation that suggested he'd been through the routine before. As he did, Daniel could see the stubby flashlight in the man's latex-gloved hands.

"Drop the flashlight."

After a few seconds where Daniel wondered if the guy would try to rush him, the five-inch Maglite rolled down the man's back and across the floor to Daniel's feet. The insolently slow compliance added a spike of anger to the adrenaline already flushing under every inch of Daniel's skin. He had to keep a tight grip on the desire to pick up the flashlight and smash it over the guy's head. This was his family. His house. Even if he avoided both as much as he could, this wasn't just any crime scene.

Pistol leveled for a headshot, Daniel moved around to face the kneeling man and stared into a ski mask.

Men in ski masks. That's all Trey's dad ever remembered about that night. The .22 still lodged in his brain had left him as confused and incoherent as a stroke victim. This ski mask didn't have to mean anything. Masks were an efficient tool in these days of facial recognition software and omnipresent security cameras.

"Dan?" Scott's voice came from the stairs.

Daniel never took his eyes or his gun off the kneeling man. "For Chrissakes, Scott, go back upstairs. I got him. I'm fine. And keep everyone else up there too."

He waited until Scott's footsteps faded. Pistol aimed directly at the eye socket a few inches away, Daniel said, "Clearly this isn't your first time at the rodeo, so why pick a house with a federal agent in it? Don't tell me you didn't case the house first."

No answer came from the tightly pressed chapped lips visible in the faint light from the window behind the desk.

"You know, I haven't been at the firing range in a month or two. Maybe I've forgotten how to handle this." Daniel waggled the pistol in the man's face, making sure he could see Daniel's finger on the trigger.

Only the man's eyes moved.

"The silence is getting to me. And I am definitely out of practice."

Daniel brought his free hand up to cradle his grip, shifting his aim lower, as if looking for just the right spot.

The man licked his lips. "I'm getting paid well enough to take a hit. But you like your job too much to risk it, don't you, Agent Gardner? Pull the trigger, and see how big the players in this game are. Your call."

Between one breath and the next, Daniel could see it. Could feel his finger tighten, feel the kick, see the jerk as the bullet hit, blood forming on the man's chest seconds before the sound would echo through the house. And then Scott, his mother, and Robert running in.

But a knee to the guy's chin wouldn't make nearly as much noise.

"Dan—Agent Gardner?"

Maybe it was the blood rushing in his ears or maybe Trey could move silently when he had to because Daniel hadn't heard him get into the house.

"In here." Daniel stared hard into the burglar's eyes, the smirk he read there making him wonder if Trey would help him put a couple of dents in the guy before the patrol car got here.

His own pistol drawn and aimed at the floor, Trey flicked on the light when he got to the den, making Daniel's eyes water. He kept his aim steady, though.

Trey pulled out a set of cuffs and jerked the man's hands down before snapping his wrists together behind the man's back. Daniel never lifted the gun.

"Danny?"

Until Trey said his name Daniel didn't realize his arms were aching with the tension of rigidly held muscles. He spared Trey a glance.

Trey didn't speak aloud, mouthing the words at him. "Stand down."

Daniel looked down again. "I'm just waiting to hear why the fuck this asshole broke into my house."

Despite his large frame, Trey was completely silent as he stepped around the man, reaching for Daniel's two-handed grip. Another smirk crossed the burglar's barely visible lips.

Shifting his aim to the floor, Daniel thumbed the safety on. "You're not worth the paperwork."

The arrival of the patrol officers triggered the exodus of Scott and Daniel's family from the upstairs.

Scott took one look at Trey and said, "Of. Course."

Trey pulled Danny out into the garage. "What the hell is going on?"

"I don't know." His body ached, nerves wrapped with barbed wire, muscles burning as the adrenaline faded.

"What do you mean you don't know? I seriously thought you were about to shoot him."

"I seriously thought I might. Jesus, it's my mother's house, Trey. There are kids sleeping upstairs. What if one of my nieces thought it was Santa..."

"But they didn't." Trey reached out and squeezed his shoulder. "He say anything?"

"That he was hired. Made an interesting threat, like he had major players as backers."

"Major how? Gang? Mob?"

Daniel shook his head. "Neither. I don't know. In the shop? Political? Like someone in the Department."

"I can't see your stepfather having that kind of connection."

"I don't think it's about him. I think—"

"Detective Eriksson?" Officer Acevedo stuck her head into the garage.

Daniel jerked his chin toward the door. "Go. I'll tell you later."

As Trey went up the few steps into the kitchen, Daniel sucked in big frosty gulps of air, trying to cool the rage he could still feel pulsing like hot needles under his skin. Would he have actually shot someone—someone unarmed? He looked down at his pistol, the safety back on. His hand tightened on the grip, felt the weight. No. But he sure as hell would have kicked the shit out of him if Trey hadn't shown up.

He made his way back into the house, where Trey and the uniformed officers were standing around the still-kneeling and temporarily lucky intruder.

"Do you need me to come to the station now?" Daniel asked.

"Later today would be fine, Agent Gardner," Officer Acevedo said.

Without the protection of his ski mask, the burglar demonstrated a keen awareness of his right to remain silent, saying nothing beyond a "yes" when asked by Officer Acevedo if he understood his rights.

"I'm going to head over for his processing, see if I can't find out what's going on." Trey nodded as the two patrolmen took the man out.

"Certainly you must have time for a cup of coffee." Mother headed for the kitchen and then paused. It appeared nothing had broken her polite veneer, but Daniel had seen the tremble in her hands before she hid them in the pockets of her bathrobe. "Unless you need to dust for fingerprints?"

"That won't be necessary, Julia. Danny's testimony should be everything we need. Anything missing this time?"

"Not that I can tell." Once she was in the kitchen, Mother opened the drawer where she kept her emergency cash. "Why on earth is our house suddenly so interesting to criminals?" And there it was again, a light tremor only someone who knew her well could have detected.

Robert must have heard it too, since he went over to attempt a half-embrace that Mother eluded with grace.

"Good question, Julia. It's why I'm afraid I'll have to skip the coffee and head over so I can talk to him as soon as he's been processed."

"And on Christmas," Mother said, as if such behavior was the absolute limit in terms of criminally bad taste. "Does that mean you won't be joining us for dinner?"

Daniel caught the look Trey shot his way.

"I can't be sure, Julia. I'll call, of course."

"Of course. Thank you so much, Trey, dear."

"I'll get you a drink, Mother," Robert offered.

"That would be kind of you."

"I'll walk you out." Daniel followed Trey to the door.

It was colder than last night, the winter air that had felt so refreshing in the garage now clawed into Daniel's lungs. The black Charger was in the lower third of the driveway, and Trey leaned against the driver's door like he had last night.

"So the guy was a pro. High-end lock picks, magnet on the door alarm. Probably'll find him in the system." At least Trey was treating him like he knew what he was doing now.

"What the hell's going on?"

"I don't know." Trey folded his arms across his chest, the leather of his jacket creaking in the freezing air.

"I think it has something to do with your parents." Daniel hadn't meant to throw it out there like that, wanted to wait until they were someplace where they could talk about it, not in the driveway when it was three in the morning and five degrees outside. But as he said the words, he knew they were right, believed them. It was the only explanation that made sense.

Trey laughed, but there wasn't any humor in it. "And exactly what do you base that craziness on?"

"C'mon. A pro? In our house now, at Christmas, and he takes nothing of value? Twice? He's looking for something specific."

"And from that you think it's something connected to my parents?"

"Remember what we said? What we knew? Your dad was onto something. Something big and someone needed to keep him quiet. Something that got your mom—" Daniel stopped. He didn't have to say it. It wasn't like Trey didn't know his mother had been murdered, but every time someone brought it up, Daniel saw a fresh hit of pain in Trey's silvery eyes.

"Careful there, Agent Gardner, people will think you're as crazy as me."

Daniel pressed his face against the tinted glass to peer into the empty backseat. "Crazy enough to have taken a hundred pounds of art books into your house this afternoon?"

Trey's lips curved. "So what is it, this something specific?"

"Something small, but whatever it was the killer has to get it back because it's proof. Something your dad had that moved from your house to ours."

"You sound like you've been thinking it out."

"And you haven't? Why the hell else would you be spending so much time on a simple B and E?"

Trey looked at him steadily, and the floodlight over the garage let Daniel see exactly how intent those light eyes were.

"Shouldn't you be getting back to your warm boyfriend? I'm sure he wants to give you a hero's welcome."

"Jealous?" Daniel would never have asked if Trey wasn't

looking at him like that.

Trey opened the door of the Charger and then turned back, ending up close enough that Daniel could feel the moist warmth of Trey's breath on his face. For a second he thought Trey might kiss him. Daniel wasn't obsessively closeted, but it was not the kind of thing that would get him a promotion at work. If Trey were out enough to kiss guys on the street, even at three in the morning, Daniel definitely would have heard it from his mother. But Trey didn't kiss him.

Instead, he let his gaze move slowly over Daniel's body. "I've got no reason to be jealous. But I would be if I were him."

"Why?"

"Because there isn't anything I don't want to do to you, Danny." Trey swung into the car and shut the door.

Chapter Four

When Daniel got back inside they were all having coffee, the kids sipping on mugs of sweet milky tea. He was certain his mother's mug held a liberal application of Bailey's Irish Cream.

"There's no getting the girls back to sleep after this," Mother said.

No kidding. The girls' eyes looked stretched open, pinned wide by a combination of excitement and fear. They sat on the couch in their brand-new Christmas-themed pajamas, wedged between their robed parents, who exchanged frequent unreadable glances over the girls' heads. Though Daniel couldn't be completely certain, he'd bet money no one in that Gardner family would regret heading home to Harrisburg.

Scott was at the opposite end of the love seat from Mother, looking as comfortable as if he were sitting on a bed of nails. The pile of presents dwarfed the small artificial tree trimmed like a magazine picture in cranberry garlands with cream ribbons and balls. When Samantha and Ashley finished their tea, their eyes looked a little less wild and they slid from the couch to sit cross-legged in front of the presents. At ten and twelve, every muscle strained with the urge to dive headlong into tearing through the color-coordinated wrapping papers, but they were still Gardners, bound by the force field holding them back until the signal from their grandmother.

"Let's see what we have this year," Mother said, catapulting the girls forward into the pile of presents.

As they dug through, reading tags, they flung back adult gifts, and Daniel calculated them by box shape and size. Shannon: blouse from Mother, obligatory jewelry from Rob, the sin of the unimaginative gift card from Daniel. He winced. If he'd known Scott was coming, would he have added his name to the gift tag? The invitation to come to Easton for Christmas had been issued a month ago, before Scott had ambushed Daniel with the conversation that had made them take this left turn into Awkwardtown.

Of course, Shannon opened Daniel's gift first, thanking him and then glancing at Scott who smoothed it over with a smile and a nod. Rob cradled his bottle of Chivas Regal with a quick thank you, and Mother exclaimed over her present with generalized gratitude. By the time Samantha and Ashley made their round of formal thank yous, Scott was signaling Daniel with his eyes.

Daniel followed Scott into the den. Tension flooded back just from being back in that room, anger that some bastard had been in this house twice and Daniel hadn't been able to force a reason out of him.

In front of the big leather chair where Daniel's dad had put down more single-malt Scotch than the populations of Glasgow and Edinburgh together, Scott turned and faced him. "I'm exhausted. I'm headed back to bed."

There was no invitation, no demand in it, and Daniel had the feeling again that when Scott went back to D.C. tomorrow, it'd be a lot longer than the time it took to close Mother's house before he saw him again.

"Good idea, babe."

The endearment seemed to piss Scott off in a way nothing else had. "And I'm headed back after dinner tomorrow—today—whatever."

"But the office is closed until Monday."

"It has nothing to do with work. Dan..." Scott looked down at the oriental carpet. "I know I said I'd give you however much time you needed, but we both already know what your answer's going to be."

Daniel wanted to argue, just for the sake of proving Scott didn't always know what Daniel was thinking, but since Scott was right, he didn't see the point. Daniel's feet carried him a step forward anyway, because comforting Scott had kind of become a habit, and when Scott finally looked up from the carpet, his brown eyes looked a little wet.

"Look. I'm not mad."

Daniel raised his brows.

"Okay. Not much. I'm not going to throw your stuff out on the street. And I'll return your calls and we can pass back keys and all the other civilized stuff. Not that you'd be anything but, right?"

"What does that mean?"

"I mean." Scott dragged both hands through his hair. "Fuck. I'm too tired for this shit right now." He took a deep breath. "I see where you get it from, okay? But you're—you just shut down, push people away. When's the last time you felt something, for anyone?"

"You expected that I'd start crooning love ballads because you think we should buy a house together?"

"I expected you might tell me how you feel about me instead of getting sarcastic."

"I guess I'm too civilized for that."

"I guess so. Like I said, Daniel, I get it. And it was my fault for expecting something you—"

"I what?" If Scott wanted Daniel to feel something, he did now. And God, the anger felt so much better than guilt.

Scott's lips pressed in a thin line before he spoke. "Something you can't or don't know how to give."

"I never realized what a martyr you were to my cruelty."

"Jesus, Dan. I didn't say that. Look, I want to be in a relationship. You don't. So the best thing for both of us is to just move on."

"Sure. Besides. You haven't gotten laid for two weeks. Move right along."

"You too. Go ahead and fuck your cop buddy. I'm sure Trey would be happy to give you a do-over. But don't think that's going to end any differently."

After Scott went upstairs, Daniel sank into his father's chair. Wow. He'd just been dumped. On Christmas. And he really was a selfish asshole since his sense of relief was a hell of a lot stronger than his sense of regret.

His stepfather must have liked this chair enough to keep it. As he slid his hands along the satiny arms, the leather released a rich scent. Daniel would have thrown the chair out with his father, but his mother had kept it, kept the surface conditioned. Why?

Why would anyone want the reminder of failure?

He tried to pinch away the headache he could feel forming between his eyes. Pinching didn't help, so he tried rubbing, making his eyes bleary enough that he remembered he was supposed to swap out his contacts two days ago.

But they were upstairs. In the room. With Scott. So his irritated eyes could wait. Daniel got up, deciding to try something useful, like actually figuring out if there was anything in the den worth stealing. He moved behind the gigantic oak desk—thank God getting it out of here would be the movers' problem—and opened all the drawers, finding nothing but empty space, not so much as a leftover paperclip or pencil.

He looked around at the walls. There was no safe, and nothing but a few old paperbacks in the glass-fronted bookcases. He could only wish the thief had taken the stuffed grouse on the credenza, a relic from his stepfather's outdoorsy fervor.

He crawled around, wondering if there was something he was missing, or if the burglar had been just as frustrated by the barren space. And then under the desk, through the one eye that wasn't watering, he saw a shred of white.

A scrap of paper stuck out of the bottom drawer. He pulled it out, finding an opened envelope with a handwritten letter inside, addressed to his father. Given its sixteen-year-old postmark, the letter must have been wedged between the back of the file drawer and the desk frame and missed his mother's purging and packing.

He looked at the postmark again. "Holy shit."

With the sudden rush of excitement and discovery buzzing like whispers under his skin, he had to force his hands to carefully unfold the old paper before he tore it in eagerness.

Dear Dr. Gardner,

My name is Maureen and my father is a patient at the VA hospital in Altoona. He shares his room with Howie Irving.

I hope that name is familiar to you. Mr. Irving was a member of your unit in Vietnam and he is dying. He has been begging the nurses to contact members of his unit as he says he has something important to tell you. I know the nurses have made calls, as despite his condition he is well-liked by the staff here.

My father and I are disappointed by the idea that anyone could ignore the dying request of a soldier who they served with in wartime. It's obvious from his condition that Mr. Irving has made some mistakes, but he wishes to atone for his sins. I beg you to reconsider his request out of loyalty and charity.

Respectfully,
Maureen Flynn

Holy double shit. He had to get this letter to Trey.

After dumping the offending lenses and adding a liberal quantity of Visine in the bathroom, he crossed the hall and flicked on the light. Scott sat up, an expectant look on his face. Daniel held back a wince. Scott didn't think Daniel had come running up to ask him to change his mind, did he?

"I forgot to change my contacts and now I need my glasses." He pulled the case out of his briefcase.

"Oh. What's the rush, then?"

There was no point in lying, since the rest of the family would know when he went back downstairs. "I need to head over to the police station."

"Damn. I told you to fuck him but that was fast." Despite the words, there was hurt in Scott's voice.

"As you're so fond of pointing out to me, for once, this isn't about you."

"No, it's about you. Like always."

"I found something. And—I can't explain it all now. Ask Rob about Trey's parents if you really need to know." Daniel stopped at the door and turned back. Scott blinked like he was still trying to adjust to the light, and again Daniel wanted to offer him something, even if the longer they kept trying the more it was going to hurt. "I'll be back by dinner. Get some sleep."

"I don't want to insult your mother's hospitality, but I don't think I'll still be here for that."

Daniel pushed his glasses up, though there hadn't been time for them to slide down his nose. Like everything else about coming home, the old habit was easy to pick up. "Scott, I'm sorry. About all of this."

Scott sighed. "I know, you civilized bastard. So you want to turn out the lights or do you want to have me driving home with no sleep?"

Daniel flicked the switch and shut the door.

"What the hell dragged your ass in here?" Detective Sergeant Jankowski greeted Trey when he came into the station.

"It's the Gardners again." Trey nodded at the still-black-clad, still-nameless intruder being led through booking.

"Lucky you." Jankowski leaned back against the wall.

Lucky me is right. Trey wished anybody but Jankowski was on tonight. Everybody loved overtime, but not for the graveyard shift on Christmas. Jankowski had seniority, but he didn't have family so it figured he'd volunteer for the bonus. Jankowski wasn't an asshole, but he'd been Trey's dad's partner. He hadn't wanted to testify against Trey's dad, but the D.A. had dragged him to the stand anyway, manipulated Jankowski's testimony to make it sound like Ron Eriksson was unstable, secretive and obsessed. Jankowski had come to Trey to apologize to him after the trial, but Trey hadn't wanted to hear it. Now Trey understood how the system worked, knew Jankowski hadn't wanted to make Trey's dad look nuts, but at the time it had felt like the last betrayal. But Julia Gardner had taken him in, even when his mom's sister wouldn't.

"I can take over if you want. Judge won't be in for hours." Jankowski pushed away from the wall. "You got plenty of time. No need to be here on Christmas." Like Jankowski didn't know Trey had less than no family to spend the holiday with.

"I know. But I want to talk to the guy now."

Jankowski shrugged and waved at one of the interrogation rooms. "This guy's a pro. Not gonna get anything out of him."

"Probably not. But I'm gonna try."

"Your case, kid." Jankowski popped a handful of sunflower seeds and chewed. He was putting in his second twenty, six years to go, with no ambitions beyond Sergeant. He actually seemed to like the job. Without that twisted memory between them, Trey would have looked up to him. Now he just tried to avoid him.

"Let me know when the prints cough up a name."

"You got it."

The suspect settled in, as relaxed as he could be, cuffed to the loop welded on the table.

"You want to give us a name other than Santa Claus?"

"It's more fun if you guess."

"You know we're going to nail you on those prints and then—"

"Is this where you say if I cooperate you'll try to help me out?"

"If you know the drill, why don't you just save us all some time and you can be comfy in your cell in no time."

"Maybe I'm comfy here."

Trey was beginning to see why Danny had almost plugged the smug prick. "Why did you break into that house?"

"I didn't break in. I was lost."

"With your lock picks?"

"Lost my keys." A one-shouldered shrug.

Trey tried the question again. "Why did you break into that house?"

"I was looking for my dog."

"What's his name?"

"Scruffy."

And again.

"I thought it was a twenty-four-hour Walmart."

After a knock at the door, Jankowski stuck his head in and jerked it toward the hall, calling Trey out for a conference. "There's a fed here, says he needs to see you. Your buddy in there is Derek Bartos, last known address in Camden."

Trey went out to find Danny at his desk, practically rolling up onto his tiptoes in excitement. What the fuck did he want? Trey had said he'd call him.

As Trey got closer he could see Danny's glasses. They made him look younger, almost the sweet, innocent geek he'd been in high school.

"Check this out." He slapped an envelope into Trey's chest like a process server as soon as he got close enough.

"What is it?"

"Read it. I found it in my father's desk."

Trey scanned it quickly. "So?"

"Look at the date."

"July 2, 1993." The words echoed around in Trey's head. "A week before my mom was killed."

Danny nodded. "I know. So when do we call her? I already checked out Howie. He died July 15 that year. Do you think he's in that picture we found?"

"Whoa, Danny. We don't know that any of this—"

"C'mon, Trey, when's the last time you had a lead like this?" Danny leaned in, moss green eyes bright under the glass lenses. Trey would have sworn at that moment Danny wanted a pat on the head and a "good dog."

Trey's neck itched, feeling Jankowski's stare. "Thanks for this information, Agent. We'll take a look at it and I promise I'll let you know what we turn up."

Danny's face looked like a kid's who's just been told he's not tall enough for this ride. Then his eyes flickered around the room and his jaw tightened as he nodded. "I appreciate your cooperation, Detective."

Trey watched him go. As Bartos was rebooked under his own name, Trey thumbed a quick text to Danny: *581 Spring Garden St. 2 hrs.*

It still wasn't light yet when Danny pulled up to the curb in the black Navigator. Fucking car must have cost half of what Trey paid for his house, he thought as he went to let Danny in.

Each of Danny's hands held a cup of coffee from the one open convenience store in town, but that didn't slow him down. As soon as he crossed the threshold, he asked, "Do you have an address for her yet?"

Trey took one of the coffees and nodded. "But I am not bothering this woman on Christmas Day."

"So she is still alive? Awesome."

Trey wanted to shake his head. This wasn't Danny's case, not his fight, and what the hell kind of federal agent said "awesome"? He handed Danny the print out. Maureen Flynn had divorced and retaken her maiden name. No children. She lived near Altoona and was a medical receptionist.

"What about her father?"

"James Flynn is seventy-eight, still alive. I haven't gotten the VA records yet about his stay. I can't get clearance yet."

"I can get that." Danny grinned, the sight hitting Trey in his gut all over again. "Take me to your computer."

He led the way through the house to his basement office, the familiar dampness and burnt-coffee smell hitting him as they were halfway down the stairs.

"Holy shit." Danny sucked in a quick breath.

Trey hadn't thought about what the cellar might look like to someone else. No one but him had ever been down here. Corkboards covered almost an entire wall, full of clippings and pictures and notes, anything and everything he could find out about his father or mother.

"You realize this looks a little serial killerish, right?" Danny said over his shoulder.

He wasn't wrong.

"Yep. You nervous?" Trey asked.

"Terrified."

Danny walked up to the walls, closely scanning the yellowed newspapers, the faded photos. He stopped in front of the picture they'd found yesterday in the garage. Trey had slipped it into a plastic sleeve before tacking it up.

"Chronological arrangement?"

"Yeah."

Danny looked at the pictures, then a printout of the

testimony from the trial. "I'd like to look through this sometime. My parents wouldn't let me go."

Trey wished he hadn't gone either. It'd been torture to watch his father struggle to make sense of the accusations, to try to get his words in a coherent order to communicate with Trey or his lawyer. Trey had the transcripts, he'd read them—he just wished he didn't have the concrete memory to back them up. And who knew? Maybe his perception of it all was too fucked to get anything from it. Maybe a pair of fresh eyes— And there he was dragging Danny into it. Though he didn't seem to be complaining much.

"Sure. Take 'em. I've got other copies."

Danny went back to the picture of their dads' squad.

"So do you think it was something that happened during the war?"

"If it was, I haven't turned up shit." The sudden force behind his words startled even Trey, but Danny only smiled.

"We will."

Trey thought of Danny standing over that guy, gun leveled and intent in his eyes. An icy rage so different from everything he remembered about the sensitive teenaged Danny.

"So." When Danny spoke Trey realized he'd been staring. "Computer?"

Trey powered it up and typed in his password before relinquishing the chair to Danny.

"What do we want first? Howie's records or James Flynn's?"

"Howie's."

Danny clicked through a few screens, fingers zipping over the keys. "Here we go. The life history of Howie Irving."

Trey looked over Danny's shoulder. "Jesus, that's scary." As a cop, Trey had access to a lot of information through police databases with nothing more than a license, but what Danny could do with just a name...

"We're the government. We know everything."

"I guess so."

Howard LeRoy Irving had squeezed a diploma from Elizabethtown High School in Kentucky with a D minus average. And then managed a few part-time jobs until after a court appearance on a misdemeanor D&D he joined the Army in 1969.

"What's that?"

Danny exited the screen and another governmental firewall came up, demanding a password.

"Fuck. His service record is sealed. I can't access it through here."

"Could you at work?"

"Why? Planning a road trip to D.C.?" Danny's tone was light, like everything they were doing was just a holiday game.

"No."

"I don't know if I could get in there. Getting past that takes clearance I don't have. I could try to get it, but it might attract some attention."

"Can you get his VA records?" The first lead he'd had in years and it was sealed.

"Everything to do with his military service is blocked." Daniel clicked through another screen. "Wait. I've got a police record."

"I could have gotten that."

"We've got possession 1975, possession with intent to distribute 1982, possession 1990."

"How much time did he serve?"

"Wow. Who the hell was his lawyer? Only eight months on the intent to distribute. And that was for a couple of ounces of heroin." Danny spun the chair around and looked up. "So I think I can guess what the VA records would say. And maybe explain that part in the letter about Howie's mistakes in the past."

"He was a junkie." Trey's brain had jumped on a train of

61

thought that was leaving the rest of him at the station with a hollowed-out gut.

"Looks like."

"What would it take to get records sealed like this?"

Danny glanced back at the computer. "Friends in high places, I'd guess."

"So your bad Santa meant it about the big players?"

"You know what this means?"

Trey shook his head. He knew what Danny was about to say. And he couldn't. Because no matter how much he'd wanted this, been waiting half his life for an answer, he couldn't believe it.

Danny grinned. "Your dad was innocent. He didn't kill your mom."

Chapter Five

"Sealed records and a break-in. That's what you're calling proof?" Trey wished he had Danny's confidence, but nothing justified that leap of logic.

"Two break-ins." Danny held up his fingers.

"Proof of what?"

"It's what you've been looking for. And all we have to do now is talk to Maureen Flynn and confirm it. Then—"

"Confirm what? That my dad ended up on the bad end of a heroin deal?"

"Is that really what you think?"

Trey didn't know. After all these years of wild supposition, clinging to the idea he and Danny had hatched long ago about a conspiracy worthy of a John Grisham novel, the cop in him said it was drugs. So his dad hadn't killed his mom. He hadn't pulled the trigger, but he might as well have, involving himself in that shit.

"I don't," Danny said with all the conviction Trey couldn't find. "Your father didn't get those records sealed. It's something big, just like we thought. And I'm betting it has something to do with the war." Jumping to his feet, Danny pulled the Polaroid off the wall and flipped it over, still inside its plastic. "There. You think that's Howie?" He pointed at a faded squiggle of ink. It could be Howie. Or Harry. Or Hank, for that matter. Only the *H* was still clear.

Danny counted off the names across the bottom with a

finger and flipped the picture again. "Him?"

An indistinct blob of a face under curly hair growing out of the military buzz cut. All Trey could tell was the guy was white and wore a goatee.

"We should take this when we go to see Maureen Flynn tomorrow. We could see if she recognizes him."

"Tomorrow?"

"Altoona's only three hours away."

"Four. Exactly how fast do you drive, Agent Gardner?"

Danny cocked his head in a half-smile. "All right, three and a half. But we could still do it in a day."

Trey felt the pull deep in his gut, like Danny's excitement was some kind of gravitational well. He stuck his hands into the front pockets of his jeans, as if that would help ground him. "Stop. Just stop."

"What?"

"Danny, this isn't a game."

"I never said it was. I thought you wanted answers."

He did. But he didn't want ones that ended with his dad dealing heroin. And right now that looked like the best answer. "I do. What the fuck do you think I did all this for?" He jerked his head at the corkboarded walls.

He could see the excitement leave Danny's face, like someone had unplugged the lights. His shoulders drooped.

"I get it," Danny said.

"What do you get?" Trey couldn't look at him anymore, couldn't stand the dose of guilt Danny'd always been so good at dishing out. Stepping over to the desk, Trey clicked out of the sites Danny still had open.

"You just don't want me helping you."

"Maybe I'm trying to figure out why this is suddenly so interesting to you. You haven't spoken to me in fifteen years. So why now?"

"You know why."

There was none of the playfulness in Danny's voice now. Just a familiar need. Familiar from the wakefulness on those dark nights when he'd sneaked into Danny's room. Familiar because it was the same earnest voice that had welcomed him under the blankets. Familiar in the way Danny was waiting for him to make the first move before he'd kiss Trey back like it was his only hold on life. But they weren't seventeen anymore.

Trey looked up. And that was a huge mistake. Because Danny was close, so close Trey would know how hard the muscles were under the soft black sweater if he took one more step.

"Ah, fuck it." Trey reached out and grabbed Danny's head, pulling him into a kiss.

Hard, like it had been then, when neither of them had known what they were doing, a quick thrust of tongues, Danny's teeth dragging over Trey's bottom lip, pulling his mouth open.

And then it was nothing like back then, because they did know what they were doing now. Knew the right pressure, the way to ask and get what they needed.

Danny gripped Trey's shoulders and shoved him back into the wall, long lean frame pressing against him, grinding hard.

They shouldn't. Trey shouldn't. But Danny had always pulled Trey in like iron to true north. That pull wouldn't let up until the fucking world stopped spinning. Saying no to Danny was about as easy as saying no to oxygen. Mouth opening wider, Danny ground his hips in harder, the rough urgency as familiar as the strength of the body pinning him was new.

Trey tilted his hips, the growl in his throat trapped by the force of Danny's tongue licking deep into his mouth. Damn, Trey needed skin. One hand on Danny's spine to keep him close, Trey slid his other hand between them, working first on his fly and then on Danny's. His hips eased back enough to let Trey shove their jeans down, then Danny's hot dick slapped right into Trey's hand.

Trey grinned at Danny's gasp. "You always walk around so ready, Danny?"

Danny tipped his head to look at Trey's face. "Busy chasing bad guys. No time for underwear." He lifted the elastic waistband over Trey's heavy cock and then circled Trey's wrist with his fingers.

Danny used his grip to move Trey's captured hand, a few quick strokes on Danny's dick, and then he pulled Trey's hand up, pinned it to the wall over their heads so their cocks rubbed together. Skin. Hot silky skin, and God, just a bit of slick.

And that's why he'd always known. Even as a teenager. Cock to cock with Danny, no way to pretend it was anything but another guy. No matter what else he tried, he couldn't forget how good it felt like this.

Now he knew a whole lot more than just a quick grind in the dark. And he wanted everything he couldn't let them have back then. Wanted it *now*.

Danny arched, making their cocks drag together. His sweater clung to the soft cotton of Trey's faded Henley shirt, dragging it up until their bellies touched. Trey jerked his hand free of Danny's grip and yanked the sweater up over Danny's head, running a hand down his pecs, thumb rubbing hard across a flat brown nipple until Danny groaned and jerked his hips, sweet friction on their dicks.

Danny shoved Trey's shirt up, pulling hard enough to rip the thin cotton when the buttons stuck on Trey's head. A button pinged off the metal desk and then their chests came together, the dusting of hair on Danny's scraping against Trey's nipples, muscles and skin hot in the chill of the basement.

Trey moved his hands down the tight muscles in Danny's back until he cupped the even tighter muscles of his ass, lifting him, sealing their bodies together. Danny's weight drove him back against the wall and everything was hot and rough and still damned close to perfect. Hard wet kisses as their dicks dragged against each other with enough friction to push Trey close to an embarrassingly quick orgasm.

He shifted his grip on Danny's ass until he could slide a finger along the crease. Danny groaned and pressed impossibly closer, like he could somehow fit them inside each other with force alone. Trey rubbed his dry finger around Danny's hole, pushing just enough to dip the tip inside.

Danny dropped his head onto Trey's shoulder, panting, hips pumping, a shock of heat flooding between them. Danny's come dripping hot on Trey's dick sent him over, fingers tightening on Danny's ass while long spasms jerked the heat from his own body, adding to the come smeared between their bodies.

Trey let his head fall back against the corkboard with a deep thud, but it didn't seem to restore his common sense. He still wanted to take Danny upstairs, into his bed, where they could try some of those things they'd missed out on fifteen years ago. When Trey had been too scared, scared of himself and scared of Danny to let it go that far. Trey had plenty of time off in the bank. He'd take a few days leave and they'd live on pizza and sex until the lube ran out.

And he didn't care if Danny had a boyfriend waiting, that in a few weeks Danny would be back in D.C. and Trey would still be here with his Post-Its and pictures and printouts. He just wanted. He hadn't let himself want anything in so long he could actually feel it, like some animal rolling around in his guts, clawing a hole Trey had to find a way to fill before he bled to death.

He forced a memory of his father into his mind. "Promise." It was one of the last coherent things his father had said to him, before the mini-strokes had eaten away the rest of his language skills. Trey didn't have any business taking a week off to fuck his brains out. And then there was the realization of how much smaller his life would be when Danny left it again.

"So you were saying?" Trey licked his swollen lips.

"That's it?" Daniel stepped away, pulling his jeans back up

over his ass.

"Well, that's it for at least fifteen minutes." Hitching up his jeans, Trey reached for his torn shirt to rub at the come turning sticky on his belly.

Daniel picked up his cashmere sweater. "You really haven't changed at all."

"You have. You're a much better kisser." Trey threw the shirt at him.

"Fuck you."

"I'm sure you've picked up some experience at that too."

"Why the hell are you acting like this?" Danny looked up from wiping his stomach.

"Acting like what?"

"An asshole."

"Danny, we don't know a thing about each other except that we used to like to get each other off fifteen years ago. Maybe I am an asshole."

"We could fix that."

"Mc being an asshole?"

"Not knowing each other. I only want to help."

"And get off."

"That just happened."

"Is that what you're going to tell your boyfriend?"

"He's gone." Danny flashed a quick smile, hiding its lack of conviction under his sweater as he pulled it over his head.

Trey didn't want the little spark of *good* at Danny's words. Didn't care. Except. "What happened?"

"He dumped my ass and went home."

Trey wanted to know why. Danny would tell him if he asked, he knew that, but what if Trey liked the answer? What if he liked it enough to start thinking pizza and sex could be back on the schedule?

"Merry fucking Christmas," Trey said.

"Yeah. I guess. Whatever." Danny didn't seem too upset, and Trey liked that even more than hearing about the breakup in the first place. "So are we going to do this?"

For a second, Trey thought Danny was talking about the headboard-slamming sex running on a loop in his brain, and then realized he meant the case.

Trey cleared his throat. "I'll call Maureen Flynn tomorrow. If you still want to—"

"I want to."

"Just don't get all—like you get. It's probably nothing."

"I don't know if you've noticed, but I don't really get like that anymore."

Trey thought of Danny bouncing with excitement in the police station, his immediate insistence on some ancient letter being the key to everything. The hell he didn't get like that anymore.

The next morning Daniel got his mother packed off in the van with Rob and the kids. Shannon pulled out behind them to drive Mother's Audi down to Harrisburg. Of course, his mother had reminded him to call if he had any news about the break-ins at least a dozen times. Before he shut the minivan door, she told him she was sure the local police would have no difficulty handling things, a not-so-subtle suggestion to not go chasing burglars himself.

Daniel was just glad he could finally take a deep breath. The sight of the cars backing out of the driveway seemed to take fifty pounds off his shoulders. There was nothing he had to do until the house inspection scheduled for the third of January. Enjoying a second cup of coffee, he opened his laptop and stared at the expanse of white space on his Outlook calendar. He couldn't ever remember having ten days free before. Even back when the family took vacations, there was always something scheduled, usually on the hour. He wasn't answerable to a single soul for the first time in his life. He'd gone from school to the bureau to the department, trying to please teachers or supervisors or in the case of the last year, a boyfriend.

He let himself waste time clicking around online, landing on a message board argument about a movie he hadn't even planned to see, and then got bored when he started being able to predict the next level of name calling and irrational assertions. He looked up and realized he'd wasted ninety minutes, and felt a jolt of panic until he remembered the blank space on the calendar.

The landline rang, and he tried not to think of how pathetically happy he was to be ready to talk to anyone less than two hours into the vacation he'd thought he needed. He answered without even caring who was calling.

"Hi, dear. I wanted to remind you that the inspector will be there at one on the third."

"I remember, Mother."

"I'm sure you do, but I wanted to tell you if you need anyone to do repairs, there's a list of people we use in the drawer next to the kitchen phone. I wasn't sure you would find it."

Because of course, he couldn't look in a phone book, or heaven forbid, use a tool to conduct a repair on his own.

"I'll—"

"Maybe you should just look, to make sure it's still there."

He took the necessary two steps and opened the drawer as noisily as possible. Without even looking down he said, "Yes, it's here."

"Well, that's good. If you run into any problems—"

"I'll call."

"Thank you so much for taking care of this, dear."

As much as you'll let me. "You're welcome, Mother."

He'd just put the phone back in the charger when his cell chimed on the counter next to his laptop.

"Hey. So Maureen Flynn would be happy to meet with us tomorrow."

Tomorrow. Daniel thought of all those blocks of white.

Trey misunderstood his silence. "Unless you don't want to come with me."

"I do. What time?"

"She said after church, so I'm guessing one would be safe. I'll pick you up at nine."

"All right." He'd only have to fill nineteen more blocks of white space. "You get anything out of that guy that broke in?"

"Derek Bartos? Nothing. He's got a couple of priors. Small stuff. Never more than a month or two in county. Last address was Camden. Did you run him through the federal databases?"

"I didn't have a name yesterday." *Probably because of that whole thing where we were half-naked against the wall. Things kind of slipped my mind.* But of course they weren't talking about it. Some things would probably never change.

There was a sound like a quick breath, and Daniel swore he could hear Trey running a hand up from the back of his neck like he did when he was nervous or embarrassed or about to spring a big lie. Finally, Trey said, "Yeah. We got Derek Allen Bartos, 1791 State Street, Camden."

"I'll see if anything comes up."

"See you tomorrow."

Daniel flipped his phone closed, but he didn't start accessing the databases. Because he was still seeing Trey running his hand up through his hair from the back of his neck. It had always made the longer pieces in front fall in his face, like that would be enough to hide what was really going on behind those silver blue eyes.

He'd done it a lot that night he'd asked Daniel to meet him

at eleven thirty in Bushkill Park, behind the roller-skating rink. The park wasn't open for the summer yet, but jumping the fence wasn't hard. Everybody did it. It was the three-mile bike ride that had made Daniel hesitate. But Trey had kissed him the week before. Kissed him and then pushed him away like Daniel was the one who'd jumped him.

In early April with the ground almost liquid from the spring melt and rain and his hands freezing from the long winding ride along the creek, Daniel leaned against a tree behind the corrugated metal walls of the skating rink. Staring at the ground thick with cigarette butts and beer caps, he wondered if Trey had changed his mind, or never planned to meet him there. Then he thought about how much shit he'd catch if his parents found out he was riding his bike down here at midnight on a school night.

The first sound of the fence jingling made Daniel's heart kick hard against his ribs. And then it clanked and shook as Trey dropped over the side.

"Sorry. Took longer than I thought."

Daniel just nodded and blew on his hands.

Trey ran his hand up from the back of his neck. "Danny."

Daniel stuffed his hands in the pockets of his sweatshirt, shoulders hunched. He could barely see Trey's face. The light from the road out front didn't really do much back here. Everything was shadows and guesses.

"Thanks for meeting me."

"It's all right." It wasn't. It was miles back—uphill, getting colder, and he had no idea if Rob would rat him out because he knew Rob had seen him getting his bike out. Of course, Rob got to take the car whenever he wanted. Daniel had hit the mailbox the first week he'd had his license and his father had said he could take the car out alone when hell froze over.

"I just—" Trey got closer, close enough for the smoke his breath was making to puff against Daniel's cheeks. "Last week. I—I shouldn't have shoved you. But I—I don't know, all right?"

"I do." Daniel didn't know he was going to say that until the words got out of his mouth. He wondered if he looked as surprised as he felt. "I know. I'm sure."

"How do you know?" Trey dragged his hand up even more forcefully. The long strands stuck way out, catching the little bit of light before they flopped back down.

"I just do." It wasn't something he'd decided, it just was. And there didn't seem to be anything he could do to change it.

"Well, I don't want to. I don't want to know. And I don't want to feel like this."

Daniel shrugged, hands still deep in his pockets. "So don't." He'd come all this way in a cold wind that had him wiping his nose on his sleeve so much he almost ran off the road so Trey could tell him he didn't want to be gay.

"Whatever." He started back toward the part of the fence where he'd left his bike.

Trey grabbed his arms, yanking him back and then pushing until Daniel's back slammed into the rough bark of the maple tree.

"I can't." But he was leaning in, and Daniel's stomach was in free fall, and it kept on falling because Trey moved his hands from Daniel's shoulders to his head and held him while he kissed him, not soft and tentative like last week, but hard, wet and messy.

Daniel could taste the cinnamon gum Trey always chewed, smell the cigarettes his dad smoked on his clothes. The kissing went on for awhile, and finally Daniel figured out what to do with his own tongue, and he was so distracted by that he wasn't exactly sure how he ended up with a hand on his dick that wasn't his. It felt so amazing it only seemed right to return the favor.

Trey stopped the kiss long enough to pant "Danny" in his ear, which was somehow wired to his dick because that's when Daniel came. He kept stroking Trey though, wishing he had enough nerve to move enough to see what he was doing, see his hand on Trey Eriksson's dick, or maybe even kneel on the muddy ground and put his mouth on him.

The dick in his hand twitched, the skin tightening, and Daniel worked his hand faster, daring to tip his head and lick the broad jaw, kiss and suck and finally bite the soft skin right beneath Trey's ear. Trey jerked before grabbing Daniel's shoulders again and groaning as his dick spat come over Daniel's fingers.

He wanted to taste it, see if it tasted like his own, mostly to taste Trey, but didn't want to gross him out. They just stood there for a minute, heads on each other's shoulders, their breaths fogging Daniel's glasses.

Trey lifted his head and pulled his hand back, wiping it on the seat of his jeans. "I should go."

"Me too." Danny wiped his own hand off on his jeans.

Trey reached up and pushed his thumb against Daniel's lips. He could smell himself, and after a minute he licked Trey's thumb, tasting the bitter salt on the damp skin.

"Jesus. I still don't know, Danny. But—fuck." He moved his thumb and kissed him again. "You—it feels good."

Daniel wanted to think of a reason for them to keep standing there especially if it would keep Trey saying his name like that, at least a million more times, but Trey was already stepping back.

"See you tomorrow, Danny."

Pumping his bike all the way back up College Hill didn't seem so bad that night.

But then Trey didn't see him the next day. Or if he did, he ignored him. He was always looking the other way, talking to somebody when they passed in the hall. In U.S. History, even alphabetical order didn't help, since Trey was at the back of the first row and Daniel at the top of the second. After two days, Daniel waited by Trey's locker as soon as the last bell rang.

He should have known from the way Trey started rubbing his neck.

"I don't think we should hang out anymore."

"Is that what it was? Hanging out?"

Trey looked around, like anyone could hear them in the Friday-before-spring-break crowd. "Keep your voice down. Jesus. I can't."

Daniel was past being cool, past being something Trey could use to try to figure himself out. "Yeah, I remember that's what you said just before—"

Trey slammed his locker shut loud enough to make everyone stop and look. When nothing else exciting happened, traffic started again.

"Well, I'm not going to again." It was a furious whisper. For someone who didn't want people staring, Trey was making a pretty good scene.

"Yeah. Go ahead and keep telling yourself that. I'm sure it'll work." Daniel walked away. And they didn't talk again until two months later. When Trey moved in after his mom was killed.

Chapter Six

Trey was early, but Danny must have remembered that about him, because he came out of the garage as soon as Trey put the Charger in park in the driveway. He could see grey slacks and a dark green sweater under the long black wool coat Danny had open despite the low-teens wind chill. He had a bag slung over his shoulder and a silver thermos in his leather-gloved hand.

Instead of getting into the car, he came over to the driver's window. Trey slid the window down halfway. "You want to take my car?" Danny jerked his chin back at the Navigator waiting behind him.

"This is fine. I just filled it up."

Danny stared inside, probably comparing all the luxury add-ons, like heated seats and heated cupholders and whatever the hell else they came up with to justify charging fifty grand for a passenger car. "But there's more room in mine."

Yeah, but it wasn't like they were traveling with a hockey team. "There's only two of us."

"I'll even let you drive." With that patronizing tone in Danny's voice he was lucky Trey had been cold enough to only roll the window down partway or he'd have smacked him.

He kept his voice even. "It's police business. Police car."

"Is that what you're calling it?"

"Relevant to your break-in. And I'm sure there's no one in Altoona to impress with your big expensive car."

"You think that's why I have that car?"

Why the fuck else? Danny had always sworn he was going to leave their "shit town and get rich."

You've always been rich, Danny.

My parents are. This is going to be for me.

Trey let himself smile a little. "Well, after yesterday, I'm pretty sure you're not compensating for any...shortcomings."

Danny didn't return the smile, but came around to the passenger side. He seemed confused about the shield between the front and back seats, but swung his bag into the back and shut the door before climbing in himself.

"What did you bring?"

"My computer."

"Why? Planning on playing solitaire?"

"In case we need it." Danny buckled himself in.

"Can't go anywhere without it?"

"Is this what we're going to do for seven hours? Snipe at each other like an old married couple?"

Trey stared straight ahead, wishing there was something more distracting than the sight of the Gardners' driveway through the windshield. "I'm used to working this alone."

It was true. Except for Danny, he'd never talked about his parents with anybody. When he was in the service, it was so good to finally not be that poor Eriksson kid that he'd never said anything about his family. If he hadn't promised his dad, he'd never have come back, never have tried to retrace his father's footsteps all the way to the end. And now. What if he was there and the end was only a stupid mess with drugs?

He put the car in reverse, but didn't take his foot off the brake. "It's supposed to snow."

"Your father wasn't dealing heroin. You'd have known. And you would have found something before now."

He turned his head to back down the driveway. "That mind-reading trick probably comes in handy at work." They swung out on to Paxinosa Avenue and he put it in drive.

"It doesn't work all the time. Or on everybody."

As Trey looked left to turn on Cattell Street, Daniel's eyes seemed greener than Trey remembered. Like a picture Trey had of the Gulf of Mexico off Florida. The one he kept hidden behind a picture of his parents. Because sometimes he thought about just chucking it all, disappearing somewhere and running a fishing boat. He could learn how to fish. How hard could it be? When Danny cocked his head in question, he realized he'd been staring. He shook his head and turned down Cattell toward Third.

He wished Danny were wearing his glasses. Maybe that Gulf-of-Mexico color was from contacts.

When Trey started on 22 going east instead of west, he waited for Danny to question his route, but he only held up the thermos. "Want some?"

"What is it?"

"Coffee."

"Just coffee?"

"Even we big-city fags can occasionally leave the house without our lattes. Yes, just coffee. Black. No sugar." There wasn't any anger in Danny's voice, it was almost the patronizing tone he'd used when he'd offered to let Trey drive.

"I've got some." He pointed at the cup he'd gotten at the convenience store before picking Danny up. "Doesn't that bother you?"

"What? Being called a fag? What do you call it? Tell me they don't use that word at the cop shop in good old Easton."

Yeah, so lots of the guys used that word. And a lot of other ones besides, for pretty much every minority in the country, even when that minority worked a desk in the same room.

"I don't use it."

"Use it for what?"

Jesus, didn't Danny know? Did he have to say it? "Me."

"So you go around saying what, 'I'm gay'?"

"I don't say anything. I fuck guys when I want, and since the bar on Thirteenth closed, I usually go down to Philly if I want to get laid, but if you're asking, yeah. I'm gay. I don't fuck women anymore. Tell me you go around wearing some kind of *I'm Gay Ask Me How* button at the Department of Homeland Security."

Danny made a choked laugh and washed it down with some coffee. At least he wasn't going to try to lie and say federal law enforcement was some kind of enchanted land of tolerance for diversity.

"When?"

Trey considered playing dumb and asking Danny what he meant, but that would only buy him a minute. Danny had him trapped in the car for the next seven hours and they were apparently having this conversation now.

"I stopped fucking women after I got out of the service. It wasn't like I didn't know. It was just easier then."

Danny drank his coffee in silence.

"Fine. I was a shit to you junior year. But you already knew that. Are we done catching up?"

"I didn't ask for an apology."

"So what do you want?"

Trey didn't look over, since they were flying around a semi on one of the mountain curves on 33, but he could feel Danny shift, body falling back against the seat, attention going to the scenery outside. "I don't want anything."

"Bullshit."

"All right. I want to know what happened back then. It wasn't my life—I know it wasn't—but didn't you ever wonder why the hell I decided to go to the best school for criminal justice in the country?"

"I thought you were going to be a lawyer."

"Lots of easier places to get into than John Jay. Cheaper

student loans to pay back too."

Trey dropped his speed under seventy and glanced over. Daniel met his gaze and Trey looked back at the road.

"I loved going over to your house. Even when you were a dick to me in middle school. Your mom was always nice to me. Things were different there," Danny said.

Trey never really talked to Danny about how much Bill and Julia drank. He remembered riding home in the car one night, his dad saying to his mom, "I'd hate to be the poor sucker who ends up on Bill's operating table tomorrow."

"So I want to help you catch the fucker who killed her, all right? Because it wasn't your dad."

Trey pushed the speed up to seventy-five again. "Thanks."

They were taking the ramp onto I-80 West before Danny asked, "So. How often do you get down to Philly?" There was a sly teasing in his voice Trey couldn't remember hearing before.

"Not enough."

"I'll bet. I went there once, to that bar on Thirteenth, when I was home one summer. It was a little creepy."

Trey thought of Danny's College Hill upbringing and pictured the old bar. "You just had to get to know it."

"When did it close?"

"Two thousand two or three. There's still a gay bar over in Bethlehem, a couple in Allentown. But the crowds are more mixed now."

"Hard to tell the breeders from the queers?" But Danny was laughing when he said it, and Trey felt the tension ease from his shoulders.

He set the cruise on eighty, holding the car steady against the wind. He thought of changing the subject, but he really wanted to know. "So what happened with that guy Scott?"

Danny drank a lot more coffee before he answered. Trey wondered if he was going to get an honest answer. Maybe Daniel wished he had something stronger than coffee. Did he drink like his parents?

"He wanted things to get more serious. I told him I'd think about it. He got tired of waiting."

Danny didn't seem like the fuck 'em and chuck 'em type.

"How serious?"

Trey heard a smile in Danny's voice. "Mortgage serious."

There was a lot more Trey wanted to know, and he cared too much about the answers to ask all of them, but he said, "How long were you together?"

"Two years."

Yeah. Trey probably didn't want to know that. Didn't want to know that if he did manage to get Danny in his bed, Trey wouldn't be much besides a rebound fuck before Danny went back to his life. Maybe even back to Scott. What did Trey want with Danny anyway, besides scratching an old itch? It's not like he was looking for anything mortgage serious himself.

He tried to think of something to say that would get things back to the comfortable way he'd felt when they were talking about the bars. The fact was, other than work, Trey didn't really talk to people.

But he didn't have to. Danny said, "You know, there's a case we studied about Altoona. The FBI and early terrorism. The Nazis used subs to drop off eight guys who'd lived in the U.S., just dropped them on a beach. One of their targets was the Horseshoe Curve outside of Altoona, the big railroad pass to Pittsburgh, they were going to blow it up and cut off the Northeast's steel supply."

"What happened?" Trey didn't care. He remembered enough of U.S. History to know nothing in Pennsylvania had been blown up in World War II, but Danny's interest made it worth hearing. He got into his story, and Trey let himself listen. He couldn't remember the last time someone told him a story he didn't have to pick apart for alibis, weigh each word for truth.

"One of the saboteurs got spooked and turned himself into the FBI. The FBI decided he was nuts and sent him away. The guy finally had to come back with about eighty grand of the money the Nazis had given them. Dumped it right on the agent's desk. They decided to listen then. Of course, federal bureaucracy has only gotten better at ignoring the obvious since."

"It isn't any better on the local level. Some guys would have to get shot in the ass before they'll bother to do more than file a report."

After that the conversation bounced everywhere. From work to how unrealistic movies about cops were to the stuff guys they worked with ate. By the time their exit came up, Trey almost missed it, talking about this stain on Mancini's desk that just seemed to grow bigger and bigger on its own. There was talk of an office pool on when it would cover the entire desk. Somehow they'd clocked over one hundred and fifty miles without touching their personal history.

His ears popped as they came over the mountains outside of State College, and Trey chomped hard on his gum. Even with the wind throwing gusts of snow at them, it beat knowing there were mountains waiting to fall down on top of them in the tunnels on the turnpike. Out of the corner of his eye he saw Danny working his jaw.

"I forgot what it was like out here."

A snowy gust vibrated through the car.

"When were you ever out here?"

"My dad wanted me to go to Penn State like he did. Dragged me out here junior year for a week. In February. That decided me on anywhere but here."

The mention of fathers seemed to drag tension back into the car, or maybe it was the way Trey needed to concentrate as they took a couple of mountain passes before getting back on an interstate.

Getting stuck behind a tractor-trailer on the state road before they could get on I-99 ate up their time cushion. Daniel had hoped they'd have time to check out the VA hospital before heading down to the Flynn house in Hollidaysburg. People were impressed enough with the actual federal badge that a personal visit might get him access to what hunting online couldn't.

It was one thirty and snowing harder when they finally hit Altoona and Trey took them straight on south, pulling up in front of the row house where Maureen lived with her father.

Trey had a cop's knock, solid even rhythm, even on a friendly call.

The door opened quickly, and Trey had his badge ready.

Maureen Flynn had black curly hair, betrayed by the smallest amount of silver at the roots. Her blue eyes were candid and friendly. She wore a white cable-knit sweater, a gold cross dangling from the collar.

She looked right at Trey. "You must be Detective Eriksson."

He did have that Nordic look, broad shoulders, blond hair, wintry eyes.

Her gaze was still welcoming when she looked at Daniel. "And?"

He held up his badge. "Agent Gardner, Department of Homeland Security."

Her eyes widened. "Goodness, I didn't realize it was that urgent. I'm so sorry to have kept you waiting."

They stepped back as she opened the storm door. Daniel did his best to shake off the snow from his coat and scrape slush off his shoes before following her through the small hallway. Trey's brown leather jacket didn't seem to have picked up any snow. He probably had some instant snow-melt, cold-repellant in his Viking genes.

Maureen had already moved into the living room, where an old man struggled up from his seat as they came in.

"Dad? Here's the policeman I told you who wanted to talk to us. And someone from Homeland Security."

Daniel handed his badge to James Flynn before he could

ask for it and Trey followed suit. Flynn studied the badges carefully and then studied them, eyes sharpest on Daniel. He felt out of uniform without a jacket and tie, and read the accusation in the old man's gaze.

"So what can we do for you gentlemen?"

Maureen went into the kitchen and came back with a coffee set, complete with saucers and creamer. The blue pattern on the china matched the wallpaper in the living room. As he tried to fit a finger through the small hook on the cup he was handed, he felt like he'd been compelled to play tea party with his nieces. Although Flynn kept staring at Daniel, he let Trey take the lead.

"Mr. Flynn, you were at the VA Hospital in Altoona in July of 1993?"

"Triple bypass. Want to see the scar?"

"That won't be necessary, sir." Trey's body language shifted, bearing military-straight. "Where did you serve?"

"Korea. Triple Nickel Artillery. But you fellas knew that."

"We did. I went into the infantry myself."

"Gulf War?" Flynn sat a little straighter.

Trey shook his head. "My stint was between the two of them. Did a rotation in Kuwait, though. Heat's brutal."

"Yeah but you got the dry heat." Flynn actually managed a smile.

Daniel had never really thought about Trey in the Army, just how angry Trey's stubbornness had made him. But if Trey had gone in later, he'd probably still be in Afghanistan or Iraq, if he hadn't gotten killed. The cup slipped on the sudden burst of sweat from his palms and he placed it back in its saucer.

Flynn was a lot friendlier now, leaning toward Trey as they spoke, initial suspicions disarmed.

"Well, we don't want to take up too much of your time, so let me explain what brought us out here. As I explained to your daughter on the phone, we needed to ask you some questions that might be able to help us in an investigation over in Easton. During the investigation of a current crime scene, we found some evidence that might be linked to an earlier crime."

Daniel could hear the absence of the word "unsolved" in Trey's speech. Of course, in the eyes of the legal system the crime was solved. Punishment levied and served.

Trey took the plastic bagged letter from his pocket and handed it to Maureen. She glanced down. "We found a note written by you, Ms. Flynn."

"Me?"

She rose and found a pair of glasses before returning to scan the old paper. "Yes. Yes. I remember that. Dr. Gardner."

She looked up at Daniel. He bounced the question to Trey with a light lift of his brows and read the answer on his face. They'd be better off with the truth.

"Yes, ma'am. Dr. Gardner is my father. Someone broke into my family home on Christmas Eve."

"To steal this note?" Her brow wrinkled.

"We don't know," Daniel said.

"Eriksson," she said suddenly, turning to Trey. "Your father. Howie Irving wanted to see your father too."

"Yes, ma'am. Dr. Gardner and my father and Mr. Irving served together in Vietnam. Did you write to my father as well?"

"No."

"Mind if I ask why?" Trey's voice was soft but strong.

He was good at this. Daniel hadn't worked an interrogation since he moved out of the Bureau.

"Mind if I ask what you want to know for?" Flynn broke in. "You didn't come all this way because of a break-in, even if it was in a federal agent's house. Sorry, Agent Gardner."

"You're right." Trey shifted again so he was at a perfect eye level with the shorter older man. "Back in '93, right after this letter was sent, someone broke into my house and shot my mother and father."

Trey's voice remained calm and strong, as though he were talking about any case, any mother and father instead of his own. Even Daniel couldn't find the hesitation he was so familiar with when Trey spoke about his mom.

After the expressions of shock and sympathy faded, Maureen spoke with the urgent air of someone who's just remembered something important. "Your father was a policeman too."

"Yes, ma'am."

"Dad wouldn't remember. He'd just come out of surgery, but Howie got a call. And it was all he could talk about. I think it was from your father."

The only tension Trey's body betrayed was the tightening of his fingers where he gripped his jeans. "What did he say?"

"Mr. Irving used a lot of colorful language, always, though he was apologetic. From what I recall and could parse out, he was certain now that he had the ear of the police, he could right some wrong."

Daniel saw that hit Trey, knew he was back to thinking his father was in something dirty up to his neck, but Trey was wrong.

Trey's eyes had gone flat. "What was wrong with Mr. Irving, ma'am?"

"His kidneys were failing. He refused dialysis. And of course, he was on heavy doses of methadone for the addiction."

"Did you see my father?"

"If he did visit, I'm afraid it was after Dad was discharged. And one of the nurses called to let us know that Mr. Irving passed away two days later."

Trey's full mouth pressed into a thin line. He wasn't thinking his father had killed Howie, was he? Daniel became convinced Trey was going to leave without another word.

To forestall him, Daniel said, "Do you think you might recognize Mr. Irving from a photograph, ma'am?"

"I could try." She put her glasses up on her nose again.

Trey sent a glare Daniel's way, but got the plastic-wrapped photo out.

She held it under the light, studied it closely, and then shook her head. "I'm sorry, Detective. It was long ago, and the faces are so blurred. Maybe Dad?"

Flynn passed the picture back to Trey without glancing at it. "I wouldn't know, honey. I was more out of it than Irving most of the time. Sorry, gentlemen."

Trey tucked the picture and the letter back inside his jacket and stood up.

Flynn pushed himself out of his own chair. "Since you're here, I figure they didn't catch whoever killed your parents."

Daniel wondered if the Altoona papers had covered the case, if a not-so-simple murder-suicide was enough to stick in the Flynns' heads for sixteen years.

"Someone served time for it," Trey said after a pause.

"Not the right someone?" Flynn asked.

"That's what we're trying to find out," Daniel said as he rose, because he wasn't sure how much more Trey could take.

Flynn shook Trey's hand and clapped his shoulder. "I'm sure your father would be proud of you keeping at it, son."

Daniel turned back to wave at Maureen Flynn as she saw them off through the storm door. "I think we should check out the VA."

"What for? Even if we had a picture of my dad, there's no chance some nurse is going to recognize someone she might have seen sixteen years ago visiting some junkie on his deathbed."

"No."

"No what?"

"Your dad didn't have anything to do with Howie's death."

"Like he didn't have anything to do with my mom's?"

Daniel didn't care that they were standing in front of the

Flynn house in Hollidaysburg. He grabbed Trey's arm before he could walk to the driver's side door and spun him so they were face-to-face.

"What is this? You've never doubted him before."

Trey shook him off and stepped out into the street. "Get in the car, Danny."

"What happened to make you—?"

Trey jerked open the driver's door. "Get in the fucking car or find your own way back."

He glared at Daniel across the black roof, eyes sharp and metallic hard. Daniel had seen friendlier looking bullets. Trey's hand was fisted where it rested on the roof, never moved to rub his neck. He wasn't bluffing.

Daniel was pissed enough to test the asshole, but he got in the car, mostly because his computer was still in there and he didn't trust Trey to toss it out to him before leaving him standing there in the snow.

"Can we talk about this now?"

"It's snowing harder." Trey pulled out into the street as if that explained everything.

"And?"

"I don't want to get stuck out here."

Daniel was pretty sure the rest of that sentence was an inaudible *with you.* "If we'd brought the Navigator, it wouldn't matter."

"You never could let anything go, could you?"

"Me?" Daniel should have let Trey take off with the fucking computer.

"You."

"I'm not the one who arranged his entire fucking life to do exactly what his father did."

"Didn't you just tell me you went into criminal justice because of what happened?"

"I did. But *I* didn't come back to Easton. I didn't keep

hitting my head against the same fucking wall for fifteen years with nothing but a scummy bar and trips to Philly to keep me warm."

"That's right."

"What's right?"

"You didn't come back."

"I told you I wasn't— Holy shit! Watch out for the plow!"

Trey didn't break and send them sliding, instead he tapped them into a swerve and dragged the wheel enough so they fishtailed around the plow that had just backed out to make another pass to clear an intersection.

When Daniel got his breath back, he glanced at Trey and nodded. Anything they managed to solve wouldn't matter if they got killed trying. He tightened his jaw and shut his mouth.

Chapter Seven

"Jesus fucking Christ."

Trey's words broke the tense silence they'd maintained since their close encounter with a Blair County snowplow. Daniel held his breath as Trey managed to get the car to shudder to a stop just before it tapped the bumper of the Highlander in front of them. The snow was thin, but coming down as fast as rain. There were already a good three inches on the ground and visibility was for shit.

The stretch of I-99 that had taken twenty minutes on the way down had taken more than an hour on the way back. With coffee intake consisting of a big mug at the house, the thermos in the car and a just-to-be-polite cup at the Flynns, Daniel really needed to piss. He could only imagine Trey had an iron bladder. Damn it. He should have gotten out when Trey fueled up on the way into Altoona, but it had been so fucking cold he'd stayed in the car.

Trey tapped the radio. After the recitation of his name and badge number, the state police dispatcher gave them info on a tractor-trailer overturned up at Port Martha. Just as Trey put a new route into the GPS, the state police dispatcher crackled in with "Interstate 80 is closed in both directions between exits 192 and 199 due to white-out conditions. We expect to issue a bulletin limiting non-emergency travel at eight p.m."

Trey turned off the radio before muttering, "Fucking hell." He swerved out from behind the Highlander, testing the limit of the barely plowed shoulder and the all-season radials, and reached for the GPS again.

Daniel felt the car slew, saw the guardrail flying toward him and turned the GPS back his way. "Let me do it."

"I got it."

Daniel could see the exit approaching, and Trey triggered his emergency lights before other cars could join them on the shoulder.

"Where are we going?"

"I'm getting off on that road." Trey pointed, both out the window and on the little screen. "Whatever the fuck it is, the one that goes south to 22."

Daniel looked at the skinny line on the GPS.

"Why don't we turn around and get on the turnpike? Maybe it's not as bad a hundred miles south."

"This is fine."

"A tiny mountain road in the middle of a blizzard?"

"It's not a blizzard. You've been living in the South too long."

"That's why the State Police are closing the roads."

"Okay. It's a storm."

"A blizzard."

Trey cut the flashers as they cleared the exit. The road wound up around a mountain as soon as they left the interstate behind. Daniel would almost have preferred it completely unplowed. Instead it was a blend of packed ruts, slush and enough clear patches to give false hope.

They skidded again on a switchback. Daniel held onto his bladder and the dashboard. "What the fuck are you trying to do?" he demanded.

"I'm trying to get us the fuck home."

Going back down the mountain was worse than climbing it. Daniel couldn't see any drop-offs, but there were lots and lots of thick trees to crash into once they left the road. Of course, sliding into a tree was better than getting drilled by a tractor-trailer if one lost control coming the other way.

"Wow. I didn't realize it was worth risking death to avoid spending any more time with me than necessary."

"Jesus, Danny. Could you pretend to grow up long enough for me to get us out of this mess?"

"And what's your grown-up reason for not taking the very well-maintained Pennsylvania Turnpike? A minute in a fucking tunnel?"

"You know why."

Daniel did. And he felt like a total shit. That was low—even as pissed and tense as he was, he knew what it had cost Trey to tell him about that. About the dreams.

A few months after his mom died, the second time Trey had snuck across the hall and into Daniel's bed, Trey had woken up from a nightmare, shoving off the covers, punching at Daniel, clawing at the air and gasping for breath.

The sweat-soaked sheets had been trashed anyway from them both coming twice before they fell asleep, so Daniel slipped into the hall and got fresh sheets from the linen closet, tossing the old ones down the laundry chute.

He half expected Trey to be gone when he got back, but Trey was standing by the window, shivering. He helped Daniel put the new sheets on.

"Did I punch you?"

Daniel's jaw was a little sore, but he'd live. "Nah."

"You know, they thought my dad was dead." Trey didn't look up from tucking in his side of the sheet. "And he was in a coma for a week. I know it's stupid but..."

He sat on the freshly covered mattress while Daniel gathered the comforter. It was November and his mom kept the house a chilly sixty-five at night. He wished he knew what to do. If he should touch him or stand in front of him or try to say something.

Trey kept talking, his voice a hypnotic drone despite the agonizing words. "I thought maybe Mom wasn't dead. Like it'd been a mistake, like with Dad, and sometimes I dream about her trying to get out. Trying to dig her way back out. And sometimes it's me. And the dirt..."

He wrapped his arms around himself. Daniel climbed in behind him and put a hand on his T-shirted shoulder, felt the damp chill from his sweat. Trey shook him off and stood up.

"C'mon. It's freezing."

Trey didn't leave, but he didn't sit down.

"I'll make a list of all the things that freak me out."

"It's not a naked-and-late-for-a-test thing, Danny." But he sat back down and let Daniel pull the comforter up over both of them. Trey shoved it to his hips, and then let Daniel put an arm around his shoulders, turn him in toward his side.

Daniel couldn't believe he'd made that crack about the tunnels. He looked at Trey who was glaring out at the snow like he could melt it with laser eyes.

"Sorry. I guess being called a selfish brat brings out the selfish brat in me."

The corner of Trey's mouth quirked in a half-smile. "I never said you were selfish."

No, that was Scott's complaint. Selfish and cold.

"Just immature." Daniel smiled. "We do seem to regress to sibling squabbles."

Trey shook his head. "I might have lived with your family, but we were never brothers, Danny." His voice dipped lower. "There's nothing brotherly about the way I think of you."

The dizzy rush in Daniel's gut had nothing to do with the fact that they'd crested another mountain. It was the same yo-yo feeling Trey always gave him. The way he pulled him in, let him think for a minute—or a night—that Daniel mattered, and then he'd push him away as if nothing had happened at all.

Trey had let up on the speed, but there was only so much

traction snow-caked tires could maintain. Trey turned the wheel around a curve and slowly but inexorably, the back end swung out, sending them sledding down the mountain, sideways-on. No violence—instead of a Tilt-a-Whirl, the spin was Ferris Wheel gentle—the snow cradling and cushioning them. The pine trees, however, looked a lot less friendly. The tires caught briefly as Trey tried to steer them out of the slide, but the best he could manage was to keep them on the road, even if the back end was intent on getting down the mountain first.

The road straightened, flattened and they bumped up against a bank that swung them back straight.

As soon as he got the car back in the right lane, Trey shot Daniel a quick look. "Okay?"

"Aside from almost peeing myself, I'm good. Can we surrender yet or do you need to try to kick Mother Nature's ass again?"

"No. I'm done. Next sign of civilization we're stopping."

The next sign of civilization was a few stoplights, a Sheetz convenience store and mercifully, a blue neon sign for Motel 22.

Daniel nodded as Trey flipped on the blinker.

The snow was deep enough in the parking lot to whisper against the car's undercarriage, the bumper breaking through like a ship's prow.

Daniel was popping open the door before Trey put the car in park next to a van in the parking lot, at least it looked like a white van. It could have been a Mini Cooper piled with snow. He wasn't going to give Trey a chance to change his mind and if he didn't get to a bathroom in the next five minutes, things were going to be embarrassing. "I'll get us a room."

Trey waved and Daniel turned to look at him, snow halfway to his knees, soaking into his slacks. "Unless you want two?"

Trey gave him that twisted smile again. "I think one's good."

Room 14 was on the second floor. With the rate of snowfall, a second-story door might be the only one that would open tomorrow. Motel 22 had no keycards, just old-fashioned metal keys hanging from big plastic room numbers. Daniel fumbled with the lock and then tore off to the bathroom, ignoring Trey's mocking laughter.

"Didn't your dad ever tell you to go before you left?"

"I left seven hours ago."

"Don't drink it if you can't hold it."

Daniel staggered out and flopped on the nearest bed.

Trey took his turn and then simply stood in the bathroom doorway, facing Daniel.

"So now what?"

Daniel's crunches paid off as he sat up so quickly it was a testament to his personal trainer. "What do you mean?"

"I don't know about you, but I'm starving."

"I passed starving a long time ago." Maybe that was the reason for his headache, instead of the stench of mold which seemed to come from every corner of the room—or from the whiplash he got trying to track Trey's moods.

"I'm going over to that convenience store. You want anything?"

"Anything. Everything. Tastykakes. And beer."

"You got it." Trey waved as he slammed out of the door.

Daniel hadn't planned far enough ahead to stuff anything useful in his computer bag, like a change of clothes, but he was cold and wet and there was at least a decent chance of a hot shower. He could just crawl into bed in his undershirt and briefs.

He cranked up the heater before going into the bathroom, and wished he'd thought to pack other things that could make an overnight stay more comfortable. Like lube and condoms. Trey might push him away when he tried to help, might be the moodiest bastard on the planet, but he wasn't hiding the fact that he wanted more than just a quick hump against a wall.

Daniel's hands remembered the feel of those arms under

his palms as Trey had lifted him. The warm glide of skin over hard muscles, the tiny shifts and jumps as Trey had gripped him tighter. Too fast, too rough in that moment to see, but he tried to imagine Trey's cock from the feel of it grinding against his own, hot and thick and heavy. Lips parting under the shower spray, Daniel could picture it sliding over his tongue, the weight, the taste.

As he soaped his stomach, his dick thickened, tightened. He reached down to cup his balls, sinking into arousal, the buzz sizzling along his nerves. One soap-slick stroke on his dick and then another, and his belly was already clenching, the rush making him grab blindly for the wall. Being in the car with Trey all day had him right up on the edge. It wouldn't take much. And if Daniel took the edge off now, maybe he could think around Trey so they could do something more than have everything go off fast and rough between them.

Giving his dick one last stroke, he tugged down his balls and reached for the shampoo. He was thirty-two, not seventeen. His dick might still be driving half the time, but he was old enough to at least have it take directions.

The motel had better cable than he got for an absurd amount of money in D.C., but no wireless internet. He contented himself with flipping through a hundred channels, half of them premium, until he found some historical drama he'd missed in the theaters.

Trey came back in with a cold wet blast of air and three full bags.

"Now *that* is a convenience store." He dumped the bags on the desk and started throwing things onto the bed where Daniel was wrapped in a blanket. A plastic-wrapped ham and cheese sandwich, a bag of chips and a package of Tastykake Butterscotch Krimpets landed on his chest with the accuracy Trey had always shown shooting free throws. "I'm not throwing the beer, so you're going to have to come get it yourself." He lifted a six-pack out of the bag. "I've got a bottle of water and some sodas too." Peeling off his leather coat, he stomped over to the heater. "Jesus, Danny, it's like a hundred and fifty degrees in here."

"So turn it down." Daniel looked down at the Krimpets and tried not to smile. Did Trey remember or was it nothing more than a good guess? "You can get these in Maryland but they're stale." He waved the package.

"I never saw anybody inhale those things like you. You could eat a box in three minutes."

"My one true talent."

"I doubt that." Trey popped the top off one of the beers, full lips curving in a smile.

Daniel concentrated on unwrapping his sandwich. Fuck if Trey didn't make him feel like that idiotic teenager, hopeful and desperate at the same time, the exact feeling he tried to avoid by spending as little time in Easton with his family. He could feel the moment Trey's attention shifted from him to the TV.

"What's this shit?"

"I think it's *Seraphim Falls*. Post Civil War revenge thing."

The word revenge seemed kind of loud.

"Well, that sounds thrilling." Trey's voice was dry. Hooking the desk chair with his ankle, he tugged the chair forward and sat down to eat his own sandwich. "Did you want turkey instead?" He offered a half to Daniel.

"Split." Daniel passed over half of his ham and cheese. Letting the blanket fall to his waist, Daniel sat on the edge of the bed, the bag of chips between them.

On the screen Pierce Brosnan dodged a bullet by rolling in the snow.

"He's lucky the guy has to keep reloading." Trey passed Daniel the beer and dug out a handful of chips.

They ate in a companionable silence, broken only by Trey's occasional comments about the movie.

"You don't go to the movies a lot, do you?" Daniel asked.

"Why?"

"Because you're not supposed to talk."

"No one complains in my living room."

Daniel couldn't stop a grin. "Remind me not to go to a movie theater with you."

"Why, you wanna date?"

Daniel took a swallow of beer before he realized Trey was teasing, not mocking.

"Depends on whether or not you expect me to put out." Daniel chased away the last of his sandwich with another swallow of beer.

Trey stood up and kicked the chair back. Digging in one of the bags he'd brought in, he came out with a small bottle of lube and a box of condoms. Tossing them onto Daniel's lap, Trey said, "Sheetz really does have everything for your convenience."

"You've got big expectations."

"Thanks for the compliment." Trey pulled off his shirt and unbuttoned his jeans.

Daniel tossed the lube and condoms backward onto the bed and shoved the blanket onto the floor. "I didn't eat dessert yet."

"You didn't used to play hard to get." Trey took the beer bottle from Daniel's hand.

"As I recall, being easy didn't get me far."

Trey picked up the remote and switched the TV over to a football game.

"I was watching that."

"It was distracting."

"And you get turned on hearing the announcers talk about defensive line penetration?"

Trey shoved down his jeans and pushed Daniel backward. It wasn't exactly a tackle, but it was close to offensive holding. "Watching your mouth turns me on. Wanting to see what you've got under that T-shirt turns me on. Thinking about putting my dick in you turns me on."

Daniel supposed this wasn't the time to bring up how he'd begged Trey to fuck him. Back when adolescent stupidity created Daniel's conviction that actual penetration would mean something.

Would make Trey want to come to New York. Instead his pleading had sent Trey sprinting for basic training.

"Who said you were putting your dick in me?" Daniel asked.

"I did."

Trey's weight settled over him, into him, muscle on muscle. With all the lights in the room on, Daniel could see every detail of the light irises of Trey's wide-open eyes. The dark silver edge, the bronze striations around the pupil, and the smoky blue in between. He could hypnotize people without even trying. No wonder he was good at interrogations. Trey didn't try to kiss him, didn't even rock his hips. "So? Are we doing this or what?"

"That's romantic."

"Your dick thinks so."

"Our dicks don't lie? Could be our song."

Trey looked at him in confusion.

"It's a pop song, 'Hips Don't Lie'? Never mind." Daniel reached up and yanked Trey's mouth down to his. Trey slid his hands down to get under Daniel's shirt, sending a groan vibrating into his mouth. The silky hair around Trey's lips tickled until Trey pushed their mouths wider. The yeasty taste of the beer melted into the taste of Trey's mouth, still heated with that hint of the cinnamon gum he always chewed.

Tightening the grip in Trey's hair, Daniel thrust his tongue deeper, grinding his hips up as his cock got desperate for friction. Fuck. He should have taken the edge off in the shower.

Trey didn't pull away, just eased back from the kiss, slowing Daniel's urgency with a soft response, until they were barely tasting each other's mouths, breaths quick and shallow.

When Trey lifted his head, his eyes were darker. "This time there's no rush."

He sat back, pulling Daniel's shirt over his head, leaving his arms tangled, pinning his hands in a tight grip of cotton. With a quick glance up at Daniel's face, Trey started licking and kissing all over Daniel's chest. A warm wet suck on his nipple made Daniel's breath catch, but the second Trey used his teeth, Daniel gasped and arched closer.

Trey looked up and smiled. "Oh really?"

He sucked tingling bites all over Daniel's pecs, back up to his shoulders, before scraping his nipples with teeth and beard and nails until Daniel was panting. When Trey put a line of dark red bites on Daniel's stomach, he groaned and started rubbing his cock along Trey's neck, getting just enough warm pressure through the cotton of his briefs to ease the ache.

Finally freeing his hands from the shirt, Daniel reached down to thread his fingers through the soft spikes of Trey's hair, trying to get his mouth to move lower. But Trey just nipped and licked his way back up, leaving a wet circle around Daniel's navel and a hard hot bite just under his left pec that turned cold when Trey raised his head, dragging shivers onto Daniel's skin.

He laid another lick on Daniel's neck on the way to his ear. "I'm gonna make you come so many times there won't be room in that busy head of yours for anything but how bad you want it. Need it."

"Need what?" Daniel ran his hands up along the hard lines of Trey's back, sliding back into his hair.

"My cock in you."

Trey kissed him, hard, but not rough or messy, just with the kind of thorough possession that made Daniel think maybe coming "so many times" was not going to be an exaggeration.

Trey rolled over onto his side. "Get naked." He pulled down his own bright blue boxer briefs.

"Squash my Butterscotch Krimpets and I will kick your

ass." Daniel threw his briefs in the direction of the chair where his pants were.

Trey rescued the package and lofted it onto the other bed. "Good idea. Gonna need the energy."

"A lot of talk, but not a lot of— Jesus Christ."

Trey's mouth closed over the head of Daniel's dick. He let himself think about that for a second. Trey Eriksson's mouth on him, a million adolescent jerk-off fantasies come true. And then reality got lots better. Trey took him in deep and then backed off to lick the head, hand stroking down.

Daniel hadn't been fully hard, but hadn't was now the operative word. As soon as Trey groaned around his mouthful of cock, Daniel's skin got so hot and tight he had to pin his hips flat to keep from fucking straight down Trey's throat.

Trey shifted his grip, hand pulling hard on the head while his mouth sucked hot wet kisses down the shaft, an alternating prickle and then glide from the hair of his beard. He licked the inside of Daniel's thighs, sucked on the sensitive line of his groin and then dipped to run a flat tongue all over his balls.

Daniel was trying to think of something clever to say that would get Trey's mouth back on his cock without coming out like a pathetic adolescent whine. All he managed was to tug on Trey's head, trying to guide him. Trey pushed Daniel's hand off and then wrapped warm lips tight around the head of his dick, sliding down until a hard tongue flicked steadily on the bundle of nerves right under the head.

Trey's hand slid up and down his shaft, moving where his mouth wasn't so that everything was hot and tight and oh-shit-I'm-going-to-explode good. His tongue flattened on the shaft and then he pulled up with that hint of teeth he'd already figured out made Daniel nuts, and Daniel reached out, trying to find something to hold onto, to slow his slide into orgasm, because he wanted Trey's mouth on his cock forever. Christ, Daniel had been waiting for this forever. He should be able to last longer than two minutes.

But then Daniel lifted his head and Trey looked up. And that was it.

The sight of him, cheeks hollowed, eyes dark as pewter, lips swollen around Daniel's cock. *Trey* groaning as his tongue worked Daniel deeper into a hot silky throat. Trey forced Daniel's hips flat against the mattress with both hands and swallowed him all the way in.

Daniel couldn't even gasp a warning.

His eyes snapped shut, head thrown back as the sparks rushed from his balls and out of his dick in a white-hot flood, pouring shock after shock of it into Trey's throat. Trey sucked him dry and licked him soft, right through the too-sensitive part where he only wanted to lie there and stare at the mold on the ceiling until he could remember how to breathe.

But Trey kept licking, rubbing his beard on the inside of Daniel's thighs, a silky scrape that should have tickled but there was too much sensation running through his nerves. And all those neural pathways were working on just one thing, getting his dick hard again. Trey's fingers lifted Daniel's balls with a feather-light touch while licking from the inside of his thigh all the way up to his hip where he left another dark bruising bite.

Jesus, Trey was relentless. Daniel wanted to tell him to stop, that there was no way he could go again so soon, but Trey's hand turned so he was still rolling Daniel's balls gently across knuckles while rubbing a thumb behind them, pressing on his perineum just hard enough to send little flashes of pleasure pulsing from inside. Daniel moved his legs farther apart.

Trey kissed his stomach again and laughed, reaching up to stroke Daniel's dick, which apparently had decided it was still seventeen and a thirty-year-old's standard refraction time could go fuck itself.

"You've got a beautiful cock, Danny." Trey pressed a kiss on the shaft and the head. "Sweet and so pretty getting hard for me. I can't wait to taste your ass."

Daniel's vocal cords sent up sound and his tongue did its best to turn it into some kind of words, but all he managed was an indistinct "Oh fuck" as Trey spread him wider and licked down the underside of Daniel's cock, following the ridge over his balls and under to flick hot and wet at his hole.

Trey held him open, gripping both cheeks and making his tongue pointed and then soft, and Daniel flushed hot and cold with shivers. His throat let out a sound he knew his brain didn't approve when Trey let his teeth scrape the sensitive skin. Rough and then soft, back and forth, Trey's beard dragging against the inside of the crack of Daniel's ass with every movement.

Daniel's belly softened, melted as the tension flooded into his dick and balls and ass. He arched down, trying to get Trey's tongue inside, finally got a little pressure from Trey's finger and then the point of his tongue. So hot and *oh fuck,* Daniel did need it.

"Please."

Trey lapped Daniel's balls and the root of his cock before looking up into his face. "Please what?"

Daniel's fingers dug deeper into the sheets. "Fuck me."

Trey didn't smile. He loomed over Daniel, fast enough to make Daniel's heart kick with a rush of adrenaline, but all he did was grab the lube and crawl back down between Daniel's legs.

Trey rimmed him again, a finger holding Daniel open for a harder stab of tongue, and Daniel stopped trying to edit what was coming out of his mouth.

"Christ. Just do it. Please."

Trey pressed up over him when he pushed two lubed fingers inside, tongue and teeth on a nipple. "God, Danny, you're so tight. How long's it been?"

Daniel couldn't quite remember. It wasn't that Scott didn't like to top him, he just came so fast when he did the arrangement fell out of their repertoire. "Long enough."

And with Trey looking down as he worked his fingers in and out, Daniel started to wish he was on his knees, so he could avoid that hypnotic stare. It hadn't been long for Trey, or he had a good enough memory because it took him two strokes to start rubbing Daniel's prostate, the deliberate kind of prodding that had precome slipping from his dick as his body started craving more. He hoped to hell Trey could back up everything his slow deliberation was promising because if he got in and shot off in a minute, Daniel might have to kill him.

He shut his eyes against that knowing stare and jerked them open to the whisper of his name. "Danny. You want it? You ready?" Trey pulled his fingers out.

Despite his name in there, Daniel couldn't help wondering if Trey was like this with all the guys he picked up to fuck. Did he whisper to them? Drag it out until they were out of their minds? Did he watch their faces so closely?

Or maybe Trey was treating Daniel like he was the virgin he'd been when he left home with those same smooth lines he'd used to coax cheerleaders out of their panties.

"Just fuck me." Without Trey's fingers scissoring inside, Daniel could get some force behind his words.

Trey rolled off him, wiping his hands on the sheets before he tore into the box of condoms. He didn't say anything else as he rolled the rubber over his cock, lubed his sheathed dick and pulled a pillow down under Daniel's hips.

Trey pushed inside, stopping when he'd just stretched Daniel wide, holding still so Daniel could feel the ridge under the head of Trey's cock. As Daniel let out a tight breath, Trey nudged his way in deeper. Now Daniel really wished he was on his knees, because he didn't want anything of what he felt showing on his face. Didn't want Trey to know that he was hanging suspended between ache and want, too much and not enough. Didn't want Trey to know how close Daniel was to forcing himself down onto Trey's cock, so he could stop the way

Trey was making him aware of the empty space inside.

He kept moving deeper with little thrusts until he was in all the way and Daniel wasn't empty anymore. The want was gone, leaving nothing but the ache of too full, too stretched, too sensitive to Trey's breath, his pulse.

"Oh God, that's good, Danny."

The words rolled from Trey up Daniel's spine. He pushed back, trying to make him fit. And then Trey shifted his hips from side to side, making his own room, making Daniel soften and open. Heat bubbled from his loosening belly through his ass, his balls, his cock, even his thighs as Trey kept shifting and pushing.

Daniel lifted his legs until his ankles were high up on Trey's back. "Yeah. It's good."

Trey held Daniel's hips and started thrusting, deep and hard and fast. The slap of their thighs together was louder than the pattern of collisions, whistles and commentary from the TV. As Trey's balls pounded against Daniel's ass, the bed shifted and began to thump against the wall.

Trey stopped for a second, reaching up to grab the headboard and then kept driving the breath out of Daniel, forcing out moans so loud he didn't think stopping the thudding headboard would do much good. Trey bent down for a hard kiss and that shifted his cock so he was rubbing perfectly, driving against Daniel's prostate with every stroke of his hips.

He reached out, hand slapping against Trey's chest, but it wasn't to push him away. He just needed something to hold onto. Trey let go of the headboard and gave Daniel his hands to grip, kissing him. Hips shifting to shorter thrusts that dragged Daniel deeper into the heat spilling from inside his ass, flooding his cock and balls. Maybe he'd be happier if Trey couldn't go for long because his body was riding that edge—with or without his consent. If Trey kept nailing his gland like that...and then he straightened again, urging Daniel's legs higher while Trey went back to trying to slam the headboard through to the next room.

The urgency faded just enough for Daniel to watch the flush on Trey's chest, to feel the blood burning down his own neck to turn his chest dark red. Trey groaned each time he bottomed out inside, Daniel's throat adding its own deep sound. He pried one of his hands free to drag it to his cock, desperate to hit the top and fall over. The build so intense it filled his head with white noise, until he knew Trey's name was the only sound he could make.

Trey kissed him again, dragging Daniel's head and shoulders up off the mattress with one arm, the other locked wrist to wrist with Daniel's. Trey's belly pressed Daniel's dick against his own, so his hand could only make tight quick jerks on the head, but with the pleasure pouring out in burning pulses from the movement of the cock in his ass it didn't matter how much friction there was on Daniel's dick because he was coming. Long bursts of it lacing his fingers, shooting up on his chest.

Trey groaned and—Christ—fucked harder, faster. As the last spurt ripped through Daniel's dick, Trey's head went back and he let out a long chokcd groan, hips jerking and then stilling as he pumped away.

Daniel felt Trey ease out, felt the sting of letting go from muscles no longer flying on endorphins. And then Trey was back, his weight and the drag of exhaustion landing on Daniel like snow sliding off the roof, and just like that he was asleep.

By the time Trey woke up enough to lift his head off Danny's shoulder, the football game had given way to a sitcom loud with canned laughter. Trey straightened up enough to slap a hand out for the remote and shut it off. Danny didn't stir.

Asleep, he looked younger, more like the earnest kid he'd been. The kid Trey had fallen for all those years ago, though he'd been a little too late figuring that out. Only what happened to his parents hurt as much as Danny leaving and never coming back.

Danny's lips moved in his sleep and Trey stopped himself from kissing him awake, from licking along the dark stubble on his jaw to his ear and whispering how much he wanted back in that tight ass. He wanted both, Danny's mouth to kiss and his ass clenching like a fist around Trey's cock, but right now Danny asleep was easier to handle than Danny awake.

Danny awake was full of questions, ideas, plans. He'd been back in Trey's life for three days and already had him dragged across the state for answers Trey was getting pretty sure he didn't want to find anymore. Danny awake was overwhelming.

Trey lowered his head back onto Danny's shoulder and Danny's hand rode lower on Trey's back. Their legs were tangled together, but the bigger tangle was in Trey's head. Just being with Danny had been enough of an uproar in Trey's life, fucking Danny had only made it all much more complicated.

Tangled up in Danny's legs, tangled up in everything Danny made him feel. Want, frustration, even a whole big dose of fear. It wasn't fear of doing something that would make him irrevocably gay, the way he'd been afraid at seventeen, but fear kicked up by knowing exactly how easy it would be to start wanting things Danny couldn't give him.

Why would Danny want to? He had the life he'd always wanted. And now that they'd finally scratched that itch what the hell else was left?

Trey lifted his head to check the alarm clock. Ten after ten. He wished he could get a weather report as easily, but for that he'd have to get up. Peeling himself free as slowly and carefully as he could, he managed to roll off the bed without Danny doing more than making an annoyed grunt and flopping on his side.

In the light from the motel sign, the snow still fell, slow lazy spirals instead of the sheets that had been falling when they left Altoona. Looking back to Danny curled up on his side, naked in the motel bed, Trey was still glad they hadn't driven the

Navigator. The car was an indistinct lump in the parking lot. They weren't going anywhere at least until the motel lot was plowed.

After he pissed and cleaned up in the bathroom, he started the tiny coffee machine on the desk. He'd bought another bag of chips and some beef jerky, but Danny's package of Tastykakes was looking really good. Given how much Danny had loved those things, he probably would kick Trey in the balls if he ate them before Danny woke up.

Trying to hold the two Dannys in his head gave him a really weird sensation, almost disorienting, like he was trying to see both images in an optical illusion. Two different Dannys except they were the same. The man superimposed on the boy. As Trey had said to Danny, they didn't really know much about each other except that they'd liked to get each other off fifteen years ago. After the last few hours, Trey could add to the information that they were better at it now. And he wouldn't mind doing it again.

The Weather Channel still showed heavy bands of snow when Trey dumped a couple of sugars in his coffee and sat on the other bed in his underwear. Danny finally pushed up from the bed and shivered.

"'S fucking cold."

Trey wasn't sure if that was an invitation to come warm him up again so he said, "So get under the blanket."

Danny reached down and yanked up the blanket they'd kicked onto the floor. "Better not have eaten my Krimpets."

Trey jerked his chin at the package on the nightstand. Danny grabbed it and tore it open. Whatever manners Julia had drilled into Danny's head apparently didn't extend to the consumption of Tastykakes. Trey's cock twitched as he watched Danny cram the first rectangular cake into his mouth whole. Oh yeah. That itch could use some more scratching.

"Still snowing?" Danny mumbled around cake and frosting.

"Yep." Trey waited for Danny to remind him they should

have taken the Navigator.

Danny got up and went over to the window, leaving Trey with a nice view of a tight, biteable ass before jumping back under the blanket.

"Want some coffee?" There might be about half a cup left in the carafe, but Trey could make more.

Danny shook his head and wrapped the blanket around himself like a robe before going through the second Krimpet in the package more slowly, savoring each bite. If he licked icing off his lips one more time, Trey was going to cross the space between them and drag a taste out of Danny's mouth. Danny finished and licked his fingers, ending with a long suck on his thumb, and Trey launched himself onto the bed.

Just as Danny's head hit the mattress, Trey saw the gleam in those eyes.

"You were doing that on purpose."

Danny shrugged, the corner of his mouth twitching in a half-smile.

Trey lowered his head to taste the sweet butterscotch on Danny's lips, licking it off his tongue and feeding him what he hoped was more coffee-flavored than sleep-stale mouth. Danny grabbed the back of Trey's head and wrapped an arm around his shoulders to roll him under.

Trey held Danny's face in his hands to slow the kiss, to make every stroke of their tongues count, so each suck and tug of lips or teeth made things deeper and darker. Danny's hips bucked and he lifted his head, licking under Trey's jaw, moving slowly to his ear.

"What are you after, Danny?"

"Maybe I was just cold." Danny licked and then kissed, dragging shivers onto Trey's skin.

"I think you want me to fuck you again."

"When do I get to fuck you?"

Trey felt Danny's smile against his skin. "When you really

want to."

Danny rolled away, grabbed the lube and tore another condom off the strip. Trey raised his eyebrows, but Danny pressed the bottle and the packet into Trey's hand before rolling belly down.

Trey tried not to smile in case Danny had eyes in the back of his head, but Jesus, Danny on his stomach was a hell of a view. He'd filled out since high school, yeah, but now those narrow hips made his shoulders look that much broader, accentuated the muscles along his spine and his ass. Damn. Trey'd often been drawn to a nice rounded ass, but Danny's was sheer muscle, still perfectly rounded, but tight enough to bounce a quarter off of. It'd look even better with the mark of Trey's teeth in it.

One hand trailing from Danny's shoulder to the curve of his ass, Trey whispered, "Like this?"

Danny arched into his hand. "Yeah."

Trey leaned in to nip the top of Danny's ear. "Like it on your knees?"

"You don't have to seduce me, Trey. I'm not a girl."

"I thought we cleared that up. I wouldn't be in bed with you if you were."

"So stop treating me like you have to ask permission. Like you're trying to charm me into bed. I'm already here."

Bastard could hold onto a grudge like he had Superglue hands.

Trey had been an asshole. Okay. He got that. He'd been confused and scared, but he never should have treated Danny like that. Using him, jerking him around. But Trey thought that last summer he'd made it pretty obvious what he wanted.

Now he knew why they'd never move past scratching an itch, never get to the point where things were okay between them. Because Danny couldn't let them be.

Frustration made him rougher than he'd normally be,

popping a lube-slick thumb into the tight ring of muscle, following right away with the other so he could rub them together and hold Danny open. Danny didn't seem to mind. Raising his hips off the mattress, he groaned and pushed back against the pressure.

After Trey rolled down the condom, he remembered the rattle of the headboard. Grabbing the comforter off the floor, he wedged it behind the fake wood bedstead.

He lifted Danny up on his knees. One hand on the small of Danny's back, Trey used his other hand to guide just the head of his cock in, leaving Danny panting.

"You want it? Come get it. Fuck yourself on my dick."

Danny started working back onto Trey, breath coming in tight grunts, almost as tight as the grip his ass had on Trey's cock. Muscles shifted and shook under Trey's hand as Danny rocked back and forth, sliding down more each time until he drove his hips back hard, a whispered hiss breaking from his lips.

Danny didn't stop there. He dragged himself forward and back, neck arching until Trey could see that pretty face, the taut muscles in his neck that needed biting. Yeah, Danny liked the hard edge of teeth on his skin, the sharp touch bringing deeper groans from his mouth. And Trey liked knowing he was the one to get Danny to make those sounds.

Trey draped himself over Danny, hooking an arm over his shoulder and across his chest to hold him steady against the thrust of Trey's cock in his ass. He licked the spot before setting his teeth to it, a small patch of skin that would sting under the sucking pressure. Danny's ass tightened on Trey's cock as he bit him, quick pulses that made Trey reach around his hips to see if Danny was coming, but his cock was hard and hot, silky with precome leaking steadily from the slit. He fisted Danny's cock, nuzzling sweat-damp hair out of the way for a bite right on the back of Danny's neck, earning a groan and another clench of Danny's muscles as Trey pushed deeper into the hot grip of Danny's body.

Trey ran a hand through Danny's curls, tightening fingers in a stinging grip, pulling his head farther back so he could get at Danny's mouth, thrust in a tongue in time with his cock.

Danny groaned a "C'mon, fuck me" into Trey's mouth, and Trey released his grip.

Leaning back on his heels and twisting Danny onto his side, Trey used his arm to hike up Danny's knee, coming into him sideways, moving deep and fast.

Trey kissed away the protest on Danny's lips.

"Want to kiss you." And he did. But even more he wanted to watch Danny, watch his mouth soften as the groans escaped him, watch to see when Trey found the angle that would make Danny fall apart and beg to come.

He found it in the soft shout of "Fuck" he swallowed in a kiss, in the way Danny's eyes slammed shut and he tore away his mouth to breathe, in the bruising grip Danny had on Trey's thigh as if to drag him deeper, harder.

Trey leaned in for another kiss, hips still working in fast, hard strokes. Danny's tongue soft and hot in Trey's mouth when with a pop, the lights went out.

Trey froze in surprise and then Danny chuckled. "Damn. You *are* good. Nobody's ever fucked me blind before."

Trey laughed. "Nah, not that good."

Danny groaned. "Still not complaining. You could move again, or just keep laughing because damn, that felt nice."

Trey laughed again and Danny reached his other hand between them, finding a way through the knot of legs and arms. Trey leaned his chin on Danny's biceps, wishing he could see more than just shadows as Danny started to strip his dick with his fist. Trey felt it a second before he saw it, felt it from the way Danny's ass got softer, hotter right before the muscles clamped down on his dick in a tight flutter. A second later Danny shot onto his belly, their thighs, warm quick spurts. Trey tried to get in one last kiss but the pressure around his dick was too much.

His mouth opened and he panted as Danny's ass dragged the heat from his dick, pulled it into his body.

He eased out while his dick was still twitching and flopped on his side. Danny's leg shook as Trey gently let it down. In the pitch black of the room smells and sound were stronger, Danny's breath coming in wobbly pants, Trey's lungs full of the smell of them together, come and sweat. He liked it, wanted to breathe it all the time. Wanted to lean over and lick Danny clean, lick him hard, see if he could go again because, no way was that itch scratched enough.

Trey heard Danny sit up. "I'm gonna shower, in case the water heater's electric."

Before Trey could offer to join him, Danny added, "I'll be quick."

Trey tossed the condom in the trash and grabbed his wet jeans. "I'll go out to the car and get a flashlight."

By the time he got back, Danny was under the covers in the other bed, a fresh beer in his hand. Moving that fast in the dark must have meant those changeable eyes were part cat. Guess Danny wasn't much for cuddling.

Trey set the flashlight on the bathroom counter and showered quickly, the tiny motel soap almost a sliver already.

When he toweled off and went back into the room, he swung the flashlight between the two beds. "You sharing or do I have to sleep on your wet spots?"

Danny gave a put-upon sigh and then patted the spot next to him. "Just don't hog the bed or steal the covers."

"Okay." Trey stole Danny's beer instead. "Shit. It's warm."

"That's what happens without refrigeration. Maybe we should put it out in the snow."

Trey grabbed a towel and clutched it over his dick and balls before he stuck his head out of the door far enough to put what was left of the six-pack in the snow.

Danny took the flashlight when Trey handed it off and

placed it on the nightstand. As Trey scooted under the blanket, his icy thigh brushed Danny's hot one.

"Asshole."

But Danny didn't kick him away, just put the beer on the nightstand and flicked off the flashlight before turning on his side to face Trey.

"What?" Trey asked.

"This. It's just weird."

"And familiar."

Danny laughed. "Yeah. That too."

Trey rolled toward him, doubling up the thin pillow under his head. Danny handed him one of the extras he'd been using to prop himself up.

"We didn't always screw around." Danny's words dropped into the space between them.

"No." Sometimes they'd talked. And sometimes, Trey had only wanted to touch him, something warm and alive.

"Your dad wasn't dealing heroin."

"I don't want to talk about it."

"He was onto something. Remember? You said he was suddenly spending a lot of time on a big case."

"Danny."

"What's got you so spooked all of a sudden?"

"I said I didn't want to talk about it." Trey rolled on his back.

"That's all right. I'll just sit here and watch the blank screen of the TV in a pitch-black room. That should be entertaining. Since we're stuck here for who knows how long."

Trey wasn't going to get into this game with Danny. The escalating blame. He clenched his teeth and stared at the darkness in the direction of the ceiling.

"That's right, Trey, because it always has to be where and when you decide. Just you."

"For Chrissakes, Danny, let it go."

"Why? You don't."

Trey rolled off the bed. "Listen to me, you little shit, what happened to my family had nothing to do with what went on between you and me. And you do not get to make comparisons like that."

Danny took a sharp breath. "Fuck." Trey heard Danny sit up, found the glitter of his eyes. "You're right. I— Shit. I never should have said that."

He didn't think he'd ever heard Danny—or any Gardner—admit he was wrong. Maybe it was easier to make confessions in the dark, when you didn't have to see someone's face. That's probably why the Catholics had those nice booths with the screens. Trey found his way around the room and sat on the other bed.

"You don't have to sleep over there."

"Maybe I do. I thought..."

Danny didn't interrupt, he just waited.

"I think this was a mistake. Just raking up shit we're better off forgetting."

"Which? Driving out here and asking questions or me letting you fuck me?"

"Both." Trey stared hard, trying to read an expression in Danny's eyes. Was he serious? "Let me?"

Trey saw a hint of white teeth flash.

The little shit was making a joke.

"If by 'letting' you mean getting up on your knees and jamming your ass down on my cock, yeah I guess you let me fuck you."

Now he could clearly see Danny's grin. "See. It doesn't have to be that serious. Now come back here and keep me warm."

Trey picked up the flashlight, found an extra blanket in the closet and threw it at Danny.

"That should do it." It wasn't that he didn't wish it didn't have to be that serious. Or that he didn't wish to hell Danny Gardner could just be another fuck. But there was no way they could sleep in that small bed without touching and once they did...

Danny picked up the flashlight from where Trey had set it on the nightstand and flicked it on again.

"Did you get anything else to eat?"

"Beef jerky."

Danny broke into a grin that crinkled all the way up to his eyes and slipped out of bed, tearing into the package of Slim Jims. He sat back on the bed, gaze roving over Trey's body before focusing on his cock just as Danny stuck the end of the beef stick into his mouth.

"That's all, huh?" Danny said with his mouth full.

Trey's cock really should have known he'd had enough. But apparently where Danny was concerned, there was no such thing as enough. Or the word no. No matter what the consequences.

"Move over." Trey gave in. "I'm cold."

Danny handed off the flashlight and slid over. "Shit. This side of the bed is freezing."

"I know." Trey grinned and tucked his arms under his head. "Think going to college made you smart, Agent Danny?"

The Slim Jim whipped his unprotected biceps hard enough to sting, but Trey laughed and grabbed it.

"Time to share again, Danny."

"Just don't say that about my Butterscotch Krimpets."

Chapter Eight

Danny might not want to share his Tastykakes, but he was all for sharing a blow job before they got out of bed in the morning. Trey opened his eyes to find a pair of dark ones watching him, a long-fingered hand stroking down his chest in a leisurely inspection made up of light and hard touches, a firm tug on a nipple, a tingling fingertip caress on the tight skin beneath his navel.

By the time Danny's hand was an inch from the base of Trey's cock, Trey was arching to meet it, his dick having left simple morning wood behind for God, suck me off now. Those mind-reading eyes crinkled at the corners as Danny wrapped a hand around the shaft and his lips around the head.

A long growl escaped a throat too rough from sleep to moan. Danny's eyes slitted like a cat's, still watching as those dark lips slid down, cheeks hollowing in a tight suck as he pulled off. God, Danny Gardner giving head made for a hell of a visual. Trey thought if Danny had his glasses on, those familiar geeky frames around his eyes, Trey would have come from the first flick of Danny's tongue under the head.

As it was, he had a hard time not grabbing the curls and holding Danny there to fuck deep into his throat. Danny combined that ruthless suck with a wicked tongue, and yeah, there was a lot to be said for doing this once they both knew what the fuck they were doing.

Danny was angled sideways over him and Trey tried to pull

him up. "C'mon up here. I want some too."

Danny was shifting, swinging his leg over Trey's shoulder when Trey's cell started ringing. Danny didn't stop, his lips got tighter, mouth hotter and softer as he let the head of Trey's cock rub on the velvet at the back of his throat.

"Danny, c'mon, man. It's the shop."

Trey started digging on the nightstand, realized his phone was in his jacket the fuck across the room and finally had to drag Danny off his dick by his soft black hair.

"Hold the thought, okay?"

He hobbled awkwardly to grab the phone as it stopped ringing.

The time on the screen read 9:30. He was so fucked. The phone rang again and he slid it open.

"Eriksson."

"Where the fuck are you? The chief—"

"Is that him?" Trey heard the demand over the air as clearly as if he were in the station.

It wasn't Jankowski in his ear anymore. "Eriksson, what the fuck are you doing in Altoona?"

"Chief, I called last night. There's a foot and a half of snow—"

"I get the Weather Channel, Eriksson. But I want to know why you are halfway across the state when the ADA needs to talk to you about your case. And you had better not be chasing ghosts again."

"No, Chief."

"Do you like being a detective, Eriksson?"

"Yes, Chief. I'll be there."

The chief hung up on him.

"That's interesting," Danny said from the bathroom doorway.

Trey spun around. "What?"

"You go all military, eyes front, rigid at attention. Even now your face is a total blank."

"Well read it now. We're leaving if we have to push that damn car across the state."

"Guess it would be a bad time to mention that we should have taken my Navigator?"

"Unless you want my foot up your ass."

Danny's gaze was clear and assessing without a trace of his eye-slitting smile. Yeah, Danny still got too excited when he thought he'd solved something, but in everything else he had learned to hold himself back. Now, the way he looked at Trey was as if that brain was calculating plusses and losses, weighing it all out before he said anything. Despite everything, when Danny let a hint of his smile curve his lips as he looked at Trey's softened dick, the chief's threat didn't seem as menacing. If Danny wanted to finish what he'd started...

"All things considered, I think I like your dick in my ass better." Danny ducked back into the bathroom.

"Didn't you go before we left?" Daniel teased, leaning toward the open car door.

Trey flipped him off and slammed the door shut. As he jogged away toward the service station, he looked kind of adorable, broad shoulders hunched like a guilty child's, hands tucked deep in the pockets of his leather coat. Trey's hands had suffered as they exhumed the car this morning, and now looked as bruised and scraped as if he'd been in a bar fight.

Daniel's own hands, even protected by his lined leather gloves, ached. Trey had produced a folding shovel from the trunk of the police car and along with the one provided by the motel owner, together they'd managed to clear enough of a path to push and coax the Charger out of the motel lot and onto the plowed and sanded highway. Once they cleared the mountains, the roads were only wet.

His hands weren't the only thing that ached. Every time he shifted in the bucket seat he felt the echo of Trey pounding inside him. Daniel didn't think it was possible he could want Trey with anything as powerful as that overwhelming combination of lust, envy and adoration Daniel had suffered as a teen. But that was before.

It wasn't only the novelty of a lover with some endurance when Daniel wanted to get fucked. No, this was Trey. That fiery intensity focused on Daniel. Even when Trey got angry, just having so much of Trey's attention was a hell of a rush.

Daniel didn't want to get on that ride again. Life was better—everything from work to sex to dealing with his friends and family was much easier without that heady sensation confusing him, making him stupid enough to buy into the kinds of fantasies he gave up a long time ago. He was never going to be that pathetic kid again, the one who'd begged Trey to come with him to New York, spinning stories about an apartment and part-time jobs and school.

It's not like Daniel was completely cold to the idea of relationships. Scott wasn't the first guy he'd had a long-term thing with. It was only, when it started to get messy, to get involved, it seemed like too much effort.

The door popped open, and Trey jumped in. "It's going to rain, maybe snow again, I can smell it."

He pulled back out onto the highway, following the signs for the interstate around Harrisburg.

"Don't want to get stuck again, right?" Trey glanced over, the look in those silver-blue eyes under his sandy lashes made a thick heavy pulse of blood hit Daniel's cock and his ass at the same time, had him shifting in his seat.

"All right?" Trey's voice was that soft, reassuring tone Daniel had already told him to drop.

"Fine." There was one thing guaranteed to capture Trey's

focus. "Can I see that picture again, the one of our dads' squad?"

The sleet that had started making a silvery rattle against the windshield looked warmer than the gaze Trey shot him this time. "Why?"

"I want to look at it."

Trey reached into his jacket and handed over the plastic sleeve with the picture in it. Daniel tried matching up some more faces and names. One name stood out quite clearly on the back, even though his image was obscured by the mosaic-like crack running across his eyes where the photo must have been folded at one time. Lieutenant Kearney stood in the back left corner, a cigar clenched in his teeth.

"Hey." Daniel looked up. "The old chief—Mr. Vice President-Elect Kearney, he was always on your dad's case about smoking, wasn't he?"

"I guess. Dad was always promising Mom he was going to quit."

"So why is he smoking a cigar in this picture?"

"They were getting shot at all the time. I don't think he worried much about getting lung cancer. People do a lot of stuff during a war they wouldn't do at home."

"I remember one night at your house and your dad had cigars and the chief said he hated them."

"Maybe he did."

"So why does he have one here?"

"How the hell would I know? You want to call him and ask him? You've probably got clearance. Go for it. Call the guy a couple weeks before inauguration and ask him what cigar he was smoking in a forty-year-old picture."

"Maybe I will."

"Jesus, Danny, it's just a fucking picture."

"I don't think so."

"Well, it is. And I'm done with this shit. I am not losing my job over it. I don't know what the hell I was thinking letting you talk me into coming out here."

Trey honestly thought his dad was to blame for what had happened. That was the only explanation Daniel would believe for Trey being willing to chuck the case he'd made his life's work.

Daniel looked back down at the picture as if sheer force of concentration could make the lieutenant's features clearer. As if he could make that broken blob speak.

"Gimme that." Trey put his hand on the plastic sleeve.

"Why? Why do you care? You're done with it."

"Because I want to make sure you're done with it too. I know you, Danny, you don't let anything go."

Except you. I couldn't hang on to you.

"This is my shit, my family. I need you stay the hell out of it."

Daniel released the picture. Neither of them spoke again until Trey dropped Daniel off on Paxinosa Avenue.

He grabbed Daniel's arm as he got out. "Danny—Daniel."

God, it must be serious. His full name sounded weird coming from Trey. Did it feel as strange to say it as it did to hear it?

Trey let go of his arm when Daniel stopped. "I've spent my life looking for this, for answers and—I guess I don't like the one I found."

"But—"

"Please. Just stay out of it. Okay?"

"All right."

"Call if something's wrong in the house again or—" And there was that look in Trey's eyes again. Hot. Intent. "If there's anything else you want."

"Yeah. There was that other thing you offered."

"Whenever you really want to." Trey waited until Daniel had pulled his briefcase from the backseat before speeding away.

Daniel waited until Trey turned the corner before speeding to the nearest electronics store for the best wand scanner he could find.

Chapter Nine

When Daniel called Trey at seven that night, it wasn't only so Daniel could sneak that picture away long enough to scan it. And even that plan wasn't just because he couldn't resist a puzzle, a code, a mystery. Trey's mom and dad had always been nice to Daniel, never made him feel like the awkward geek he knew he'd been, but actually asked him questions and talked to him like he was a person and not his parents' baggage. But even more, there was no way Daniel was going to let Trey spend the rest of his life believing his dad was mixed up in some drug trafficking that had led to the shooting.

That wasn't all of it. There was also the whole getting to have sex with Trey again. And they'd see how much Trey liked being sweet-talked into getting fucked. All afternoon, Daniel had talked himself into a plan. A fuck-Trey-stupid, find-the-picture, leave-with-his-puzzle-piece-and-get-the-hell-out-of-Dodge plan.

Trey derailed the whole thing by meeting him at the door with two twenties in his hand.

"Sorry. Thought you were the pizza guy."

"Danny?" a familiar voice called from inside the house. He hadn't heard it in years, but he'd know it anywhere.

"Ginny?"

She was on him in a minute, a soft press of a curvy short body and the herbal scent of her hair. He hugged her back until she pulled away. Only to punch him in the shoulder. Fortunately, at her height it didn't do much damage. He decided to fake it before she got serious.

"Ow."

"That's for not calling me for ten years. But this"—she punched him again, this time in the ribs and he didn't have to fake the grunt of pain—"is for not telling me you were in town for a month."

Daniel would have thought up an answer, some kind of vague "I planned to as soon as things settled down," but he was still fighting for breath.

"You guys catch up. I'm going back to watch the rest of the movie. Or the news. Or whatever else I can find that's not so violent." Trey stepped aside.

Even if Trey wasn't offering much in the way of protection, Daniel decided there was safety in numbers and started to follow. Ginny grabbed his hand and dragged him down the hall, pulling him into the bathroom.

"The bathroom?"

"I'm not going into a strange guy's kitchen."

"Trey isn't a strange guy."

"Oh no? He calls me out of the blue and says 'Hey, I know you were good friends with Danny Gardner and he's in town and we thought you might like to hang out. Want to come over at eight?' That is seriously fucking weird."

"I notice you came anyway."

"Well, it's obvious it's the only way I was going to see you again this lifetime."

Maybe the darkness had kept her from landing another punch, but Daniel flicked the lights on anyway. He felt ridiculous crammed into the bathroom, whispering in the dark. Of course he felt ridiculous. That's what being in Easton did to him.

Ginny's copper-bright hair hadn't dimmed at all since high school. It still fell in frizzy spiral curls to her waist. Her skirt was brighter than the ones he remembered, purple and green gauzy swirls more suited to a gypsy Halloween costume than a December night. But that was his Ginny. She did what she wanted and didn't care. He remembered her mantra. It had helped him out a lot that first year in college until he found his footing. "Fuck 'em all." He hugged her again, scooping her up off the ground.

"I'm sorry."

"You ought to be, you asshole." But she hugged him back. "So what the hell is going on?"

"Where do I start?"

"You could start with that gorgeous piece of man you've got out there. So, you finally get somewhere with him?"

"You knew?" He'd never told her. Never talked about Trey with anyone, though Daniel and Ginny had both talked about what it was like to realize you were gay in high school.

Ginny rolled her eyes. She'd really hit the recessive gene jackpot. One hazel eye, one dark blue. It wasn't too noticeable if you didn't stare. "Of course, I knew."

"It's complicated."

"How complicated could it be? Do you need a manual? I'm sure we sell one."

"No thank you. I heard about the store. My mother told me."

"Oh, your mother told you. So you knew exactly where the fuck I was and you never bothered to call me? Wait. Don't tell me. That's complicated too."

"I'm sorry," he said again.

"So if you guys are finally having complicated, wish-I-had-a-camera-in-the-bedroom sex, *finally* after all those heated gazes senior year, why am I here cock-blocking?"

"I don't know. When did he call you?"

"Around seven. Is he still...?" Ginny lifted her hand and wobbled it back and forth.

He wasn't going to ask how she'd known that Trey had

trouble figuring out his sexuality.

Daniel gave her a quick smile. "He says he's not. Really. I don't have any idea why he called you."

"Well, I'm glad he did. Damn, I missed that smile."

Danny gave her the whole works.

Ginny laughed. "You're the only person I know who had adorable crow's feet by the age of fifteen."

With Ginny here, his plan got a whole lot easier. "Hey, do you think you could help me out with something?"

"Relationship help? Oh, honey, just because I'm a dyke don't think I got a social work degree. Hell, I can't keep a girlfriend longer than three months."

"Mother told me you were running the bookstore with a *friend*. You know, in that tone she uses to mean I-don't-know-what-else-to-call-it."

"Yeah, my mom has that tone too. But Joanna and I are much better business partners than lovers. She runs the café and I run the bookstore."

"How's it going?"

"Oh now you want to ask?"

"Exactly how many times do I have to apologize?"

"I don't know. Let's see, there's at least two or three holidays a year you must have been in town and didn't call me, so three a year? Thirty? And never underestimate the power of a grand gesture. Expensive gifts, public humiliation."

Daniel gaped at her.

"Catholics and Jews might have invented the guilt trip, but lesbians are the true masters."

"Don't you mean mistresses?"

"Sexist pig."

"Huh?"

Ginny was smiling, her tiny white teeth poking over a pale pink lip. "The mere fact that you have to make a gender distinction implies gender bias."

127

"Do you all constantly change the definition of politically correct just to humiliate the unwary?"

"See, 'you all'. Exclusive language. This is what we can expect from employees of the federal government. Don't *you all* take sensitivity training?"

Daniel knew enough to walk away from a fight he couldn't win, which was basically any fight with Ginny. "How's the store doing, Ginny?"

"Great. The rent's killing me up there on the hill but being close to the college means we get lots of traffic. So what is this thing an independent bookseller could help you with?"

"Nothing like that. I need you to do something sneaky and underhanded."

"I can do that. Just ask any of my ex-girlfriends."

"Slut." He grinned.

"Cocksucker." She stuck out her tongue.

"Need lessons?"

People who smelled something dead before their first cup of coffee made less unpleasant faces. "No thanks. So what underhanded thing do you want me to do?"

"After we eat, I'm going to go to the bathroom. You keep Trey in the living room. No matter what, all right? Keep him talking."

"About what? I haven't seen him in fifteen years and we were never exactly friends."

"Dazzle him with a rant about the patriarchal structure of the police department."

"And while I'm doing this what perverted thing are you going to be doing in the bathroom?"

"I won't be in the bathroom."

Ginny could make her different-colored eyes work for her in a piercing stare.

"I'll be in the basement."

"I am not starting an argument with an Easton cop until

you tell me what the fuck for."

"All right. You remember Trey's parents."

Her expression softened. "Of course."

"Well. I've been trying to help Trey find out what happened."

"But I thought his dad—"

"I knew his parents. They weren't like mine. Or yours. His dad would never have done that. Not in a million years."

"If you're supposed to be helping him, why do you have to sneak into the basement to do it? Is it some kind of twisted I-found-the-murderer surprise?"

Daniel had a gruesome mental image of greeting Trey while wearing a birthday hat and holding a grisly crime-scene photo. "No, no surprise. Actually he kind of told me to stop helping him."

Ginny shook her head, sending the copper spirals of her hair twisting and bouncing. "Oh, Danny. You never could let something go, could you?"

Jesus, what was it with everybody? He let lots of shit go. He was civil to his father. He'd just been very civil to a boyfriend who dumped him on Christmas Day. He didn't even call his brother an asshole half the times he deserved it. But this really mattered. Especially to Trey.

"Are you going to help me or not?"

Ginny leaned back against the sink, giving Daniel a flirty look from under her lashes. "Mmm. I'll bet Trey's a hell of a fuck."

"And you base this on your experience fucking how many men?"

"Hey, just because I don't want to fuck him doesn't mean I can't see that he's gorgeous. And he's got this..." She gave a little shake of her shoulders that made the sequins on her top shimmer. "You know?"

"Yeah, I noticed."

"God, how was he?"

As Daniel looked away, he caught a glimpse of himself in the mirror. Jesus. He looked like a lovesick teenager.

"C'mon," Ginny persisted. "I had to watch you drool over him for four years. At least you could give me a little peek."

He wasn't going to tell her how he could still feel Trey in him, the weight of his hands, the heat of his mouth, the brush of soft deep whispers in his ear. Wasn't going to tell her how quickly Trey learned the pressure of teeth on Daniel's skin sent a jolt of electricity along his nerves.

"He's...intense. Ummm, focused."

"Oh." Ginny licked her lips. "Focused is really good." She shook herself again. "And you're going to risk—*umm*, blowing all that?"

"God, you could never resist a pun, could you?"

She waved that off. "Well, you've gotta know he's not the forgiving kind. If he knows you're digging up this shit behind his back you won't be getting laid tonight—or ever by him."

"I do. Which is why you're going to help me, right? If you don't screw it up, he'll never know."

"Oh so whatever happens will be my fault?"

Trey's voice sounded out in the hall. "Everything all right in there? Do I need to call an ambulance?"

"I'm fine. Thanks for giving her enough time to kill me," Daniel called back. He lowered his voice to barely a breath. "So, will you?"

"Are you sure?"

"I'm doing it for him."

She shook her head even while saying, "All right."

Daniel smiled and opened the door.

"Hey." Trey walked back in from the kitchen, carrying napkins and cups. He smiled at Ginny. "Everything he told you is a lie."

"So you don't have a ten-inch dick?"

Trey dropped the cups.

Daniel bent to pick them up. "You'll get used to her—unless you want to kick her out. After the abuse I've taken that would be fine with me."

"Hey, I'm only trying to establish some ground rules." Ginny grabbed the napkins from Trey. "I have a filthy mouth and a dirtier mind. I don't expect anyone to put on good manners for me."

"Message received." Trey still looked a little shell-shocked. "I just wanted to tell you guys the pizza was here."

Trey and Ginny got on better than Daniel would have expected, though some of their bonding came at his expense. He didn't care as long as it meant he got to sneak his scanner down to Trey's office.

Maybe the better plan would have been to wait until Trey was asleep, but at least this way, Ginny would find some way to give him a warning.

His stuff wasn't in the hall where he'd dropped it when Ginny attacked him. God, he hoped Trey hadn't looked in the bag. What if he'd felt the shape of that wand scanner and taken it out, thinking it was a sex toy Daniel had brought?

Daniel peered into the first dark room off the hall, took a step in and tripped over his bag. He gave himself thirty seconds to consider all the ways this could go wrong, and then thought of Trey spending the rest of his life believing his father was a drug dealer. He plucked the scanner out of the bag and snuck into the cellar.

Of course the picture wasn't tacked back up on the corkboard because that would have been too easy. He yanked open the top desk drawer.

Jesus. Long, black, lethal. The Luger. The souvenir Trey's dad had brought home from Vietnam. The antique pistol that had killed his mom and left his dad with scrambled brains. Daniel reached out, running one finger along the barrel. Jesus fuck. The thing was freshly oiled, looked ready to fire. He lifted it and saw the clip.

Trey wouldn't be that melodramatic. No. No matter what Trey believed about his father, Daniel knew Trey would never leave a scene like that for someone else to find. But why the hell had he kept the gun—and kept it maintained? Why the hell would he even bother to get it back? Daniel would have left the thing gathering dust in the evidence locker.

Right. *Daniel* was the one who couldn't let anything go.

He checked a couple of other drawers and the cabinet, one eye on his watch, ears tuned to the lilt of Ginny's voice upstairs. He'd bet the damned Polaroid had never left Trey's jacket pocket—the jacket hanging on a hook in the hall where there was no way he could get to it with Trey in the living room.

Ginny shot him a look with one raised brow when he went back into the living room. Daniel lowered his gaze.

"I probably don't want to know," Trey said with a smile in his voice.

Shit. Daniel didn't know how he'd forgotten Trey was a cop, and very far from oblivious.

"No, you *don't* want to know," Ginny said.

Daniel shot her a warning look. She blinked and tried to look innocent. If he didn't know her, it might have worked.

"Do I have to send you two to separate corners and tell you to have a clean fight?" Trey asked.

"I don't think that's necessary, now that you've given me Danny's number I can call and abuse him any time. Which reminds me, it's time I hit the road. I've got to open the store at nine tomorrow. The joy of Christmas returns."

As she hugged Daniel at the door, she whispered, "Let it go, Danny. I actually think he cares about you. Try not to fuck it up."

But they were just fucking. Expecting anything else from this was crazy. There was too much shit behind and between them to ever be something as simple as friends, let alone lovers.

They watched through the open door as Ginny waved again before she climbed into her green Jetta.

"She's a trip."

"Yes, she is."

Trey turned that gaze on him. In the streetlight, his eyes were an impenetrable flat grey. "Why'd you guys lose touch?"

"Just happened. Always meant to call. Didn't." He should have though. He'd forgotten how much fun Ginny was. How much she'd always known without him saying anything. "Why?"

"No reason. You guys seemed so tight back then."

"Do you still hang out with people from high school?"

Trey shrugged. "Handed some of 'em tickets when I was driving a patrol car."

But it wasn't his being a cop. People hadn't known how to treat him—after. It was like tragedy was contagious. He'd missed a lot of school, going to the trial. And then he'd gotten kicked off the basketball team for fighting. In those days, it hadn't taken a lot for Trey to come out swinging.

As Trey locked the door and leaned back against it, Daniel looked over at the brown leather jacket hanging from a hook in the hall next to his own coat. If the Polaroid was still in the pocket, he'd be done in a minute. If he didn't find out anything new, Trey would never know.

"Uh." Trey's voice was hesitant, almost diffident. Nothing like his usual confident tone.

Daniel shifted his focus, wondering how long he'd been staring.

Trey dragged his hand up from the back of his neck through his hair. The blond strands were too short to flop now, a grown-out brush cut, spiky on top, but the gesture was so familiar, so Trey, Daniel's stomach tightened.

"I kind of thought when you brought the bag, you wanted to stay, but if you want to leave..." He jerked his chin at the coat rack.

"No. I don't want to go anywhere. Unless you—"

"No." Trey's usual confidence reasserted itself, voice dipping lower to say, "So. Is that a toy bag, Santa?"

"Just my toothbrush and shaving stuff." Daniel leaned against Trey's body pressed against the door. "Disappointed?"

"Yeah." That single word held a smile to match the one on Trey's face. "I was hoping you were a lube connoisseur. Thought maybe I was worth something special."

"I wouldn't know yet, would I?"

"I think you know plenty." Trey spread his legs as he leaned, enough to let their cocks grind together. Daniel reached up to cup Trey's face and dragged him into a kiss, the sweet lick of tongues growing wetter, messier as they rubbed together.

When he raised his head, Trey murmured, "We seem to end up against a lot of walls."

"Trust me. You'll like the wall there in a second."

Tugging at Trey's belt, Daniel dropped to his knees. His fingers brushed the worn spot on Trey's jeans where his holster rode, a nail catching on the frayed threads as Trey helped Daniel shove jeans and briefs out of the way. Trey rocked his hips forward as Daniel lifted the thickening length to his lips. A big, heavy hand sifted through Daniel's hair while he rubbed his face over the soft skin, stroking and kissing, fingers teasing under Trey's balls.

"God, Danny. So good."

Pizza and beer and laughter made Trey easy. Daniel hadn't even started. He splayed his hands over Trey's hips, thumbs rubbing across the jut of bones, lips sucking the head, tongue lapping the slick drops from the slit. Tilting his head, he licked his way down the shaft, using his tongue first to trace the vein underneath and then making ice-cream-swirl licks as he kissed his way back up and down, feeling the silky skin tighten under his lips.

Heavy, salty-slick cock on his tongue and the twitch of muscles under his fingers as he sucked the strength from another man's legs. The familiar rhythm made his own dick press hard against the buttons of his fly, but the pulse under his skin, the not-completely unpleasant tilt and lurch in Daniel's gut, that was all because the man nudging his cock into Daniel's throat was Trey. No matter what Daniel told himself, Trey was always going to be able to do this to him. And right now, Daniel didn't even care if Trey knew it. Letting a groan vibrate his throat, Daniel stretched to take Trey deeper.

Trey made a hoarse gasp and then his fingers twisted in Daniel's hair, pulling his head back. Daniel looked up.

Trey rubbed a thumb across Daniel's lips. "Want you in my bed." Hooking Daniel under the arm, Trey hauled him to his feet. With his jeans barely hitched up on his hips, he led the way down the hall, stopping every couple of feet to kiss Daniel's mouth.

Trey ducked into the still-dark room that held Daniel's bag and brought it back out. "Sure you didn't bring anything special?"

Wrestling Trey for it would have made his nervousness obvious. "Are you implying there's something wrong with my basic equipment?"

As Trey backed into a room near the kitchen and flipped on the lights, he reached out to slide a finger under a belt loop on Daniel's jeans. "I'm going to need to make another inspection." Trey stroked his cock while nodding at Daniel's jeans.

He peeled off his sweater and T-shirt before undoing the top button of his fly, watching the slow slide of Trey's hand on his dick. When he stepped forward, intent on getting another taste, Trey stopped him with a hand on his chest.

"You don't want a blow job?"

"Well, when you put it like that..." Trey yanked off his shirt and shoved his jeans and shorts down, kicking them away once he'd sat on his bed. At least, Daniel thought there was a bed under that mess of sheets and blankets. He wondered if Trey still got nightmares and then he didn't wonder anymore. He knelt and took Trey deep right away, hand tight around the base while he bobbed quick and tight with his mouth.

Trey cupped Daniel's head, not forcing him deeper, just a gentle rub at the base of his skull that suddenly became an urgent tug.

"Fuck. Don't—"

Daniel flicked his tongue underneath the head, hard and steady along with the pressure of his lips, throat open and waiting, body humming with the power of knowing he'd taken Trey further than he'd planned to go.

Trey dragged Daniel off with an eye-watering grip in his hair and lay there panting for a minute. Slipping off his jeans and briefs, he stretched out on the bed next to Trey.

Trey rolled on top, pinning Daniel's wrists over his head. "Christ." He dropped his forehead to press on Daniel's. "Slow down."

Until Trey said that, Daniel hadn't realized how much of what flared up between them was still driven by those quick-before-we're-caught,   hurry-he's-going-to-change-his-mind impulses. Rough urgency had always seemed to be a part of sex with Trey. But now, there really was no rush. There was time to savor every second of sex with Trey, with Trey's intensity reaching into Daniel until it burned through him from the inside out.

Daniel nodded.

Trey gave him a quick smile and bent his head. Despite his *slow down* he dove into Daniel's mouth like he'd eat Daniel alive. Teeth scraped across lips already swollen from cock-sucking as Trey pulled Daniel's tongue deep into his mouth, a growl vibrating up between them.

Daniel twisted, trying to get Trey's head down to his neck, eager for the sweet sting of teeth drawing the sensitive skin between them. One sucking bite on Daniel's neck and his cock twitched, hot-tight skin rubbing on Trey's belly, slick beads of precome spreading along their skin to ease the friction.

With his hands still pinning Daniel's over his head, Trey nipped from neck to chest. The clamp of his teeth in the stretched-tight muscle under Daniel's arm made him jump, wrists twisting as he tried to free his hands. Then Trey was licking and sucking a nipple to a hard point before his teeth closed tight, pleasure and pain fighting for control of Daniel's nerves on a loop to his dick. He arched up, trying to feed more flesh into Trey's mouth to ease the sting of that bite. Trey just sucked harder and the pleasure won, burning down to Daniel's balls.

Trey lifted his head, eyes scanning the marks he'd left on Daniel's body. "God, look at you, Danny." Trey's voice was rough, like he'd downed half a bottle of whiskey in one gulp.

The lurch in Daniel's stomach became a slow burn. "Fuck me."

"Yeah?" Trey bent his head to leave a throbbing mark near Daniel's collarbone. "What else do you like?"

It was that coaxing whisper again, despite the whiskey-hoarse voice, but just as Daniel opened his mouth to protest, Trey whispered, "Nah, not trying to seduce you. Just want to know. I want to make you scream."

Warmth exploded in Daniel's gut, spilling down his legs, up into his throat. He needed to get it out somehow before he drowned in it.

"I like fucking." Holy shit. Was that his voice? It sounded like he'd gargled with gravel.

"Yeah? You like to be held down?"

He liked it at the moment—except for this heat loosening inside him, threatening to tear free. "Not as a rule."

"But you wouldn't rule it out? Because—" Trey licked and sucked the other nipple, teeth and beard rough on Daniel's skin. "I can see you, cuffed to the headboard while I ride your cock. See you going crazy trying to get your hands on my hips to speed up the fuck. You ever like to let it go like that, Danny?"

Daniel sure as hell was going to now. He shifted his weight

enough to hook one of Trey's legs and used the leverage to free his hands and flip them.

"Save the cuffs. I just need to fuck you."

Trey grinned. A perfect breath-stealing grin. The kind that made Daniel feel like he was the only one who'd ever seen Trey like this, legs dropping open, eyes summer-sky clear, free of clouds and shadows. Still grinning, Trey reached under a pillow and brought out a bottle of lube and a condom.

Daniel snapped the top and poured out the gel until it ran down his wrist and onto Trey's thigh. Maybe after he could pick up some style points—he needed this wet and messy and right-the-hell now. When he pressed a finger in, Trey reached up and grabbed at Daniel's shoulders, wrapped an arm around him and hauled him into a distracting kiss.

But not so distracting he didn't notice exactly how fucking tight Trey was around one finger.

"Jesus." Daniel breathed the word into Trey's mouth.

Trey let his legs drop wider and Daniel ran another finger around the rim, rubbing, waiting for the muscle to relax enough to let it in.

"Who's being all coaxing now? Let me see what you got, Danny. Fuck me."

Daniel wasn't going to hurt Trey just to prove something. Fingertip circling, Daniel waited until he felt the hard muscle soften and slid a second finger in. He fucked them in and out, twisting and scissoring, pulling moans out of Trey, but when Daniel crooked his fingers, found the swollen gland and rubbed, Trey came up off the mattress.

"Do it. C'mon."

But watching the way every thrust and prod of his fingers had Trey arching and groaning made Daniel's body buzz. His breath came out on a deep sigh and he had to get a grip or he was going to lose it, pour the heat from his gut into Trey as soon as his dick got into that sweet tight space. Lose his fucking mind looking into Trey's eyes, at Trey Eriksson spread open underneath him.

Daniel pulled his fingers out. "Roll over."

Trey shook his head before tearing open the condom and rolling it down Daniel's cock.

Daniel put more lube on his palm and stroked his dick. "Don't like it rough?"

"Oh, I like it plenty rough. But Christ, Danny, you're fucking gorgeous. I love looking at you."

Daniel swallowed and guided his cock to press just inside that hot, clinging muscle.

"Always did," Trey panted as Daniel worked the head in and back out.

Daniel flexed his hips and drove a little deeper. The pressure of the tightest ass he'd ever been in was draining most of the blood away from his brain, but he thought Trey had said something. Verbal function greatly diminished, Daniel managed, "Huh?"

"Al-ways. Looking. At. You."

The heat in Daniel's gut flared, filling him with the fear that he'd start babbling those stupid things you say when you're fucking deep inside, things like *I love you and want to be in you forever.* Or even worse, that fire would burn free his icy grip on those long-buried resentments like *you really hurt me, asshole* and *how could you just take off like that?*

Daniel lifted one of Trey's legs and pushed in all the way. Trey grabbed Daniel's hip, making Daniel grit his teeth against those words, trying to wait until Trey had softened enough to let Daniel move, but...*fuck.*

"Yeah," Trey whispered, even though Daniel hadn't opened his mouth for fear of letting anything slip out. "Even when I didn't want to I watched you, Danny."

"Oh fuck." Daniel reached for whatever part of Trey he could get and fucked him hard, Trey meeting each thrust, ass clamping soft and hot and tight—everything perfect on Daniel's aching cock.

Daniel's eyes were closed, but he could feel Trey's gaze like a beam of light on the lids and Daniel jerked them open. He fell into a rhythm then, deep thrusts going faster and faster, sweat soaking his hairline, tickling down his spine. He watched Trey, knew the perfect angle from the bruising grip of Trey's fingers, the quicker jolt of his hips.

"Harder. C'mon. Just..." His neck flushed bright red, tongue pushing out between his lips. "Fuck. So. Fuck."

One hand shifted to his cock, and Daniel wanted his mouth there again, wanted the taste and the thick length pushing into his throat, the hot, slick, salty burst when Trey came.

He reached out and covered Trey's hand, holding it still. "Wait. I want..."

But Trey was already coming, his ass already pulsing around Daniel's dick, slippery strands of come pumping out to lace their fingers, even Trey's chin as he kept shooting. Daniel's own orgasm scorched down his spine, heat pumping from his cock into Trey's body, even as Trey's ass still worked him in tight quick tugs. He was boneless, almost bodiless, dropping down onto Trey while muscles gave a few final twitches.

Daniel was starting to think lying here, dick still in Trey's ass while Trey's hand drifted up and down Daniel's spine was about all he wanted from the rest of his life when Trey grunted.

"Sorry, man, but you're heavy."

"Oh." He reached down, but Trey already had his fingers around the latex at the base of Daniel's dick. "Sorry." Daniel slid off.

"'S okay. Just couldn't breathe anymore."

Daniel held the condom and slipped it off.

"Just drop it."

He let it fall over the side of the bed.

Trey's non-sticky hand went back to stroking Daniel's spine, stopping at the top to lift the sweaty ends off the back of his neck. But that want-to-sink-right-into-Trey's-bones feeling was gone. Daniel couldn't fall asleep, not if he was going to sneak away and get the picture scanned. A mildew-slimed tentacle of guilt wrapped around Daniel's stomach. Trey had been so fucking open, held nothing back, and Daniel was going to use that trust to do exactly what he'd promised Trey he wouldn't do.

But Trey was just so goddamned stubborn. Everything had to be one way, his way—like when he'd decided the only way to learn what had happened that night was to retrace his father's steps as closely as possible, going from the military to the police force, no matter how many other ways Daniel tried to tell him he could look for the truth.

Trey never saw things in shades of grey. If Daniel thought it would have done any good, he'd have couched the argument again, explained why the picture was such a good lead. After talking to the Flynns, Daniel was more convinced than ever that the key to the mystery lay somewhere in Howie Irving and Ron Eriksson's shared wartime experience. Maybe the picture was exactly what the burglar had been searching for.

There was no drooling grown-up-to-sexy geek on his shoulder when Trey woke up, but Danny had dropped a blanket over him before disappearing. It was only three and cold enough to make Trey dig for a pair of sweats before he went to see if Danny was still in the house or if he'd taken off.

Two steps towards the door and the light from the kitchen made his eyes water. Danny stood in the kitchen in just his jeans. His bag was zipped up, sitting on the old maple table. The table Trey had gotten out of storage when he bought this house. The one with the destroyed finish and the one sagging end because his dad had always leaned his arms on it no matter how many times his mother had yelled at him. The table and Dad's old metal desk had been too damaged to bring anything at the auction that had helped pay for Dad's lawyer. They were pretty much all he'd been able to keep. Two pieces of furniture, a couple of his mom's books and a few pictures went into the storage shed Julia got for him when his parents' house was sold.

Danny leaned on the counter, a glass of water in his hand, staring fixedly at the side of the refrigerator. He didn't flinch as Trey came up and wrapped his arms around Danny from behind, chin tucked into Danny's shoulder. He didn't move at all, not even to lean back against Trey.

"Works better if you open the door to look in. Or do G-men get cool X-ray contacts to play with?"

Danny shook his head.

"Hungry?"

"No, just awake." Danny took a couple of long swallows before putting the glass on the counter. "I miss the taste of Easton water."

"Water has a taste?"

"Some does. Easton's is kind of metallic. Didn't you notice when you were gone?"

"Nope. How's D.C.'s?"

"Mine's bottled. No taste."

Trey picked up the glass and drank. It just tasted like water, nothing metallic about it. Well, at least there was one thing Danny missed about Easton.

"Did you want to leave?"

"Did you want me to?"

"Not even a little." Even if nothing but sex could be right between them, even if Danny leaving again was going to join all the other shit that dug at Trey's mind when he couldn't sleep, right now he'd take what he could get. Besides, saying no to Danny had never worked for long.

Danny finished the water and turned. Trey sucked in a

breath at the sight of his pale chest covered with dark red bites.

Christ.

An unfamiliar sensation burned in Trey's throat, twitched in his hands. He wanted to grab Danny and cover him with more bites, growling like some kind of animal. He wasn't used to wanting, let alone having. Suddenly those crimes people committed out of jealousy made sense, because he wanted to put a brand on Danny, prove where he belonged.

He rubbed a thumb across one of Danny's nipples, saw him flinch and lightened the touch. Danny grabbed Trey's head and dragged their mouths together, but from the first touch the kiss was soft, a brush of lips, warm licks from Danny's tongue. Not teasing, just easy and God, so sweet. Trey feathered his fingers through that wavy hair, playing with the ends as Danny moved closer.

The skin against Trey's chest was icy. How long had Danny been standing there, staring? Trey ran his hands over Danny's back and arms, trying to warm him. Moving closer and tilting his hips in, Danny deepened the kiss, still keeping it soft, but a wet smooth press Trey felt in his gut before wakening arousal sparked in his dick.

Anything. It was a good thing Danny's tongue was so deep in Trey's mouth or he'd have breathed that word out loud. He'd do anything Danny wanted. Anything to warm up that cold skin. Anything to break the distance Danny'd suddenly put between them. Danny had never been like this—so...hidden away—but now every touch, every word seemed to have as much effect as if Trey were trying to punch through a block of ice.

He let his fingers slide under the back waistband of Danny's jeans, fingertips just brushing the dimples at the top of his ass. Danny's hand tightened on Trey's neck and the phone rang.

Danny jumped and pulled away like they'd been caught making out as teenagers.

"Shit." Trey picked up the kitchen extension to hear a stream of chatter about an armed robbery at a convenience store. Giving his ETA, he hung up and turned back to face Danny. "Sorry. I'm on the shitlist already so..." He'd never minded being called out in the middle of the night before. He was almost always awake anyway. But Danny could stay. It wasn't like he had any secrets from Danny. "If you—"

"I'm going to head out." Danny picked up his bag and crossed the hall back into the bedroom.

"Sure."

Everything familiar and awkward as they dressed. Familiar since he'd dressed in front of Danny often enough when he lived with the Gardners, familiar since it wasn't the first sorry-gotta-work end to sex he'd ever issued to a guy, but awkward, so fucking awkward, because it wasn't just any guy and it wasn't fifteen years ago and something was wrong. He wanted to kiss and lick Danny back out of those clothes, pull him into bed and fuck the whole goddamned world away.

Trey didn't want it to be one of those I'll-call-you-sometime goodbyes at the door. But there they were, coats on, standing in the hall, and not much to say since Trey had five minutes to get to the convenience store on Twenty-Fifth Street. Danny hitched his bag up on his shoulder, and Trey held back the sudden relieved sigh bursting from his lungs at the realization that he'd never talked to Danny about Bartos's arraignment on the B and E charges.

"I'll call you later."

Danny looked at him, eyes dark and completely unreadable.

Trey explained. "I forgot to tell you about the arraignment. For the guy that broke in."

"Sure." Given Danny's lack of enthusiasm Trey might as well have offered to call him with the score of the Eagles game from yesterday.

He opened the door but neither of them moved, just stood

there as the freezing air snaked around them, through them, into the house. He watched the smoke of Danny's breath. Was he waiting for Trey to do something, say something? Trey would have given it to him if he could figure out what it was, but Danny's expression was still as closed as Trey had ever seen it.

"Talk to you later," Danny said at last and stepped down from the porch, steps echoing in the still air.

Daniel stared at the slowly filling download bar, controlling the irrational urge to tap at the computer screen to see if he could make it go faster. Not wanting to waste a fragment of bandwidth on an IM, he called Harris back.

"It's still downloading."

The tech's sigh was forceful. "I told you it was a big file. If the case is this old, it can wait."

"I need it now."

"Well, I've got other things to do today. I can't babysit you over this. If you need more help, call someone else."

"Thanks. Keep that in mind next time you need a favor."

After nearly an hour the photo-enhancing software finished downloading, and Daniel hooked up the scanner. He doubted even the program Harris had sent from the DHS would help. When he'd put the photo through the scanner, a piece of the lieutenant's face had flaked off, the part with the cigar.

Once the software was done, he used every enhancement it came with to clean up the image of six men on and around the sandbags in front of Can Tho. The faces became clearer, his father and Trey's easy to see. Daniel didn't look much like his dad, but the image of Ron Eriksson could have been one of Trey from their high school yearbook.

Now he could see the face of the man he'd picked out as Sergeant Howie Irving. He had a tall rangy look and cradled his

M-16 like it was a baby.

No one else held any weapons. The software had worked so well Daniel could even see the special insignia the squad had designed in country. His dad'd had a framed patch in his office until it disappeared one day. A wide-mouthed cobra, hood flared, a drop of venom from a tooth, black snake on a blue and white field, the motto "See you bastards in hell," in uneven black lettering. As he'd gotten older, Daniel wondered why they had such an aggressive slogan when his dad had said they did mostly dustoffs, emergency medical evacuations. But his dad had talked less and less about the war, cutting Daniel's questions off completely by the time he was a teen. His father must have still talked to Trey's dad about it when they got together for cards; it was all they had in common.

Daniel printed off the enhanced image of the writing on the back so he didn't have to switch between screens. Definitely Howie Irving, Bill Gardner, Tracy—maybe Terry Hunter, Brian O'Leary and Ron Eriksson. Trey's dad wasn't wearing his shirt; he had the collar hooked in his right hand, slung over his right shoulder. Now Daniel could see why. There was a white bandage on Mr. Eriksson's left shoulder. Shit. Now would probably be a bad time to call up Trey and ask him about the wound. He didn't remember anyone ever mentioning it.

Kearney. No other name. Letters dark and bold. But Daniel was sure the guy standing in the back, the guy with the brown lieutenant's bar on his shirt, had been chomping on a cigar, as much as he'd been sure the former Chief of Police hated cigars. He remembered the diatribe. Daniel had just had to do some kind of thing on smoking for his middle school health class and as usual—according to his family—he'd taken it all very seriously.

He moved the mouse over the image of the man who was next in line for the Presidency and clicked to enlarge it. Tinted orangey pink sunglasses obscured what was left of the face. He was behind the sandbags, right behind Trey's father. But...Daniel leaned forward until his nose almost touched the

146

screen...the insignia on Kearney's left shoulder. It wasn't blue and white. It was red and maybe gold. A vulture or an eagle grabbing something.

He went online and searched through about three hundred webpages full of insignias until he thought he found it. But it wasn't American. It was Australian. An Australian air squadron. Why the hell would an American lieutenant be wearing an Australian's shirt?

He looked at his cell phone. One thirty. He'd been staring at the computer for five hours. He'd known there was something important about that photograph, but now he had more questions than answers. Before she'd gotten pissed off, Harris had given him a website where he could input the Polaroid's code to get the date.

Rubbing carefully around his eyes to keep the peace between his contacts and corneas, he typed in the code from the white space at the bottom of the picture. Harris had said there was probably a seventy-two-hour window of accuracy, but according to that code, the Polaroid had been taken September 18, 1970.

There was one call he could make to ask about the picture. If he called now, maybe his dad wouldn't even be drunk.

Functional alcoholism they called it. Daniel just called it drunk. It wasn't fair Dad's liver hadn't given out yet, but Mayor Holcomb, who actually seemed to make Daniel's mother happy, dropped dead while shoveling snow.

He called his father's office in Philadelphia. Dad was semi-retired, "consulting". Which was great if it kept him from performing surgery with a blood alcohol content of .18. The receptionist put him through with a smile in her voice.

"Yes?"

Daniel didn't know what he'd been expecting. Warmth?

"Hi, Dad."

"Danny. Is everything all right?"

Disaster wasn't an unreasonable assumption. It wasn't as if

Daniel called regularly.

"Everyone's fine." Daniel paused, but his dad didn't speak. He didn't know why that disappointed him. "I wanted to ask you about Mike Kearney."

A thick, solid sound reached him, glass on wood. Perhaps assuming his father hadn't started drinking yet had been optimistic.

"What about him?"

"How well did you know him?"

"We served together, and I saw him in town before he was elected lieutenant governor. You know that."

Daniel had known this wouldn't be easy. Daniel didn't even know what questions he had and asking them of his father was even more difficult.

"When's the last time you saw him?"

"A fundraiser here in Philly before the election. Why?"

"Do you still keep in touch?"

"What's going on? Are you in trouble at work? Christ, Danny, I told you to keep that stuff in the bedroom where it belongs."

Of course his father would go there. That's all he could imagine. Not success, a big case or even some cause of personal happiness. Just his queer son fucked up and now he needed saving.

"No, Dad. It's nothing like that. You know Mother is moving to Harrisburg."

"I'd heard that from your brother."

Daniel knew Rob harbored some bad feelings toward their father. But not nearly enough. Rob hadn't been home those last few months. Of course, Rob had always been "son". Daniel had always only been "Danny".

"I'm finishing packing the house for her, and I came across an old Polaroid. Of your squad in Vietnam."

Did Dad bother with a glass or was that sound of

swallowing right from the bottle?

"And?"

Now that it was time to ask something specific, Daniel realized how pointless his questions would sound. "You and Kearney were in the same squad. A helicopter squad?"

"I've told you."

Daniel waited and his father grudgingly continued.

"Evac mostly. Kearney was a pilot. I was a medic. We did drops and dustoffs for some Green Beret units."

"In this picture, do you know why Mike Kearney would be wearing an Australian officer's shirt instead of his own?"

"What kind of question is that? How the hell would I know?"

"It's a Polaroid from September in '70. Sergeant Eriksson has a bandage on his shoulder. Do you remember him getting wounded?"

"Shrapnel. I dug it out, patched it up myself. But what does that have to do with anything?"

"You're all wearing insignia, like the one you used to have in your den, but not Kearney. If he was in your squad, he'd have the same kind."

"Ron didn't. He'd have had the main division one, but he was on the ground crew and they had their own. But he went with us to see if we couldn't fix the wiring on a slick that went haywire up in Thua Thien." His father's voice had taken on the reminiscing tone Daniel remembered from when he was a kid and his father would show him things from the war. "Unlucky sonofabitch. The one time he leaves the hangar and we take fire."

Daniel was afraid to speak to jerk his father back to the present.

"Ron had terrible luck. Except at poker. And damn, he could fix anything. Get his hands on almost anything. Poor bastard." Dad cleared his throat. "Kearney said—" He broke off.

"What the hell brought this on?"

"I told you. I found a picture while I was packing up."

"Right. The insignia."

Daniel could almost hear the scotch slide down his father's throat. No gasp from the burn. His esophagus was probably nothing but scar tissue by now.

"What made you think it was him in the picture?"

"Your names are on the back." Daniel read them off, hoping something would shake loose.

"I don't remember anything particular. Kearney probably lost a bet. Or made a bet. He—" A shuffle of papers, and then the sound of a pen scratching, forceful tight strokes.

"Did Kearney smoke while he was in Vietnam?"

"Nope. Didn't drink either. On and on about clean living." His father's voice trailed off. "Well, Danny, I've got an appointment coming in."

Dismissed. His father was under there, somewhere. But the drunken bastard usually won out. Daniel had stopped missing his father a long time ago. He made a last appeal. "Dad, did you think Ron Eriksson shot his wife?"

"He went to prison for it."

"I know but—"

"People do things you'd never expect. Happens all the time. But there's usually a reason for it. Even if you can't see it, it doesn't mean it isn't there."

What was the reason his father drank himself into a stupor almost every day? Daniel probably didn't want to know. He could see why Trey was so reluctant to find out the worst about his dad, but no matter what Trey thought, *his* dad hadn't done anything wrong.

Daniel ordered a regular coffee from the tall blonde woman

manning the espresso machine just inside the wide glass front of Ginny's bookstore on Cattell Street. As she poured it, he looked around. It seemed to be a converted tavern, the original bar forming the foundation of the café. Bookshelves lined the walls and filled whatever floor space left by the few tables and chairs at the front.

After paying and getting his coffee, he murmured a "Thank you" and moved back through the store. Around a corner made by a floor shelf, he found an area rug and some furniture grouped into a reading area. One couch held two women reading, and a man whose tweed jacket bellowed pretentious professor was taking a seat in the worn leather chair at the end of the couch. Behind the couch, stood Ginny, her nose in a book.

"Excuse me, ma'am. Do you work here?"

She looked up, startled. When her eyes focused, he could see the intent to cause him bodily harm. Daniel shot a glance at the customers, and she stalked off toward the back end of the store. He followed.

She whirled to face him in front of the science-fiction section. "Ma'am? That's harsh."

"Don't you think that the people would be more inclined to buy the books if you didn't let them read the whole thing in the store?"

"Research shows that a warm environment encourages buying."

"Isn't it stealing to read it without buying it?"

"I think I'll be fine without a federal investigation."

He smiled. Yeah, he'd missed Ginny. "It's nice. I like it. So is that Joanna?" He nodded toward the front of the store.

"Don't bother. What do you need?"

"Huh?"

She gave a half smile and shook her head. "I know you, Danny, and you haven't changed. You're looking for something."

She did know him.

"Yeah," he confessed.

"What?"

"Do you have that book Mike Kearney wrote?"

"That piece of propaganda he used to springboard into national politics? The one where he waves around a bloodstained battle flag and equates war with patriotism? Do you really think I'd carry that book?"

"I think 'hometown boy makes good' sells well, so yeah, you carry it."

All of her teeth flashed in a bright, if predatory, grin. "I missed you, Danny. You're so much fun to abuse. C'mon." She led the way to an endcap near the front and handed over a copy of *A Call to Duty*. "If you try to read it all in the store without paying, I'll have you arrested. I know people in the police department."

"It's amazing that you're still single."

He felt a sharp gaze hit the back of his neck from the tall blonde at the coffee bar. Shifting his angle of view, he used the cover of flipping through the book to take in the scene. Ginny offered a quick smile to the woman behind the bar and then walked over to the register counter on the opposite wall.

The blonde woman's gaze settled on Ginny, a little territorial and a lot wistful. If that was Joanna, Ginny was overstating the better-business-than-bed-partners thing.

"You going to pay for that thing?" Ginny asked.

"Don't I get an old-friend discount?"

"No, you get a self-absorbed-asshole markup. Seventeen ninety-five." She took the book from him and scanned the bar code. "Holy shit."

It was loud enough to attract the barista's attention.

"Everything okay?" she called.

"I'm fine," Ginny answered before lowering her voice. "Holy shit," Ginny said again. "Trey's parents. That's what you were hyped up about last night. You think *he* had something to do with it?" She lifted the book.

He slapped the book back down. "I don't think anything."

"You're like a fucking computer with a single-minded search engine."

"Ginny."

"So what does Kearney have to do with it?"

"Ginny. Shut up," he said it softly, mindful of the tall blonde's protective looks.

Ginny shook her head at someone over his shoulder. "It's all right, Jo. He's an old friend."

"Can I just have my book?"

"Not until you tell me what's going on."

"No."

"Oh, Danny. Don't tell me you're still a romantic." At least she dropped down to a whisper. "You think if you do this for him, he'll love you?"

"I thought you said you didn't get your granola-lesbian therapist degree."

"I didn't. But I'm not an idiot. And I've known you since we were six."

"I'm not in love with him. But he doesn't deserve to go through life with this hanging over his head."

Ginny looked like she was about to let loose with a taunting *are so*. God, Daniel hated Easton.

"So tell me, how did your wonderfully non-romantic desire to help someone who's only a friend with benefits lead you to *him*?" She pointed at the book.

The truth made sense when he tried it out in his head, so he said aloud, "He and my dad and Trey's dad all served in the same squad in Vietnam. It's one of the reasons Trey's dad moved here. Because he contacted Kearney about working for the Easton PD. So I wondered if there was something in here about when they were in Vietnam, something that happened there that might help me figure it out."

It was the truth. He wasn't seriously thinking the future Vice President actually was involved in Trey's parents' shooting, because huge political conspiracies made great movies and TV shows but weren't exactly a part of reality as Daniel knew it. The fact that it would have taken a lot of pull to get Howie's records sealed, that Ron Eriksson had been shot as soon as he had contact with Howie, that the burglar claimed to have big enough connections to reach into the Department of Homeland Security...

It was pretty hard not to start thinking Matt Damon action-thriller conspiracies when all that came together.

"You do. You do think it's him. He was Chief of Police then. It would have been easy enough to set up, right? And control the evidence? Holy shit, Danny. What are you going to do if it is him?"

Daniel hadn't actually gotten that far. He'd seen himself working out the puzzle, freeing Trey from the weight of guilt and then what? He supposed he'd had some idea of justice being served, and Trey being... Damn Ginny for putting ideas into his head. He was absolutely not imagining himself as some kind of white knight riding in to save the day.

Summoning as much eye-rolling disdain as he could, Daniel tried to derail her. "I told you. I don't think anything."

"You are so full of shit."

He didn't know how long he'd have stood there trying to talk her—and himself—out of wild ideas, but the pretentious professor came up to the register with a pile of books in his arms.

Daniel pulled a twenty from his wallet and handed it to Ginny. When she took it, he grabbed the book. "Keep the change."

Chapter Ten

He was almost back to the Navigator when his cell rang. Trey.

"Hey."

"Hey."

The sex was awesome. Conversation, not so much.

"I just put that case to bed," Trey said, following a lengthy pause.

"The convenience store?"

"Yep. He's sitting in County right now."

Daniel looked at his watch as he slid into the seat. "Twelve hours, not bad."

"Easton's finest. So, you want to hear about your burglar?"

"Sure." Daniel dropped the book on the seat next to him.

"I was going to get something to eat. You want to meet me?"

"For lunch?"

"Whatever. Do you like Thai?"

"Thai?" Daniel knew he was asking stupid questions, but he suddenly couldn't find his footing in this conversation. Was Trey asking him out?

"Yes. Thai. We actually have Thai food restaurants in Easton. Or Greek. Or—"

"I like Thai."

"Okay. It's on Third Street, north of Church."

Daniel still wanted to say no. He'd kind of hoped the next time he saw Trey he'd be presenting him with a done deal. *Hi. Here are the answers you've spent your life looking for.* But when he considered his options—spending the rest of the day reading Mike Kearney's biography or the chance to learn what chili and tamarind sauce tasted like on Trey's tongue—it wasn't a particularly hard decision. "What time?"

"Fifteen minutes?"

"Sure."

Trey watched Danny try to squeeze the Navigator into a space a half block away on Third Street. The Thai Palace didn't offer the valet parking Danny was probably used to. Clicking the locks over his shoulder, Danny hurried across the street, coat flapping open to reveal jeans and yet another sweater, this one a dark red. How many had he brought? He sure as hell wasn't buying them at the Clover in the Palmer Park Mall.

"Sorry I'm late," Danny said when he was close enough to not have to yell over the wind trapped on the street by tall churches and old bank buildings. "Why didn't you go in?"

"I just got here."

"It's your fault anyway. You gave Ginny my number."

Trey smiled. "She asked so nicely."

"I went over to her store. It's cute. But apparently I left without the proper goodbyes, so she called me to bitch. It's hard to parallel park when you've got an angry redhead screaming in your ear."

Trey kept his jacket on, but Danny hung his coat on the rack at the entrance. A lot of trust for downtown Easton. The black cashmere coat probably cost seven hundred and was all too liftable there by the front of the restaurant.

An uncommunicative hostess sat them and Trey

remembered why he always got takeout. The table and chairs in here were a ridiculous size for grown men. He put the chair at an angle to try to give himself some extra space.

Trey pretended to study the menu, but he got what he always got. Something that tasted like barbequed pork in a bowl with peanuts, vegetables and noodles. Thank God the menu had numbers like the takeout menu. Danny ordered something with shrimp and coconut and tamarind sauce and asked for it medium hot. He probably even pronounced the dish correctly.

The waitress took their menus and came back with a soda for Trey and water for Danny.

Trey stared at the clear plastic cups. Now that they'd ordered, what? This was probably the bigger reason Trey always got take out. Not that he did a lot of taking people to lunch. But what did you say while you were waiting for the food?

Danny took care of that. "Ginny wasn't the only one who called. Mother called to tell me she already found a place. The movers are coming on the fifth, and as long as there's no issue with the inspection we're closing on the tenth."

Trey's gut lurched like he'd missed the last three cellar stairs.

Not even two weeks. Danny had said he'd be there a month. Trey had been counting on that month. Though beyond getting those years' worth of suppressed hormones out of their systems, he hadn't really thought about what he'd been counting on doing in a month. Did they really need a month for that? Shorter was better. Less time for Trey to get used to someone who could make conversation over lunch. Someone who could almost understand what it was like to be a cop. Someone he didn't have to explain things to.

So thirteen days. If he could wrap up all his cases as quickly as the one today, there'd be a lot of time to have Danny naked in his bed. Maybe if they did it enough, it would somehow add up to a month.

"So how'd you catch the bastard so fast?" Danny dropped a straw into his water.

Someone who could read his mind. Okay. That aspect of Danny was more than a little creepy.

"Girlfriend rolled on him because he wouldn't give her a cut. He only got five hundred out of the drawer anyway. Not a lot of cash for a dime in prison."

"Not very cost effective at all. He'd fit right in at a government job."

The waitress arrived with their bowls and retreated without a word.

Danny slid the chopsticks out of the paper wrapping and efficiently scooped up noodles. "Well, if they were all smart, the job would be much tougher, right?"

"Yeah," Trey agreed.

There shouldn't be anything sexy about eating a bowl of noodles. Except watching Danny's long fingers control the chopsticks with precision—never spilling a drop on his expensive-looking sweater—made Trey want to lean in and have Danny feed him a bite, kiss a little spice off his lips and then see what those fingers could do on him, and hell yeah, in him.

Yet another reason why takeout was always the best option.

He picked up his own fork and tried to pay attention to something besides Danny's fingers and mouth. "I meant to tell you yesterday. That guy Bartos made bail."

"How much?"

"The ADA tried to have him held without. Priors, no local address, flight risk, but it was his first felony so the judge said twenty-five grand."

"Bonded?"

"Nope. A guy came in around noon on Monday. Said he was Bartos's cousin. Paid the whole thing with a cashier's check."

"Wow. I guess he does have friends in high places—or at

least friends rich enough to blow twenty-five grand on him."

"It's just bail."

"Do you think he'll make his court date?"

"Probably not," Trey agreed.

"So who do you think was behind it?"

Trey put his fork down. "Danny. I told you to let it go."

"I'm asking what you think."

"Don't jump to some kind of crazy conclusion."

"So give me a non-crazy conclusion that explains the break-in and the outside support."

"I don't know." Why did everything between them have to get tangled back up in that old shit? "Your mom had some nice jewelry." Trey shrugged.

Jesus, he hated that look on Danny's face. The one that said *I see right through your bullshit.* The same one Danny'd given him when Trey had insisted he wasn't gay.

Trey picked up his fork again. "How's your lunch?"

The look remained for a second before Danny went back to eating. "It's good. Actually, I've only had better in New York."

"Not D.C.?"

"Not that I've found."

The conversation didn't feel as simple as that. Trey might as well have been conducting an interrogation. Looking for hidden meanings, holes in Danny's story. Worse, when Danny looked at him he felt like he was the one in the chair, cuffed to the table.

It wouldn't have been like this if he'd gotten their food to go and asked Danny to meet him at his house on Spring Garden.

"I thought D.C. had everything."

"Nope. Not everything."

Danny went back to scooping up noodles and shrimp, and left Trey to figure out exactly what the fuck that meant.

The waitress came and after looking at them both, put the

check squarely in the middle of the table.

Danny picked it up. "I owe you. From our convenience-store meal." The grin crinkling his eyes made Trey feel like he'd taken a belt of whiskey instead of Pepsi. The warmth started in his throat and spread lower—though whiskey had never really had such a positive effect on his dick before.

He reminded himself that he had to get back to work before his dick could follow through on any of the ideas in his head.

The narrow street lined with tall buildings had dragged the early twilight into foggy gloom. Eyeing Danny's black coat, Trey steered them onto the sidewalk as he led the way back to Danny's Navigator.

Danny clicked the locks and stopped at the passenger door, hand on the window like he was waiting for something, so Trey threw out the invitation.

"I've got to go back in for awhile, but you could come over later. Unless you've got to pack up stuff."

"So what are my choices, exactly? Packing or—?"

"Watching a movie," Trey said dryly. "Sex, wiseass."

"Well if those are my choices, I'll take...sex. It's a tough choice over packing."

"I didn't realize I was that bad."

"Maybe I love packing."

Trey let himself smile, hoped it said *I want to kiss you right here but I can't.* Without all that other shit between them, being with Danny was fun. The problem was, all that other shit wasn't ever going to go away.

"This must be a lot more convenient than going down to Philly to get laid."

Convenient wasn't the word Trey would ever use to describe what he felt about Danny. Not easy or convenient. But worth it, yeah.

"Well, you know with the price of gas..." Trey dipped his head.

Danny moved, making a shadow over the window, blocking the reflections from the old lamppost decorations of faded garland and lights wrapped around star shapes. Through the light tint Trey could see the book on the passenger seat, the too-familiar name bigger than the title.

The warmth from flirting with Danny exploded in a hot flash of anger.

"What are you doing with that?" Trey wanted to punch at the glass but confined himself to a one-fingered jab at a space next to Danny's shoulder. Of course he already knew the answer.

Even if Danny couldn't cover his guilt, at least he met Trey's gaze.

"I told you to stay the fuck out of this. You told me you would."

"It's only a book."

Danny must have thought Trey was stupid. And maybe he was if he'd thought for one second Danny could ever let something go.

Trey stuffed his fists into his jacket pockets. "Don't fucking talk to me right now, Danny. I—I've got to get out of here."

He turned and walked back to his own car.

Since the invitation for sex had clearly been rescinded, Daniel went home and pulled out the Vice President-elect's bio.

Jesus. Mike Kearney was pompous and dull, even for a politician. Daniel forced himself to scan through the "early years of duty". Cub Scouts, Boy Scouts, Eagle Scouts. He'd been in college and left for one of the ninety-day CO training schools to get into Vietnam right after the Tet offensive. He showed enough aptitude—or lack of self-preservation—to be trained as a helicopter pilot, crash training if ever Daniel had heard it.

It was too much to hope for that there would be a section in the book titled "On September 18, 1970 I Did Something Horrible." All Daniel read was how Lieutenant Kearney never left a fallen soldier behind. Time after time he went back into hot zones because he was needed. Nineteen sixty-eight, sixty-nine, at last, nineteen seventy. No mention of his medic, or a mechanic named Eriksson, just one valorous mission after another, pausing from time to time for a detailed description of the hardships soldiers faced.

Daniel hadn't ever been under fire. And he never wanted to be. He knew soldiers faced horrors he couldn't even begin to imagine, but Kearney's experiences read like a campaign speech. Considering the book had come out right around the time the Presidential candidate was looking for a running mate, that's probably what it had been.

He flipped back to the opening, read about Kearney's parents. His dad had worked at Binney and Smith, low-level management at the crayon factory. Not exactly the kind of job that screamed money, yet by the time he was Chief of Police, Kearney had lived on the Hill. He knew because the younger of Kearney's daughters had been three years ahead of him in school and his brother had had a crush on her. Not that a chief didn't pull a nice salary, but not that nice. Their house now would go for over a million, if they hadn't already moved to Harrisburg when Kearney was Lieutenant Governor.

So he went to Vietnam the son of a factory worker who lived on the South Side and came home to buy a mansion on a cop's salary. Follow the money. He'd been taught that since college. Money always left a trail.

With nothing more than a name and address, Danny could poke into the finances of most average Americans. Credit history, income, tax returns. But digging into the financial history of the Vice President-elect was going to raise a lot of flags in the system. It wasn't something he could do out of curiosity. He'd need cause enough for a warrant and he didn't have it.

But before Kearney was picked as President Szabo's running mate, his finances would have been checked with a microscope. If there was anything off about how Kearney made his money, it would have shown up before now.

Daniel took the book, his computer and his coffee the long way around into the living room, deliberately bypassing the liquor cabinet in the dining room. He was sure it had been left stocked and he didn't need to prove his Gardner heritage by drinking away his bad mood.

He'd known how Trey would react if he found out Daniel was digging even after he'd promised he'd stop. It didn't matter if Trey never wanted to talk to him again, Daniel was still going to figure this out. He did wish they'd had more time, though. Trey was one connection to the past Daniel was just starting to think would be worth maintaining. Not only because of how seriously fucking good the sex was, but because when Trey was around everything felt different. Sharper, stronger, like Trey's intensity made life more vivid.

He couldn't live like that though. It'd be like living as a junkie, trying to find a better high, another fix, a way to feel that rush again. Depending on Trey to provide it was doomed to failure. And unfair.

Despite the coffee, Danny had almost fallen asleep in front of History Channel World War II Documentary Number 3047 when there was a knock at the front door. A cop's knock.

The sudden rush of excitement had him alert in a way coffee would never manage. Even if Trey was here for anther fight, it beat dozing over Kearney's Life of Duty. He dropped the book into his computer bag and zipped it. Besides, he had a fine upstanding family tradition to uphold of being unable to resist bad habits.

Trey stood on the front step, hands in his pockets, jaw working over his gum.

"I didn't expect you," Daniel said.

"I didn't expect to be here. I went for a drive."

"Where'd you go?"

"Down 611."

The highway to Philadelphia. Daniel felt his lips twitch. "How far'd you get?"

"Halfway." Trey's smile ghosted across his lips.

Shaking his head, Daniel stepped aside and let Trey into the foyer. Trey didn't take off his coat, didn't even take his hands out of the pockets.

"Danny, I know you're trying to help, even if I don't want you to. But Christ, just...don't lie to me, okay? Don't say you're going to do something if you don't mean it."

Now would probably be a bad time to tell him about scanning the picture. The zing in Daniel's balls weighed in with a double veto. "All right."

Trey nodded.

"Gonna stay for awhile?" Daniel wrapped a hand in the open front of Trey's jacket and tugged.

"Yeah, I think I will."

Chapter Eleven

Trey let Danny pull him forward until their noses bumped and then Danny slanted his head, kissing him slow and steady and sweet, like they had all the time they needed to get it right. Trey hooked an arm around Danny's waist, dragging them tight together as Danny's fingers moved over Trey's collar, thumb rubbing over his jaw, a teasing light pressure behind his ear before sliding a hand up through his hair.

He wanted the time to get this right. And maybe stop Danny from using a smile and a joke to make sure it never went further than a quick hard fuck. Asking Danny what he wanted hadn't worked so far, only seemed to piss him off, so Trey was going to show Danny what he needed. As many times as necessary.

Even with slow kisses, they were both panting when Danny pulled back.

"Gonna let me take my coat off?"

From the grin tilting up the corners of his eyes, Danny was a lot more likely to drop to his knees in the foyer and have Trey out of his mind before he'd even taken five steps into the house.

Trey stepped back a little, shrugging out of the sleeves and dropping the jacket on a hook. Danny kissed him backward toward the stairs, but Trey stopped.

"What?"

Trey nodded at the living room.

Danny looked through the archway. "My bed's bigger than

the couch."

"I remember." Guilt and want twisting together with every step as Trey snuck across the hall into Danny's bedroom.

"But you want to...make out? On the couch?"

"Yeah."

Danny laughed. "You want to fool around on my mother's couch? Is this some weird kind of fantasy left over from adolescence?"

"Forget it."

"No." Danny wasn't laughing anymore. "Because that's pretty much the way I feel about getting you in my bed upstairs."

"But you've had me in your bed upstairs."

"Not quite the way I wanted."

Fuck me.

I can't.

Why not?

Danny didn't know how close Trey had come to giving in. It wasn't like he was a virgin, but he'd had a feeling putting his dick in Danny was going to change a lot of things and not only because of the different hole involved. And that had scared the shit out of him.

"Sorry," Trey offered, knowing it didn't do anything to change how he'd acted then.

"I think it will be better this time."

"I know it will be." Trey dragged Danny down onto the couch.

"My parents won't be home for a few hours," Danny said from underneath him.

"That's kind of a mood killer, thinking of your mother walking in on us. I had that dream more than once."

"What'd you have in mind then?"

"Making us both feel really good." With one foot on the

floor, Trey held Danny's head steady for a kiss while rocking their dicks together. It was kind of like being teenagers again. Too many clothes, an awkward sprawl on the couch—except without the not knowing what it was you're doing or what you're going to get. There was nothing hesitant or sloppy about Danny's tongue licking inside Trey's lips, or the way Danny reached down to cup Trey's ass and settle them at just the right angle.

The pressure in Trey's jeans built to a level that was too close to adolescence for comfort. Even taking things slow and easy, Danny was a threat to his control. Trey slid down him, kneeling on the floor between Danny's legs, reaching for his fly.

Danny's voice was a little rough. "Maybe I don't go that far." But he didn't stop Trey from unbuttoning his jeans.

"I think you do." Trey tugged and Danny lifted his hips. "Yeah, you do." The pants and briefs slid down to Danny's ankles.

Danny's dick bobbed as Trey's breath hit it, like it would drag itself to his mouth, but he didn't touch it. He ran his hands up under Danny's sweater and T-shirt, fingers spread wide, stroking up and down. Danny nudged his dick closer as Trey continued to ignore it, hands gliding over hard muscles, the soft down around the navel, silky hair leading lower. And back up. Watching Danny's face, the way his cheeks got dark, the way his mouth opened when a nail flicked a nipple.

"Cocktease." Danny's voice had gone from rough to hoarse.

Trey shook his head, smiling. His hands dragged down over Danny's hips, thumbs riding deep into the grooves of his groin, stopping to make slow circles on the insides of his thighs. Wetting his lips, Trey paused, still watching Danny's face.

Danny spread his legs and arched up, and Trey pushed him back down. "Relax. I got you."

"Don't—" But whatever Danny's complaint was, it was lost in a groan as Trey licked the thick vein running up the shaft of Danny's cock.

Trey's hands kept Danny braced against the couch as he licked and kissed, using just his tongue and lips, never taking Danny inside. Danny's palm landed on the back of Trey's neck, urging him closer.

Using one hand to slowly jack Danny's spit-wet dick, Trey lifted his head. Danny met his gaze, and the way his eyes looked so guarded—almost afraid—in a face soft and flushed with arousal made Trey's throat tighten—and his jeans. He didn't know why Danny was still fighting it, didn't want to just be taken care of, but Trey was stubborn enough to get him there.

"I'm going to blow you and then fuck you."

"And what am I going to do?"

"Come."

The muscles of Danny's thigh jumped under the one hand Trey was still using to pin him against the couch.

"But if you need something to do"—Trey kissed the blood-dark head trapped in his fist—"you can put your hands behind your head and leave them there."

"What if I don't?" Danny's words didn't have much force as Trey used his tongue on the spot underneath the rim.

Trey lifted his head again, trying to gauge how far he could push. There was still resistance in those dark green eyes. "Then you don't get blown."

Danny nodded and tucked his hands behind his head, but he didn't smile.

Trey's smile was enough for both of them. Whatever nervousness was in Danny's eyes wasn't having any affect on his dick. When Trey let it go, it jerked toward his mouth again.

Trey grabbed Danny's thighs and yanked him toward the edge of the cushion, then kissed and nipped from Danny's navel down, softening the pressure at the root of his cock, licking around the base. The tension went out of Danny little by little, and when Trey looked up from sucking on Danny's balls almost all the wariness was gone from Danny's eyes.

He licked lower, using first the flat of his tongue and then the point, tracing the small ridge under Danny's balls down to his hole. A second to wonder whether Danny would get all tense again and then Trey lifted those strong legs, ducking under and letting the weight settle on his shoulders so he could get at that soft twitching skin.

Danny groaned, the muscles on Trey's shoulders tightening and then relaxing, just like the muscle under his tongue. Nose buried under Danny's sac, Trey's whole head was full of Danny's smell and taste, strong and sharp, every breath of it making Trey's dick swell and pulse in his jeans. He circled and licked, waiting for that tight muscle to soften enough to let his tongue in. He got the tip in, felt the blood pumping around his tongue and drove in a little bit more.

Danny gasped and Trey wanted to forget this stupid idea. He could climb up and fuck him and worry some other time about getting it right, about making Danny lose his maddening self-control. But how many times did they have left?

He used his mouth harder, let his teeth scrape gently and his tongue wiggle in deeper.

A few unintelligible sounds and then Danny said, "Can't."

Trey eased off, licking softly, and then used a finger to take the place of his tongue.

"You can."

Trey sat back on his heels and slicked two more fingers in his mouth, waiting. He gave him a little friction with the finger inside, slow but deep, then crooked it, stroking until the pressure eased enough for more.

He was driving two fingers deep inside when Danny said it again, "I can't."

Trey knew what he meant. All that feeling inside and nothing on your dick. It was enough to make you lose your mind and that's exactly what he wanted from Danny. He couldn't believe no one had ever done this for him before. Why wouldn't someone want to worship him, make Danny fall apart with lips and fingers and tongue?

He was a hot guy anyway, but like this, skin flushed, eyes dark and glittering, cock deep red and slick from the come leaking from the tip, Danny was fucking gorgeous enough to make Trey's dick ache just from looking. He wanted his dick on Danny, in him, between his lips, rubbing on the muscles of his chest, the groove of his ass. Wanted to paint his warm skin with come.

"You can. Let me watch you come."

"I can't, I need—"

Trey rubbed the tight skin around Danny's hole with a third finger, feeling the muscle tighten and relax with each thrust, tucked his fingers together and pushed all three inside.

"God. Trey." Danny's voice was strained. He flinched away, but kept his hands behind his head. Trey could see one hand locked on the opposite wrist, knuckles white under the skin.

"Hurt?"

"Not enough to stop. But Jesus, do something."

He waited until Danny rocked down onto his fingers and then started thick friction, turning his wrist as he drove inside. Danny's breath left him in a gasp at the bottom of every stroke. Trey didn't want to hurt him with his knuckles, so he curled his fingers up, found his gland and swirled his fingers against it, making Danny buck up off the couch.

Danny's words came slow, hissed between his clenched teeth. "Don't know what you want, but Jesus, do it. I've gotta come."

"Yeah."

But Danny was still holding back, still not giving in.

"Let go."

"Stop fucking saying that."

"C'mon, Danny. 'S gonna feel so good." He thrust and stroked, watched Danny's eyes flutter open and closed and went for more direct pressure, tapping inside.

"I can't."

Trey brushed his lips across the tip of Danny's cock.

"Fuck." Danny picked his head off the back of the couch and snapped. "Get me off or I'm going to do it myself."

A gentle swirl from his tongue, prodding with his fingers.

He licked the vein underneath, felt the pulse there and against his knuckles and shoved Danny's sweater up with his free hand.

Another lick. Danny was making strangled desperate groans that sounded almost like Trey's name, and he couldn't make Danny wait any more. As he sucked on the head, Danny made a sound like something was ripped from his body. He jerked and then froze, muscles clamping on Trey's fingers, come splashing again and again on his tongue and lips. He lifted his head and pushed with his fingers, and was rewarded with a high arc onto Danny's ribs. Danny was shuddering now, come still pumping from his dick as Trey kept pushing until Danny shoved him away.

"Jesus, Trey," Danny said over and over as he slumped sideways onto the couch.

Trey crawled to his feet and kicked off his boots to peel his jeans off, hand on his own way-past-desperate dick.

"Y'can fuck me if you want." Danny's words tripped over each other, a distinct lack of enthusiasm in his tone.

Trey shook his head. "Later."

He wanted to climb on and rub himself all over the come on Danny's belly, slide in it, grind against that slick warmth until he shot his own, their come mixing together on their chests. He'd half-decided it was worth the risk when he felt the heat curl out, untwisting inside him. He could have made a convincing lie for why he had to aim his dick toward Danny's stomach, respect for Julia's upholstery or something, but the truth was he wanted to see the white spray land on Danny's body.

Even as orgasm pulled conscious control from his muscles,

Trey forced his eyes open to watch. Saw Danny's own gaze focus on where Trey's come hit him, Danny's tongue slip between his lips as if he could taste it. The sight dragged another spurt—almost a painful shock—and Trey hung his head, panting.

After taking a deep breath of the smell of them together, he said, "I'll get us a towel."

The half-bath was across from the dining room. Trey hesitated for a second before pulling Julia's decorative hand towels off the rack. She'd probably need different ones for her new place anyway. Danny could wash them or throw them out.

He washed off his hands and came back out with the towels. Danny was pretty much where Trey had left him, except he'd kicked his jeans and socks off and made an attempt at getting his sweater and T-shirt over his head. As Trey wiped his stomach, Danny squirmed and got his head free from his clothes.

"All part of the service?" Danny dropped his sweater on the floor.

"Huh?"

Danny waved a hand at where Trey was cleaning him off. "This. Your service. I feel like I should pay you."

"Christ, I just wanted to take care of you." Trey tossed the towel away.

"I'm a big boy."

"I can see that." Trey could see Danny getting ready to hide behind a joke and a cool stare. Ignoring the warning signs—and the cyclone fencing—Trey climbed onto the couch, managing to get some of his weight onto the cushions instead of all on Danny.

Danny rested his hand on the back of Trey's neck. "I'm used to actively participating when I have sex."

"I give you high marks for participation." Trey kissed him.

"I mean, I don't usually just lie there."

"You didn't. Trust me." Trey leaned in for another kiss, but while Danny's mouth was soft, he didn't respond. "Do you want me to go?"

"You don't have to." It wasn't exactly a strong denial, but Danny's hand got heavier on Trey's neck, keeping him close.

Trey shifted to grab the throw draped over the back of the couch and pull it over them. Danny pressed himself against the back so they were almost side-by-side.

"I wish it was dark," Danny said after a minute.

"It is. Oh." A guy on the TV behind Trey was loudly selling some kind of miracle cleaning product. Both floor lamps were on. He thought he knew the answer but he said, "Why?"

"It seemed to make everything easier."

Trey remembered thinking the same thing. How confessions were better in the dark. What did Danny want to say that he couldn't say in the light? Trey lay there wondering until he fell asleep.

"Danny?"

Daniel had no idea why his dad was calling him for school instead of his mother. All he wanted was to bury himself back under warm blankets and Trey's even warmer body.

Trey's body. Dad calling him. One of those things was very wrong. Which meant one of them had to be a dream.

Daniel jerked awake, and Trey pushed up beside him.

"Danny?" Definitely his dad. Definitely in the house.

"Is that your dad?" Trey whispered.

Definitely not a dream.

"Yeah." Daniel shoved, but Trey was already off the couch and scrambling into a pair of jeans. Daniel found his own, remembered jumping into pants didn't work outside cartoons and yanked them up one leg at a time.

"Go, hide somewhere," he whispered at Trey.

"Huh? Doesn't your dad know?"

"He knows I'm gay. Do you want him and everyone else he talks to knowing you are?"

Trey shrugged.

Daniel ripped his T-shirt and sweater apart. As the material parted, static sparked bright, even in the well-lit room, sending the hair on his arms into tingling spikes. He yanked the T-shirt over his head.

While his hair gel could usually hold up to Washington humidity and keep him from looking like the victim of a bad eighties perm, it was not cut out for exigencies like having five seconds to dress before your dad caught you naked on the couch with your used-to-wish-he-was-but-now-I-don't-know boyfriend. His hair lifted off his scalp.

He heard Trey snort a laugh and spun around.

"Nice."

There was an expensive-sounding crash from the kitchen. Almost everything was packed. What had Dad knocked over?

"Just go. Hide."

"Where?"

"Go out the French doors."

"You do know it's freezing."

For someone who'd been intent on attending to Daniel's every need an hour ago, Trey was being a serious pain in the ass right now.

"Take my sweater."

With an exasperated sigh, Daniel went through the dining room to the kitchen. His father held onto a counter with one hand while he crouched over the pieces of the coffee maker on the floor.

Shit.

"Ah, Dad, not the coffee maker."

His father looked up. "I know it's late. So I thought I should make you coffee."

Drunk logic. Daniel made an assessment of his father's condition. Not completely smashed. A little challenged on balance and deceptively pleasant. Early stages.

"Tell me you didn't drive."

"I'm fine."

"Give me the keys."

Trying to keep his bare feet clear of the shattered carafe, Daniel helped his father to his feet and lifted the keys and the silver flask from his coat pocket, tucking them into his own jeans.

"Okay. Go sit. I'll make us coffee."

"That's what I've been trying to do." His father jerked away.

So much for the amiable part of his father's evening.

"All right, Dad. But the coffee maker's broken. Let me see what I can do."

His father looked up at him. Actually looked at him, dark blue eyes bloodshot and muddy, like the iris was leaking into the cornea. Well, at least Dad still had his hair. That was something to look forward to.

"God, Danny, what did you do to your hair?"

But the odd telepathy Daniel would take a pass on.

He ran his hand over the still-crackling strands. He probably looked like a demented hedgehog. Waiting for his father's criticism to hit with the usual double shot of anger and disappointment, Daniel was surprised to find he only felt pity.

"I was working and I fell asleep on the couch."

"You should cut it."

"I will." As unobtrusively as he could manage, he steered his father onto one of the stools at the center counter. He'd say his father's ease at climbing onto one was due to a familiarity with barstools, but Dad only drank at home. And in the office. In private.

He filled two mugs with hot water and shoved them into the

microwave before opening the mostly empty cabinets, hoping there was instant coffee. Not that he particularly wanted his father wide awake, but it gave them something to do. A dusty jar was hidden behind some ancient instant soup. Well, it wasn't as if his dad would notice the taste.

Leaning on the counter by the microwave, he looked at his father who was hunched over the plastic spoon Daniel had put in front of him. "Why are you here, Dad?"

His father looked up and then back down at the spoon. It was time for the introspective drunk. Followed by the belligerent, throwing-things drunk and then the passed-out drunk.

"I came to visit. I haven't seen you in a while, Danny." His tone was only mildly accusatory.

Six and a half years. His sister's college graduation. "Nice to see you."

"House looks good."

Like Dad could tell from staring at a spoon.

"The closing's on the tenth."

"So soon?"

"Mother found a town house she likes."

"Incredible."

"What is?"

"Your mother finding something she likes."

Dad sounded almost surprised when he said it. So they hadn't hit the belligerent part yet.

The microwave dinged, and Daniel put the mugs and the coffee on the table. After looking at his father's shaking hands, Daniel unscrewed the cap on the coffee jar. His father scooped some into his mug and stared at the foamy swirls.

"Why are you here?" Daniel tried again. He wanted to get this out of the way before Dad slid into angry and bitter. "Why'd you drive up here at two in the morning?"

"I know I've made mistakes."

Daniel tried not to swallow his tongue. Even at his most introspective, his father never apologized.

"It's all right, Dad."

"No. It's not. But I can't fix it. I wish I could."

Whatever had driven his father to come here, Daniel didn't think he'd be getting much information tonight. "It's all right," he said again.

"Your mother always expected me to."

"To what?"

"Fix everything. Give her everything. Make everything perfect."

Christ. Sixteen years of silence and now Dad was having remorse?

"Don't worry about it, Dad."

His father swirled the spoon. "Any sugar?"

Wordlessly, Daniel got up, found the box and put it in front of his father who grabbed five packs and dumped them into his coffee. Maybe Daniel could coax his father into going to sleep—not on the couch—but up in Rob's old room. His mom had stripped all the beds except for Daniel's but considering how many sheets his father had in the wind, Daniel doubted he'd miss the ones on the bed.

Dad slugged back the coffee like it was Drambuie. When the sugar hit, his hands stopped shaking. Maybe his father was coming off a drunk rather than rolling through one.

"I need to talk to you, Danny."

"All right."

"You know those trees." His father stared through the wall behind the sink as if he could see the trio of maples in the backyard. "Planted one for each of you. Year you were born."

"I know."

"Now they'll be here and someone else will live in the house. Maybe cut them down."

That was unpleasantly morbid. Daniel controlled a

shudder. "All right. We'll talk in the morning." *When you make a little more sense.* Daniel came around to help him up.

"You weren't a bad kid."

Terrific. The accolade he'd been waiting his life to hear. *Not a bad kid.*

"Just...a little wound up sometimes."

Even better. If his dad didn't get to belligerent soon, Daniel might beat him there.

"C'mon." Daniel put a hand on his father's shoulder. "Let's get you to bed."

His father turned with more grace than Daniel would have expected and grabbed his wrist with force, landing right over the same spot Daniel had been clutching while Trey had been— doing whatever he called it. Daniel sucked in his breath and clenched his teeth. He was going to have a ring of bruises there.

Daniel patted his father's hand and tried to extract his wrist without further damage and pain. His father held on. Daniel's wrist was going to look like he'd spent the night in handcuffs.

"Are you happy, son?"

His father must have Daniel confused with Rob.

"Yeah, Dad, I'm fine."

"I was happy for awhile. After I got back. It was good to be back."

Daniel pulled again. "C'mon. You don't want to sit in the kitchen all night."

"From Nam."

He knew his father would remember this in the morning. Remember every word and hate himself for saying it. Hate Daniel for hearing it.

"Dad."

"Thought I left it all there. But you can't. Where's that picture?"

"What picture?"

"The one you called about. I want it."

"Why?"

His father threw Daniel's hand away like it disgusted him. "I want to see it. They were my friends."

Great. He'd stirred up nostalgia with his phone call. He wondered if he could distract his father with something. "I don't have it anymore."

"Why not?"

"I gave it away."

"Away? It wasn't yours to give away." His father's hand knocked the coffee mug and when the liquid sloshed on his pants, he picked it up and threw it against a cabinet.

Daniel's heart raced, instinct telling him to do what he'd always done, run. Grab his bike and get as far away as his legs would take him so he didn't have to hear this. Watch this.

In the silence after the crash, Daniel heard the scrape of a boot in the garage, a step on the back stairs. When a shadow fell across the back door, Daniel shook his head. His father would be furious if he knew there was someone else seeing him like this, and Dad had never managed the convenience of blackouts.

"Where is it?"

Daniel grabbed at his father's flailing arm, pinned both his father's wrists in one hand. He was stronger than his father now. It felt wrong. But given the look of helpless fury on his father's face, he was glad to be able to hold him.

Forcing calm over his own anger was almost as hard as keeping his father on the stool, but he managed it. "I gave the picture to Trey. He doesn't have much of his father."

The fight left his father, and Daniel released him.

"Poor son of a bitch. That was a shame."

"Yeah. It was."

"Your mother. Never gave a damn about them and then all of a sudden she had to take the kid in."

And his father's drinking and violence had gotten worse. Not that it had been much better before. But Daniel had wondered if Trey had something to do with it. Had Dad missed his friend Ron Eriksson so much that the sight of his son had pushed him further into alcoholism?

"I'm glad she did."

His father scrubbed a hand over his face. "What a fucking mess."

"C'mon, Dad. Go to bed, or I'll let you sleep in the kitchen."

"Just like your mother. 'You'll sleep where you fall.'"

"Well, she was right. C'mon." Daniel lifted under his father's shoulder and he slid off the stool, draping a heavy arm across Daniel's shoulders.

"When did you get to be such a strong little son of a bitch?"

Daniel decided to tell the truth. "As soon as I got the hell out of this house."

His father snorted. But Daniel wasn't sure if it was disgust or agreement.

Chapter Twelve

Trey was hugging himself for warmth in the garage when he heard Danny and Dr. Gardner go upstairs. Danny was all right. He was trained. He was strong. Trey should just grab his jacket and go home, but after what he'd heard, he couldn't.

When he heard Danny coming back downstairs, Trey let himself in the kitchen door.

"Forget your coat?" Danny asked.

"Everything okay?"

Danny shrugged. "He's out. For the night I think."

"I'm sorry."

"Sorry you missed the show?"

Trey didn't know what he'd expected, but Danny was harder, colder than he'd ever seen him, the words fired from his mouth like bullets.

"You all right?"

"I'm fine." Danny bent down to pick up the pieces of the mug. And the coffee pot. And the coffee machine.

Trey didn't want to leave Danny like this. He seemed so brittle he'd snap like a branch under ice. He wouldn't. If there was one thing Trey knew about Danny, he wouldn't break. But Trey still couldn't leave him like this. Even if Danny looked like he'd punch Trey for touching him.

"You're going to cut your feet. Go get some shoes on," Trey said.

Danny went out and came back with boots on. "I'll get the broom."

Trey wrapped the shards in a newspaper he found on the kitchen table before putting them in the garbage. When he turned back, Danny was soaking up the coffee with a wad of paper towels.

"I guess I'll have to mop."

"You should let him clean it up himself."

Danny shot him an incredulous look and tossed the paper towels in the garbage.

As Trey followed their arc, he saw a splash of bright red on the stained white. "You cut yourself."

Danny turned his hands over palms up to examine them. "Looks that way." He'd sliced open the web between his thumb and index finger. Blood ran freely down his palm to his wrist.

"Are you going to wash it and stop the bleeding or just stare at it all night?"

"I thought that's what you hung around for, to pick up the pieces."

"Christ. At least I know that will never change."

"What?"

"You and your dramatic timing."

Danny made a sound like a laugh, but it was anything but happy.

"So will you take care of that? It's making me queasy," Trey said.

Danny did laugh then. A hard, dry cough. "Because I'm sure you so rarely see blood."

Not yours.

He'd seen more than enough when he went running into the house that morning. Running so fast the police couldn't stop him before he got in and saw her. He could definitely go a lifetime without having to see the blood of someone he loved again.

Danny stepped to the sink and rinsed off his hand before getting a fresh paper towel. Trey finished cleaning up as Danny put pressure on the cut.

"I've got a first-aid kit in the trunk. I'll be right back."

The bleeding slowed, and Danny propped his forearm on the counter to let Trey help him put a bandage on it. He was winding the gauze around Danny's wrist and palm when he gave one of those sharp laughs again.

"I'm not auditioning for *The Mummy*."

"It needs to stay on tight. Unless you think it needs stitches."

Danny's gaze landed on Trey's face like a touch. "Tell me that isn't the same piece of gum."

Trey lifted it with his tongue and pushed it in behind his molars. "Sorry."

"You blew me—rimmed me—with gum in your mouth?"

"Sometimes I sleep with gum in my mouth. It's either gum or cigarettes." Trey tore the end of the gauze strip with his teeth. It had been hard as hell to quit when he got out of the service.

"You can smoke in the middle of a blow job?"

"I have a wide variety of skills." Trey tied off the gauze over the cut. "And an oral fixation. I'm a perfect boyfriend."

He'd been joking, but the words lay there between them dead as the conversation.

Danny flexed his hand. "Thanks." He slid off the stool while Trey packed up his first-aid box.

"You going up to bed?"

"Nah. I don't want to have to hear him if he gets sick."

"Does he?"

"The fuck do I know. I haven't had to live with it for years." Danny walked out of the kitchen.

Trey followed him into the living room where Danny flopped onto the couch.

The couch.

Life could really change fast in an hour. Trey knew that better than anyone. He wondered why it still surprised him.

As Danny aimed the remote at the TV, Trey sat next to him. "You could sleep at my house."

"No thanks. I should probably make sure he doesn't try to drive somewhere." Danny flipped through a dozen channels before stopping on Headline News for a few seconds. He muted the volume and kept flicking through the channels.

Trey finally asked the question that had been sitting on his tongue since he heard the sound of something shattering. "He ever hit you?" Trey didn't see it when he lived there, but Dr. Gardner was already on his way out.

"A couple of backhands when I was fourteen, hurt like a bitch when I had the braces on. Mother saw him do it one time and that was it."

Danny had been one skinny kid at fourteen.

"Bastard," Trey said.

Danny shrugged and picked up the remote again, adding a little volume.

Trey took a deep breath and asked the other thing he'd been holding onto. "You asked him about the Polaroid."

Danny nodded.

"You honestly think because a guy is smoking a cigar in a forty-year-old picture that, what, he's hiding something?"

Danny clicked off the TV and turned to face him. Trey was immediately sorry he started the conversation.

"That's not Kearney in that picture."

"How the hell can you know that?"

Danny stared at his jeans and rubbed a hand down his thigh. But he looked Trey in the eyes when he said it. "That night I was at your house, I scanned it, then put it in my computer with some software to clean it up."

Trey was pissed. And then he was amazed at Danny's

tenacity. And then he was really pissed. "So, you came over and fucked me into a coma so you could have a few minutes alone with a picture?"

"I came over because I wanted to have sex with you."

"Right."

"And because I want to help. You shouldn't have to do this by yourself."

"Jesus fucking Christ." Trey hoped Dr. Gardner was out cold because he couldn't help getting loud. "How many times do I have to tell you I'm not doing it anymore? We got an answer. If you don't like it, deal with it."

"It's the wrong answer," Danny said with the irritating self-assurance of someone who didn't have anything personal on the line.

"This isn't one of your little case files to poke around in. It's real people. My parents."

"I know that. Why do you think I'm doing it?"

"I know exactly why. Because you need everything all wrapped up. You don't like messy. It has nothing to do with me or my mom."

Danny looked away. "That's funny because all I ever get is messy. Why the hell do you think I had to get out of here?" He picked up the remote and started flipping through channels again.

Trey took it from him and turned off the TV before tossing the remote behind the couch. "Because you couldn't push until it was just the way you like it."

"Yeah. And why did you leave?" Danny stared at the blank TV.

Trey had gotten them into this. He guessed they were going to finish it. "I was scared."

"Of what?" Danny actually sounded like he didn't know.

"Of you. Of what was happening between us."

"So you joined the Army?" Danny was getting a little loud

too.

"I came back."

"Six years later. It wasn't like you couldn't find me."

"I tried."

"When?" Danny finally looked at him.

"When I got out of basic, I had a few days. I got your number from Julia, went to New York and called you."

"I think I'd remember."

"You weren't home. You weren't home any of the times I called."

Male voices. Laughter.

Who is it?

Some guy for Daniel.

It's always some guy for Daniel.

He'd tried not to be jealous. Didn't have any right to be, then or now. But at eighteen he'd almost broken his hand against the brick wall next to the payphone.

"I left messages," Trey said.

"I didn't get them." Danny's eyes were that deep green again as he looked straight at Trey.

"Guess not." Or maybe he did. It was a long time ago. Did it matter? "So now what?"

"I want to help you find out what happened to your parents, help my mother close the house and then I never want to set foot in this town again. What about you?"

What about him? Trey had never allowed himself to want much beyond finding the truth. If that was gone, the only thing Trey wanted was Danny, and he wasn't on the table. "Sounds good."

"Yeah? So can I show you the picture? Unless you want to go home to bed?"

For a second there was that flash of the old animated Danny before he reined himself in, shrugging the last statement as a question.

"We both know I don't sleep much. I'll look."

Trey was impressed at how much Danny had managed to pull out of the picture, but a guy who wasn't the guy named in the picture really didn't seem like grounds for a break-in, let alone a double murder.

"Check out the writing on the back. Is it your dad's?" Daniel pushed the printout toward him, the paper spinning around on the highly polished dining room table.

"No. My dad made these funny things on his R's. I used to copy them." Trey traced it with his finger on the wood and then stopped.

"And it's not constipated enough for my father's handwriting."

Trey almost laughed. "How is handwriting constipated?"

"Like this." Danny pursed his lips and squinched up his face. "Only with handwriting. He writes like a tight-ass."

Now Trey was laughing. Danny shrugged.

Trey studied the writing again. "So if it's not your dad's and it's not mine, that leaves Howie, Terry—"

"My father said it's Tracy."

"Girl's name either way, poor bastard. And Brian."

"And Kearney. Why do you think his name's like that, just the last name?"

"Now you're really grasping at straws."

"And it's bigger. I wonder if we could somehow see if the inks are the same age. If someone added that name later."

"Don't start jumping off cliffs of logic again. I said I'd look. And you're right about the insignia but I don't know that it proves anything."

"Not jumping. Analyzing. It's what I'm paid to do. Kearney's family didn't have any money. How did he buy that house on a cop's salary?"

K.A. Mitchell

"Lots of overtime."

"I wonder if I could get the records. See what missions they had that September."

"I remember my dad showing me that scar." Trey stared at the screen. "The shoulder got more fucked up when he was in the accident just before we moved here." His throat clamped on a sudden painful swallow.

He'd lived with it for a long time. Lived with the little pieces left of his father that were almost worse than the grief of having him completely gone. So a picture shouldn't be enough to start that buzz in his ears and the heat behind his eyes. But seeing his dad, even so long before Trey ever knew him, just tore all that shit open again.

He shut the laptop and went over to the bay window. In the house across the street, someone had forgotten to shut off the Christmas lights. They were all blue, the angel, the reindeer, blue icicle-strands hanging from the eaves, blue snowflakes in the windows. Danny flicked off the lights in the dining room and the blue glow seemed to spill across the wet-black pavement to the edge of the Gardner lawn.

The lights were all blue, but the snowflakes must be new. Their deeper color made some of the other lights look almost green. The old Sesame Street song played in his head, "One of these things is not like the other..." Wrong insignia, wrong guy? Why?

God, he wanted Danny to be right. He wanted to be able to stand on his father's grave and tell him, "I got the bastard." Erase the shame he'd felt every time his father had given him that hopeful look when Trey went to visit him.

Danny came up behind and wrapped his arms around Trey. He froze for a second, resisting the comfort Danny wouldn't take earlier, but then let Danny pull him back against his chest.

"It sucks," Danny said. "It sucks that your dad is dead because he was a good man, and my dad is still here and he's

188

an asshole."

Trey didn't trust his voice yet so he nodded against Danny's shoulder.

Danny pulled him in tighter, taking Trey's weight against him. He let Danny's strength support them both. There was still that pull between them, the current that sometimes arced sharp and fast as a taser blast, but it was nice just to be touched. To know someone was there, especially when he was awake at three in the morning, when there was nothing to do but stare and think.

And then I never want to set foot in this town again.

He shouldn't get used to this. It wasn't as if Danny would ask Trey to go with him this time. Or that Trey would go. It wasn't much of a life he'd built here, with his serial-killer basement and lots of overtime, but it was his.

Danny shivered against him and Trey remembered that the sweater he was stretching out, the one that smelled like a ski-vacation on TV—fresh snow and pine trees—was Danny's.

Leaning forward, he shrugged out of it, turned and handed it back. Danny pulled it over his head. "God, it's warm."

"Hearty northern breeding stock, that's what my dad always said."

"Just so you know, I'm not carrying your child. It'll ruin my figure." Danny was still standing close, but his hands were in his pockets, the bandage on his right hand a white spot against the dark of his jeans. It wasn't only his sweater's warmth that was gone.

Despite Danny's retreat, Trey leaned in and scraped their cheeks together, breathing in ski-trip aftershave and Danny's sweat with the smell of sex still on him. When Danny put his arm around Trey's waist, he thought of asking Danny to come home with him again, but it was a loose grip, like Danny didn't care if Trey left.

"I'm going to go home and shower and shave."

The grip tightened, a press into the small of his back, and

then Danny stepped away. "Okay."

Trey stepped into the foyer and fished his keys out of his jacket pocket, taking his house keys off his ring.

Danny was where he'd left him in front of the big window. Trey pressed the keys into Danny's hand.

"Here."

Danny looked from the keys to Trey's face.

"You can go dig around all you want while I'm at work."

"You trust me?"

Trey pulled his lower lip in and then said, "You planning to secretly scan anything? Because I want the benefit of you putting me into a coma again—preferably with a blow job—first."

"I think I'm good with the all-access pass." Danny put the keys on the table next to the laptop. He smiled, but it wasn't the eye-crinkling thing that always hit Trey like making a perfect shot before getting fouled off the court onto his ass. Exhilaration and an elbow to the ribs all in one moment.

"You gonna be okay?" Trey jerked his head toward the ceiling.

Danny held up his bandaged hand. "Safe and sound. I won't be the one with a hangover tomorrow."

"Call me if—"

"I can handle him. Get some sleep. You've been up twenty-four hours."

The dining room table was between them now, so Trey said, "Night, Danny."

Daniel's father was enough of a surly bastard in the morning that Daniel almost steered him to the liquor cabinet after his father snarled his second request for coffee. Daniel put the jar of instant in front of him.

190

His father glared at it. "I'll get some on the way. Where are my goddamned keys?"

Daniel slapped them on the kitchen counter.

"And?"

With a sigh, Daniel got the flask from the cabinet where he'd stuck it before dozing on the couch.

"Don't give anything else of mine away unless you call me first." His father shoved the flask into the coat he'd never taken off. Fumes were coming off him from three feet away.

"What makes you think that picture was yours?"

"It was in my house."

"This isn't your house, Dad. You haven't lived in it for fifteen years."

"It's still—"

"How do you know the picture was yours? There were names on the back, and it wasn't your handwriting."

"Don't you use that tone with me." His father pushed away from the counter and stalked toward him. "You think you know my handwriting?"

The asshole wasn't going to make him cower. Daniel let him get close enough that the stench of stale scotch gagged him, but he stared his father down. "Yeah, I do. Whose picture was it?"

"What the fuck difference does that make? Someone gave it to me."

"Who?"

"Why the hell do you care? You don't have it anymore anyway."

"No, I don't."

"No, you gave it to Ron's kid. Christ. If you find anything of mine you call me, got it? Especially from the war."

"Why do you even care all of a sudden?"

"You just need to do what you're told."

"Dad, I haven't been a kid you could order around for a

long time. How about this? Before you set foot in this house again, you call me."

He could see the blow coming and ducked it, grabbing his father's arm and pinning it behind him, shoving him face first over the counter. As his father's breath left him on a rancid grunt, Daniel released him and walked away, hands fisted at his sides.

"You little shit." But there was a touch of admiration in his father's voice even as he gasped for breath. Great. Violence he respected.

Daniel flexed his hand. Blood welled up from the opened cut, staining the gauze again.

His father pulled the flask out and took a long drink.

Relaxing his hands, Daniel spread them out on the counter next to his father. It had been a family law. No one ever mentioned the drinking directly. Fuck that. "If you keep drinking, I will call in your license number to the cops."

"You think I can't handle it?"

"I don't care how you handle it. But I do care about the other people on the road."

"Sanctimonious little bastard."

At that point, Daniel really wished he were a bastard, but he had his father's thick curly hair. "Bye, Dad." He nodded at the door.

"You think you can do that, make calls and threaten people?"

"I'm not threatening anyone. I'm saying if you leave here drunk, I'm not going to let you get behind the wheel and take out some innocent family."

"You're not the only one who can make calls."

"What do you mean?"

His father didn't answer. Daniel had meant what he said to Trey last night. It wasn't fair that his father got to live and Trey's father didn't. Or maybe it was a lack of sleep. Either way,

Daniel was done.

"Put the flask on the counter and leave." He could take it from him if he had to, and now his father knew it.

"Doesn't mean I won't stop on the road."

"But you won't. You won't want to be seen like this, no matter where."

The stalemate went on for a few minutes before his father threw the flask into the garbage can.

"Happy now? Jesus, you're even a bigger bitch than your mother. Though we shouldn't be surprised, should we?"

"You should know, Dad. Only bitchy queens use the royal we."

Even hung-over his father wasn't stupid. His face got bright red, knuckles white on his grip on the counter. Without another word, his father picked up the keys and slammed out the back door.

Bile and spit filled Daniel's mouth and he clenched his jaw against the nausea. That much adrenaline ran up interest faster than a credit card, leaving him almost dizzy. He spread his hands out on the counter again where he'd faced his father, hoping the cold tiles would help cool down his body.

The confrontation had been fifteen years too late. He wished he'd had the guts to do it then, but it still felt good to have it over.

He threw the bandage in the trash on top of his father's flask and went up to take a shower so he could go out for some real coffee.

Daniel had never been in someone else's house alone before—except for the investigations he did before he switched agencies. It was weird. He knew Trey, but he didn't know he had the whole boxed set of M*A*S*H DVDs, or that he read a lot of nonfiction: psychology, forensics, sociology—some of the editions had been Daniel's textbooks in college and at Quantico, including a few he couldn't get through. There wasn't a scrap of Trey's high school history, not a basketball trophy or a yearbook. No pictures either, except a framed one on the TV stand of Trey's mom and dad at their wedding. And no tree or any other concession to the holiday.

Curiosity was a fault Daniel wholeheartedly embraced, so he went into the kitchen. Even in the ordered perfection of his mother's home an occasional personal touch snuck in to the dishware. A souvenir mug, a glass from an event. But there was no Go Army mug or a tenth high school reunion shot glass in the cabinets. What dishes Trey had were plain, if mismatched, like he'd gotten them from garage sales.

There was so little of him here, Trey might as well have been house-sitting. What if he was ready to move? What if Daniel asked Trey to leave Easton with him this time? No whining or begging, a simple question.

Daniel had come a long way from when he'd thought sex meant love, that because someone could get you off he was the answer to everything you needed. But even though there had always been more than sex between him and Trey, it didn't mean Trey was any more likely to come with him fifteen years later.

And what would Daniel be asking this time? *Come be my boyfriend, my best friend, my partner?* What made Daniel think that after a couple of fucks and one lunch he could ambush Trey with the same question Scott had sprung? If Daniel couldn't give the right answer to Scott—after two years—how could he even ask Trey now?

It was a hell of a lot easier—and safer—to think of Trey here, kind of frozen, just something from the old life Daniel could come back to when he needed that touchstone. Better, yeah, but his mind kept seeing Trey in the apartment in D.C. On Daniel's couch watching M*A*S*H DVDs. Dropping off some Thai takeout on the table. Stretching out in the bed and making

Daniel say what he wanted—needed.

Daniel shook his head, disgusted at himself. He hadn't changed at all from that lovesick teenager who'd thought he could solve everything for Trey if he just loved him enough. He took his coffee and his laptop down into the cellar.

Pacing along the corkboard, he knew. This was where Trey lived, tied to the past. Asking Trey to leave it, especially without any resolution, would end the same way. Daniel made space for his laptop on the big metal desk and started poking into September of 1970.

There never was a *gotcha* moment. But the more he dug, the more he was convinced Kearney and Howie were in something up to their cobra-spitting insignia. Too many repairs, too many missions logged as nothing more than "Section Number" and "drop". They flew almost twice as many missions as some of the other helicopter crews, most of whom kept better records. And given Howie's later career and leisure choices, coupled with what Daniel knew of Southeast Asia's history, he was starting to think the drops were more like pick ups of the nice brown cash-crop kind.

He'd called one of his old instructors at Quantico and was waiting for a call back when he heard Trey upstairs. When Daniel came into the kitchen, Trey was putting great-smelling, greasy takeout bags on the kitchen table, the beer and soda in the fridge. He was wearing slacks and a dress shirt open at the neck, a tie already hanging off one of the chairs.

Trey noticed the direction of Daniel's gaze. "I had court today. You like sausage calzone?" Trey indicated the bags on the table.

"Valenti's?"

"Of course."

"Awesome." Daniel peered into one of the bags.

Trey pulled out two plates, both of them white and blue. After he added a small stack of napkins, he ran his hand up from the back of his neck through his hair. "I—uh—didn't get

K.A. Mitchell

their garlic knots."

It was a symbol of the absolute unfairness of the universe that Trey could make nervous and shy look so hot, especially when he had no reason to be either. Daniel wondered if he practiced in the mirror.

"You can always go out later," Daniel said, as if the slow blink of Trey's lashes hadn't made him want to push Trey onto his knees right in front of the Frigidaire.

"Later, huh?"

"After." But Daniel was starting to forget how good those calzones smelled. Trey hadn't been in the house five minutes and already he could almost see the spark between them flare up in a blue arc. There was the pile of evidence he'd printed out and cheese congealing on paper bags. Fuck it. Trey had a microwave and the case was already fifteen years old.

Trey met Daniel halfway, grabbing his head, holding him for a kiss. Daniel lifted his hands to cover Trey's. For a few seconds, their mouths rubbed softly. A light tug on Daniel's lower lip, the brush of a tongue inside, but when Daniel let out a sigh he couldn't control, Trey groaned and drove his tongue in deep, licking and sucking. Daniel followed Trey's tongue back into his mouth, walking them backward into the fridge.

As Trey rocked against him when they hit, Daniel raised his head to lick across Trey's jaw to his ear. "I'm glad you didn't get the garlic knots."

"I almost didn't get anything." Trey's breath was warm on Daniel's neck. "Because I've been thinking all day about you here. Waiting for me. I don't think there's enough time to do everything I planned before I have to go back to work."

"Hmm. Did you make a list?" Daniel yanked Trey's shirt out of his pants and then unzipped him and reached inside. Oh yeah, Trey had been busy thinking. His cock was half-hard against Daniel wrist as he bypassed it to cup Trey's balls. Gently tugging them forward, he feathered his fingers, tracing the shapes under the sac, pressing hard with his thumb on the

196

skin behind.

"Uh?" Trey spread his legs apart, trying to tip Daniel's hand onto his cock.

"A list? We could hang it on the fridge and check things off as they get done." He moved his mouth to Trey's throat.

Trey rocked again, dick leaking precome against Daniel's forearm. "As who gets done?"

Daniel could feel the smile in Trey's voice through his throat, and kissed the spot. "Yes." Still keeping Trey's balls up close, Daniel rubbed the smooth skin under his thumb.

"Stop teasing."

Daniel covered Trey's mouth with a kiss but didn't change the motion of his fingers. Trey arched and grabbed Daniel's head, pulling him back.

"Is this some kind of payback for last night? Because I wasn't teasing."

Last night. As much as Daniel's dick had thought being "taken care of" was the best thing that could happen to it, the pleasure hadn't quite been able to chase an ice ball of nerves out of his gut. Daniel never wanted to need anything as much as he'd needed Trey last night. Because Daniel had been sure that even if he could move, he wouldn't have been able to get himself off. Maybe Trey really had hypnotized him with those eyes. He'd been so desperate for every touch he might as well have been that same stupid kid, hoping Trey would stop by his locker or flash him a smile.

"No. And I'm not teasing either." Daniel dropped to his knees and slipped Trey's belt free.

"Danny." Trey's hands cupped the back of Daniel's head.

"Wasn't this on the list?"

"Yes." The word whistled out through Trey's teeth.

"But?" Daniel finished getting Trey's clothes out of the way.

"I was lying—oh fuck—down."

Daniel put a wet kiss on the head before mouthing down,

the skin on the shaft tightening with every touch of his lips. He licked back up and took the head in, letting it roll over all the soft parts of his mouth, lapping salty drops from the tip.

Trey groaned, his hand making a heavy stroke through Daniel's hair. The sound of Trey's voice, the taste of his cock, rolled down Daniel's spine to his dick, forcing him to unbutton his jeans or lose circulation to parts he never wanted going numb.

Trey held his head tighter, and Daniel looked up. Trey was watching, teeth tugging his bottom lip, eyes soft but focused. Daniel would have given his soul to have Trey look at him like that when they were kids, like Daniel was something so magical he might disappear if Trey blinked. Daniel wanted to shut his eyes and just get lost in having a thick cock in his mouth, but he couldn't stop watching, even as he started to bob, taking Trey deep and sucking back up.

Trey's teeth pulled his lip all the way into his mouth, but he never looked away. His own dick jerked against his thigh and he dragged his fist over it, the pressure too much at first until it subsided into pleasure.

"Yeah. Get us both off, Danny."

There was no command in Trey's voice, only the deeper edge from arousal, but the words went straight to Daniel's balls. Opening his throat, Daniel took Trey in, lips riding tight on the shaft. Daniel's fist set the rhythm for them both, and Trey followed, flexing his hips to glide in and out of Daniel's mouth.

Trey seemed to know exactly how his hoarse whispers sent Daniel over the edge. "Please, Danny. Take all of it."

He did, finally closing his eyes as his lips sank all the way to the root, one hand lifting Trey's balls.

"Oh fuck, Danny."

He swallowed, felt the pulse of Trey's orgasm against tongue and lips, pulled back and sucked hard on the head, tongue flicking under the rim. Trey groaned, the sound vibrating at the base of Daniel's skull, until it felt like it would shake apart and Trey's hands as he cradled the bones were all that was holding it together. Come flooded thick over his tongue, and Daniel swallowed again. His hand jerked on his dick, and it sparked through him, the warmth in his belly shooting from his dick as Trey murmured his name and stroked a hand through his hair.

When Daniel could open his eyes, he looked up to find Trey still watching him and wondered if Trey had ever looked away.

He wanted to tease Trey about his list again, but the words fell flat in Daniel's head so he just sat back on his heels. Trey hauled Daniel to his feet and kissed him, slowly but deeply as if trying to seal the taste of them as a memory, like you do for the last bite of an amazing meal.

With a soft cough to clear his throat, Trey stepped away. "What do you want to drink? I've got beer, soda and Easton water."

Chapter Thirteen

Valenti's calzones were still good, if a bit soggy out of the microwave, but Trey had only managed two bites before Danny started mumbling through a mouthful of ricotta about mission logs and drops.

"I'll show you." Danny all but took Trey's hand and pulled him to the cellar door.

If Trey's brain were going to have to track Danny's wild leaps of supposition, the neurons were going to need some caffeine saturation. He reached into the back of the fridge for one of those disgusting but loaded piss-colored sodas and popped the top before grabbing his napkins and calzone and following Danny down the stairs.

During court, thinking about Danny stretched out in Trey's bed so he could get his mouth on every inch of skin, had the potential to be professionally embarrassing if not damaging. so Trey dragged his court-procedure-numbed brain onto a less erotic if no less wild fantasy. Turning Danny loose in the house meant Trey would come home to a basement looking like a high-tech lab, the kind they had in the crime shows on TV. With help from the perky, bantering team at the computers, the whole thing would get wrapped up in an hour.

But it was still just the same basement, a fresh stack of paper in the printer's out tray.

"I made some calls today." Danny booted up his laptop.

"What kind of calls?" Trey could hear the chief chewing him

out for chasing ghosts again. He'd be in uniform, handing out speeding tickets in a week.

"Nothing official, just someone I know who has access to Pentagon records."

"Know how?" That tiny irrational surge of jealousy Trey seemed unable to control.

"Are you asking if that means biblically?" Danny's grin crinkled his eyes. "Maybe. And don't ask what I might have promised in return for one of the files."

He had to be kidding. He'd better be kidding. Trey watched Danny shove half the calzone in his mouth before wiping his fingers on his jeans and sorting through the printouts. Fifteen and a half years since the murder. Nine years since Trey got out of the service. Seven years since Trey had bought this house and started collecting whatever he could find in the basement. Five years since his father had died in prison.

Trey had been stuck in this for so long, he'd started to forget how insane it was. Watching Danny become absorbed, playing with the papers and wasting other people's time, made Trey realize he was tired of it, sick of it to his bones.

Okay, he was ready to believe his dad hadn't been the one involved in dealing, but he knew someone who had. What the fuck good did it do to nail that guy? It wasn't going to bring Trey's family back. Wasn't going to change what everyone thought. And it definitely wasn't going to give him something to hurry home to like knowing Danny was there had.

Trey wanted to pull Danny away from his pile of papers, drag him away from mission impossible and remind him there was a bed upstairs and so many more interesting things to do.

And then Danny looked up with his too-knowing gaze and read Trey's mind.

"If we can pull this all together—finish it—what are you going to do?"

"Besides show up at the sentencing and make sure the bastard gets life?"

"Yes. I mean what are you going to do then?"

A crack opened up in Trey's lungs, cold and sharp like he'd been stabbed with an icicle. He didn't know. Hadn't ever allowed himself to get that far. He loved the job. He wanted to keep being a cop. But everything he'd done had been on this same track, no stops, direct line to the end. He thought again of that postcard of the Gulf of Mexico tucked behind the picture of his parents.

He took one painful breath after another and finally trusted his voice. "Take a month of accrued vacation and go fishing."

"I didn't know you liked to fish."

"I don't know if I do," Trey admitted.

"Then why—"

Trey shook his head. "Let's see what you bet your ass on."

Danny grinned again and spread the papers out.

It wasn't evidence that would hold up in court, or even get a warrant, but Trey knew Danny believed it. He pointed out one mission after another without corresponding orders or wounded soldiers.

"Not bad," Trey told him. It wasn't. Danny had found a lot of information in a short time. In a few days, he had more than Trey had managed in fifteen years.

"Not bad? I think the guy about to be sworn in as Vice President got rich running heroin in Vietnam and you say not bad?"

"Danny. I see it. It's still a jump, but I see it. Suppose the picture was set up as an alibi, but we've got no proof."

"We've got something. We just have to dig a little more. It's there. It's always there. If I could run a check on his money in the seventies..."

"He's had more than thirty years to cover his tracks." Trey unpinned one of the other pictures from the corkboard, the one of Dad with Kearney when he was Chief of Police.

"Then why did he need to have your parents killed in '93?"

"Jesus, Danny." Trey stared at the picture of the smiling men in their dress uniforms. If Kearney had done it, even if he hadn't pulled the trigger...

His dad had respected Kearney, trusted him. Hell, Trey had voted for him for Governor. There wasn't even a framework in his brain for that level of betrayal. He shook his head. "I can't buy it. Not without a lot more. Howie was a junkie. He probably crossed a lot of people. He—"

"You think Howie Irving was the mastermind behind some kind of trafficking ring? You saw his records. The guy could barely make it out of high school. It had to be the guy flying the helicopter."

If it was, then how was Trey supposed to make that stick? With all Kearney's power and money and connections how were they going to ever get to the truth? Trey would never be able to stand on Dad's grave and keep his promise. "And what do you think we can do with that? You think you've got anything here to convince a judge? A congressman? Even a reporter? Fuck, even I'm not convinced."

"I know. But I'm not done yet. I called someone else, one of the instructors I had at Quantico. He's an expert on the heroin trade. And I'm sure someone at the DEA—"

A million little light bulbs switching on in Danny's brain, and Trey could see them all shine in those changeable eyes. Danny would dig all right. Until he dug in the wrong spot, tripped a wire—and then Danny would be the one finding out how the barrel of a gun tasted right before someone forced his finger to squeeze the trigger.

The imagined shot rolled through Trey's brain like thunder. "No."

Until Danny started and shot him a look, Trey didn't realize he'd shouted. "No," he said again. "We've got enough. *I've* got enough. You were right. My father didn't kill my mother."

"And that's it?"

"Yeah. That's it."

"Trey, you're a cop. How could you just let it go?"

"Easy." It didn't feel easy, but it felt right. "It's not worth it."

"Not worth it? You've been doing this all your life—"

"Exactly. My life. Your life. Nothing's worth that."

Another light bulb flicked on behind Danny's eyes. "Oh, come on. No one's going to notice. It's even safer for me. I'm no one. Just an agent at Homeland Security doing grunt work."

"I've already lost both my parents. I'm not going to risk you." He stared steadily at Danny, waiting for him to connect the dots.

Danny blinked and looked away. "Trey, it's only a few phone calls."

"No. You get that?" Trey stepped toward him and grabbed his shoulders. "You win. You're right. And this ends here."

"No."

"I swear to God if you don't stop I'm going to tell your mother."

"Tell her what?"

"Everything. But mostly how you're trying to get involved in something dangerous."

Danny must have decided Trey was teasing. "Just don't tell her what you did to her towels last night."

"Fine. Listen to me. I swear to God if you don't drop this, I will take out Kearney myself before I'll let anything happen to you."

"I'm a big boy, Trey. I've got my own gun and everything. I even have a badge."

"I'm not kidding, Danny."

The last bulb lit. Danny stopped protesting, eyes dark and wide, like he was trying to read Trey's mind right through his skin.

"No, you're not." Danny sounded surprised.

"Idiot." Trey yanked him in and kissed him.

Danny's fingers dug into Trey's scalp, tongue licking hot inside.

Trey pushed him away. "Don't start that down here."

Danny looked even more stunned than he had before, and there was that wounded look Trey had seen way too many times before.

Trey gave him a slow smile. "No condoms. No lube."

"Big plans again?"

Trey ran his hand down the front of Danny's jeans. "Pretty big."

As he headed for the stairs, Danny turned back to laugh, eyes clear and happy. Trey wanted it like this all the time. He gave Danny a few groping shoves to hurry him up the steps, stopping to shut the cellar door behind them. Trey leaned on it for a second, wondering what the damage would be to resale values if he bricked the whole basement off. If it kept Danny safe, he'd do it.

"You coming?" Danny called from the doorway, sweater already in his hands.

"Oh yeah," Trey said, but when he yanked his shirt over his head, he got stuck on the tight cuffs and crashed into Danny at the door.

Danny was smiling as Trey laughed through the kiss. God, he'd laughed more in the last week than he had in this century. It felt damned good, laughing with Danny. And now Danny's laugh didn't have that hollow sound Trey had gotten used to hearing, the one that seemed to tell the world to fuck off because Danny didn't care.

Trey licked into Danny's open mouth, still wrestling with the cuffs. Ducking behind, Danny tugged on the sleeves, pinning Trey's arms tighter, shoving him toward the bed.

"I'm looking forward to the frisking." Trey fell face first into the tangle of sheets.

"Maybe I'll leave you like this."

Trey swallowed hard. He'd never wanted to be on that end of things, but with Danny, he could definitely rethink it. "If you want."

Danny pressed his body against Trey's back, nothing but skin, cock barely brushing the fingertips of Trey's bound hands. He stretched them toward that soft skin.

"No." Danny's tongue flicked Trey's ear. "I want your hands on me." He lifted himself off and unbuttoned Trey's cuffs. "What do you want?"

Trey turned and pulled Danny down so he landed hard on Trey's chest, the breath rushing out of them both.

"You. God, Danny, I want you in me."

Danny groaned, deep in his throat, and kissed him with long curling strokes of his tongue, but it wasn't just the sweet slick rub in Trey's mouth that rolled like smoke down his throat, spreading warm and fuzzy into his stomach until it licked heat into his balls and dick. It was that groan. It was Danny, weight pinning Trey to the bed as those strong hands went everywhere, his face, his arms, his chest.

Swinging his legs off Trey's hips, Danny knelt on the bed and tugged at Trey's fly. "Off."

The look in Danny's eyes made Trey's dick jerk against his stomach, drops of precome beading on the head as he kicked his pants away.

Jesus. He'd wanted to see what it was like when Danny really let go. Now he knew.

Danny already had the lube in his hand and a condom in his teeth when Trey rolled back. There was nothing rough about Danny's hands on him, just an intense purpose as he lifted Trey's legs where he wanted them, then kissed him through the burn as two fingers drove inside. Trey wasn't as smooth as his hands went up to cup Danny's head. They landed heavy and Trey had to keep himself from channeling some of what he was feeling into yanks on Danny's hair.

Gentling his grip, he stroked Danny's face, cheeks, temples, thumbs scraping across his jaw where the stubble grew thickest. Danny made another groan Trey felt in his own gut and the fingers inside twisted, stretched him until he panted against Danny's lips.

"Now, c'mon, now."

Danny slipped his hands under Trey's ass and lifted him onto hard warm thighs. Pulse jumping at the brush of the thick head against his hole, Trey waited for the first sting as his muscles worked against what they both wanted, but it didn't show up. Danny pushed in, slow and steady, and then he was deep inside, touching all those places that needed it, wanted it.

Gripping Trey's hips, Danny slid all the way back and then drove forward, making Trey full and empty at the same time because as close as they were, he wanted Danny closer. Wanted inside him at the same time.

"Trey. Jesus. So fucking perfect." Danny's head tipped back, the muscles in his neck standing out in sharp relief.

"Yeah." But only a clenched-tight jaw could keep back the other word fighting its way out of Trey's throat. *Mine.*

Almost as if he heard him, Danny looked down, hands stroking Trey's chest from shoulder to cock, before digging into his hips again and dragging him on and off Danny's dick. Trey brought his legs up higher, reaching for Danny's shoulders and something in Danny seemed to tear free and he started moving them hard and fast.

The desperate want that had scared Trey all those years ago, honed by Danny's experience and distilled by his usual restraint, made for a damned near obliterating fuck. There was something in his eyes, something in his face that made Trey almost want to look away even as it kept him watching.

He gripped the forearms holding his hips and fucked back, arching so the pressure built from inside his ass, constant bursts of pleasure from the friction inside. He'd only come like this twice, both of them a nice surprise.

This wasn't going to be a surprise and it wouldn't be nice. It was going to fry his nerves and turn him inside out. It was already starting to burn as it built, a hot flood ready to drown him.

More words wanted out of his throat. They echoed in his head. *Love you, Danny. Always did. Love you. Love you.* He tightened his grip on Danny's arms and rode the feeling.

Danny lifted his hands to grip Trey's. Fingers, bodies, eyes locked.

He couldn't wait much longer, and then Danny grunted and leaned in and kissed him, trapping Trey's dick between their bodies, and he slammed hard into a long come that clouded his brain and drained the power from his muscles.

Jesus, he hoped he didn't say anything stupid.

Danny jerked and made the sweetest groan Trey had ever heard. He wanted to lift his hand to Danny's hair, push it out of his eyes and pet him through the aftershocks, but most of the systems were not yet back online. Danny's muscle control must have been better since he managed to flop off to the side.

As Danny turned to roll away, Trey summoned enough coordination to fling an arm over and block him. He didn't want Danny going anywhere. And he didn't want Danny leaving on the tenth. In case what Trey said in the basement hadn't registered properly, he was going to tell him exactly that later. When it wouldn't sound quite so much like something that slipped past numbed lips because you'd just come so hard your brain-mouth filter was blasted wide open. Yeah, later.

Trey was dreaming about skiing, and then the wet clothes were gone and he was fucking Danny in front of a fireplace in a cabin that was somehow the Gardners' basement, except for the fish drying over the fire. Sweating from the heat of the fire, Trey jerked awake.

His dick wasn't completely full, just more up than the rest of him. Danny had dragged the blankets over them, which explained the sweat and heat in his dream. He moved the blankets off, piling them on Danny then rolled toward him, running a hand through his hair and breathing in wood smoke.

The smell—real and immediate—connected in his brain at the same time the smoke detector started wailing.

"Danny." Trey grabbed for a shoulder and shoved. Rolling off the bed, he found the sweats he'd worn to the gym last week and Danny's jeans.

When the jeans landed on his back, Danny shifted and stretched like someone who knows it's way too early to get up. He reached out an arm as if looking for the alarm.

Trey yanked on the hair sticking out of the blanket. "Danny."

Danny jumped and sat up. A quick confused protest of "What the—" and then "Holy shit." He snatched the jeans and pulled them on, hopping around looking for his shoes.

"Forget 'em."

In the hall, smoke was billowing out of the kitchen, stinging, acrid and hot. They hadn't cooked anything, hadn't even turned on the coffee maker. Should he try to put it out? As Danny stepped forward like he'd go in there, Trey saw a flick of blue yellow flame at the back door.

"The front, c'mon."

It took a lifetime, running down eighteen feet of hall, and it took a heartbeat. The smoke got thicker, hotter.

If the fire started in the kitchen, how the hell did it get to the living room already?

Trey coughed as he raised a hand to the deadbolt, the metal was hot, but not burning. The cough tightened into a spasm and Danny's hand replaced his, the bolt thunking back, solid and reassuring as Danny spun the knob. But the door didn't open.

They leaned back, hands on the knob tugging with their full weight, but the door still didn't budge.

"What the hell?" Trey spat the words out between coughs.

Danny had an arm over his mouth and nose and Trey gave the door a kick before turning away.

Eyes watering, he pointed across the hall. "Window." But even in his own house, he wasn't sure he could find it in the smoky dark. Maybe they should be crawling.

Danny stopped, doubled over as coughs wracked his spine, and Trey straightened up enough to swing a chair at the dull blacker rectangle he hoped was his dining room window. As soon as the glass shattered, a roar like an ocean wave built behind them and he knew it was the fire, actual killing flames and heat. He turned to grab Danny, to push him through first, and came up with a fistful of smoke.

"Danny?" Voice thick and slow like sludge.

The answer came back like it was wrapped in wool. "Picture."

Maybe it was the smoke, maybe it was the sudden blast of fresh air from the window, but Trey's head felt oddly light, like it was floating six feet above his head. None of this could possibly be real, be happening. His house wasn't burning down and Danny had not just walked back into the fire for some picture that didn't mean a fucking thing. Nothing did. Not if Danny didn't come out of this building with him.

As he turned away from the window, an absurd thought came into his disconnected brain. *If we don't die, I'm going to fucking kill him.*

He compromised for speed over safety, running instead of crouching. Would Danny know that the picture never left his jacket pocket or would he be looking for the damned thing in the cellar? Trey couldn't see anything but the heavy burning air. Christ, if Danny had gone into the cellar...a wall of heat seared his skin as Trey turned toward the kitchen.

And then his head dropped firmly back atop his shoulders

as something solid and alive slammed against him. Solid and alive and burning the skin off his palms as he clutched Danny's shoulders. He wasn't letting go of him now.

Danny almost collapsed as another cough wracked his spine. "Down." Trey shoved and half dragged him to the broken window.

Trey pulled his sweatshirt off and laid it on the frame to keep them from severing an artery and made sure Danny went first. No discussion, he caught him around the waist and tumbled him out, tumbled them both out into the prickly holly under the window and then they were rolling across frozen ground and patches of blessedly icy snow.

Trey staggered to his feet and reached down to help Danny up. In the light of the giant campfire that used to be his house, Trey could see that Danny was clutching something against his chest.

Not the Polaroid.

He knew what it was, even as he put out his hand for the frame. Knew what Danny had gone back for.

The picture of his parents from on top of the TV.

The frame landed back in Danny's lap as Trey dropped to his knees.

He heard confused worried voices, neighbors' doors opening. And then sirens, their whine intensifying as they drew closer, but there wasn't going to be much to save. Not the kitchen table with the sagging end. Or the picture of his mom, her beautiful smile turned toward the camera even as she stood sideways to show her hugely pregnant belly the month before Trey was born.

But Danny, the stupid annoying infuriating bastard who couldn't let anything go, had managed to pull this one piece of Trey's life out of the fire, and he didn't know if that made the loss better or worse.

What he did know was that if he sat here in the snow for one more minute, even the pain of a razored-raw throat and scorched-dry eyes wouldn't be able to keep him from sobbing like a baby on Danny's chest.

He dragged himself to his feet and went out front to make sure the firemen knew no one was left in the house.

Chapter Fourteen

Daniel sat in the back of an ambulance with an oxygen mask on his face and a blanket on his shoulders. The EMTs cleaned and bandaged his cuts while continuing to recommend a ride to the ER "just to get checked out." But he wasn't paying any attention to them, or even to the spectacle of the firemen fighting the freezing temperatures and the still-burning house on Spring Garden Street. He was watching Trey.

If the ambulances weren't at such an angle, he'd have sworn it was a mirror image. Trey, wrapped in a blanket, oxygen mask on his face, the EMTs with their gauze and tape. Did his own eyes look like Trey's? Even from ten feet away, his eyes seemed to reflect the image of the flames, wide eyes in a black-streaked face.

Trey hadn't said a word to Daniel since they crawled away from the house, hadn't even taken the framed picture now sitting beside Daniel in the ambulance.

Earlier he'd let Trey convince him the case was over. Old and buried and not worth digging at. Daniel had wanted to believe him, because believing him took them a step closer to where-do-we-go-from-here and believing Trey meant *I'm not going to risk you* said a whole lot more.

But the case wasn't that old and buried if their digging had led to arson. And attempted murder. Because a fire at both ends of the house, at the doors? A door that wouldn't budge? Premeditated attempted murder.

So what had they done to set off the alarms, to scare Kearney into another attempt to cover his tracks with murder?

Not what.

Who.

The answer drove into his gut like a fist. He ripped off the oxygen mask, coughing and fighting the wave of nausea that sent his stomach lurching up his spine. Tightening the grip of his fingers on the frame of the ambulance, he managed to keep down the sausage calzone and resist the EMT's attempt to put the mask back on him. He pushed away from the ambulance and darted to Trey, bare feet burning on the frozen blacktop.

Dropping to his knees to beg forgiveness felt suitable for Daniel's level of guilt, but he didn't think Trey would appreciate it. Instead he only stood there, gasping, shifting his weight from one frostbitten foot to another.

"Fuck, Trey, I'm so sorry."

"Danny." Trey sounded exhausted, that one word heavy with an impatient *not now*.

"My dad. Jesus, my dad. He must have called him. I don't want to believe it, but oh fuck, my dad. He must have known."

Trey yanked off the mask and shoved away from the ambulance. "Jesus, Danny, will you listen to yourself?"

The EMTs hovered behind both of them.

Daniel put on his most polite smile. "Could you just give us a minute? I promise we'll be good patients after."

Trey sank back onto the frame of the ambulance and Daniel joined him, tucking up his numb feet under his jeans as he sat cross-legged. He looked down. One of Trey's feet was bandaged. The other wore a sock.

"He had to have heard it from my dad. When I called him about the picture. That's why dad came here last night. Why he wanted it back."

Trey rubbed his hands over his face, smearing soot and sweat. "I can't. Just—just let's get through this night, okay?"

"All right, but I want you to know I'm sorry. I never would have called him if I thought—God, I almost got us killed."

Trey pulled his hands down and looked at him. "You. You almost got yourself killed. Motherfucking God, Danny, what the hell were you thinking going back into the house?"

"I was thinking about saving something for you. I had lots of time." All right. He hadn't really thought it out, like he did most other things. But when they'd passed through the living room all those old morality questions flashed through his head. If you could only save one thing in a fire, what would you choose? Daniel had known Trey would choose that picture. And it had been hot, hot enough to make him feel like he was being baked in a giant oven, but he'd never felt like the quick detour had added to the danger already there. After all, there was another window in the living room.

Trey simply looked at him.

The EMTs were about to attack again when an older man who looked like he'd played offensive tackle in the NFL came up to them. His large frame was stuffed into a wrinkled suit.

"Eriksson. You all right?"

Daniel could feel Trey snap to attention, even though he never moved from his seat on the ambulance floor.

"I'm good, Chief."

"Glad to hear it." The man's eyes shifted to Daniel, an appraising stare that took in his bare chest and feet, the bandages and streaks of soot on him.

"They figure they won't be able to start the investigation until tomorrow or Friday."

Tomorrow—or—today was Thursday. Daniel had only been in Easton a week. It felt like a lifetime. It always did.

The Chief of Police went on. "It didn't take much to get them to label it as suspicious, though. You have any cases we should know about, Eriksson?"

Feeling someone trying very hard not to look at you was

almost as piercing as feeling someone glare a hole through the back of your head. Daniel knew Trey wanted him to keep his mouth shut. An EMT decided to help, slipping an oxygen mask back over his face. Now that it was easier to breathe he wanted it off. The dry overly rich air gagged like dust in his throat.

"Nothing I can think of, Chief," Trey answered.

Daniel pulled the mask off his face again. "The doors may have been jammed deliberately. Probably with a small wooden wedge so the evidence would burn. It seemed to start in the front and back of the house almost simultaneously."

The feeling of Trey not looking at Daniel turned into the feeling of Trey glaring at the side of Daniel's face with a shut-the-fuck-up expression on his face.

"And who are you?"

Daniel found himself reaching for a badge that was still in the jacket he'd hung up next to Trey's front door. And so was his wallet.

"Agent Daniel Gardner, Department of Homeland Security." Daniel offered his bandaged hand. In addition to the other cut on his palm, he now had a long slice diagonally across the back of his hand. "I'd show you my badge, but I'm afraid it's in the house. I can give you the ID number."

"That's not necessary at the moment, Agent Gardner. But I would like to know what business a federal agent has with one of my detectives and why I wasn't informed about it." Despite the words, the chief seemed somewhat relieved as he turned to Trey.

Oh. The chief was looking for a reason for there to be a half-naked guy in Trey's house in the middle of the night and was pleased to pin it on anything other than the obvious. But Trey didn't take the safety line. Daniel was about to make something up, but Trey opened his mouth.

"No official business. He was just visiting. We went to high school together."

The chief looked at Daniel again. Disappointing older

authority figures seemed to be Daniel's life's work. Unfortunately, that skill didn't look very good on a resume. After a dismissive breath, like whatever was going on was entirely Daniel's fault, the chief turned back to Trey.

"Whatever they find, you're going to need to stay far away from this, Detective, you read me?"

"Yes, Chief."

"If I see you anywhere near it I'll suspend your ass."

"Yes, Chief."

The chief was right. Trey couldn't have any personal involvement in the investigation. It would fuck the prosecution to hell.

"We'll nail the fucker, Eriksson. We look after our own. No matter what, right?"

"I understand. Thank you, sir."

The big man turned away, and then came back.

"What cases do you have open?"

"The jewelry store thing from Thanksgiving, and the assault and battery down on Washington."

"Call Mancini and fill him in. You are officially on vacation. I don't want to see you at all for at least two weeks."

Trey shifted and Daniel could sense the arguments forming on his lips. So could the Chief of Police.

"Son, you look like hell. And I know you've got the time. You're going to have enough to do just dealing with the insurance fuckers." The chief looked over his shoulder at the streams of water, smoke and flames. "You got some place to stay?"

"He's going to stay with me," Daniel said quickly.

The chief nodded. "Mayor's wife's kid, right?"

"Yes, sir."

"Leave Mancini your number when you get one. But don't come in, we clear?"

"We're clear," Trey answered.

He waved off the EMTs when they tried to get a mask back on him and then simply sat there, staring at the wreckage. The firemen had kept it from spreading to the houses on either side, but the roof had collapsed. There wasn't even going to be a burnt frame to dig through.

Uniformed policemen milled around the edges, and Daniel recognized Officer Acevedo when she stopped to bring Trey a cup of coffee and offer her sympathy. The Red Cross showed up with clothes and shoes and still more coffee. A few hours later, the fire captain came over to ask them questions.

After learning that Trey had woken up to the smell of smoke and the alarm and inquiring about the location of the bedroom, the captain turned to Daniel.

"And where were you when you became aware of the fire?"

Daniel hesitated.

"He was in bed with me," Trey said.

The captain didn't blink. He asked them about their path out of the house, what they'd seen, what made them think the door had been jammed. He gave Trey a number to call for information and suggested they take the EMTs up on the offer of a ride to the hospital.

Daniel jumped off the ambulance, wincing as the borrowed shoes pinched his sore feet. Trey was stuck in slippers since they didn't have anything to fit him.

"C'mon." He waved at Trey. "Let's go."

Trey shook his head.

"What good does it do to sit and watch this all night?"

No answer.

"Aren't you cold?"

Trey looked back at the blanket on the ambulance floor.

"I'm freezing and I want a shower."

Trey wasn't looking at the house anymore, but down at the blacktop, covered with a shining layer of fresh ice from the fire hoses and mist.

"All right. I'll come back and pick you up in a few hours."

Trey lifted his head. "Are your keys in your pocket?"

"Nope."

"So how do you expect to drive your car?"

Trey followed as Daniel grabbed the framed picture from the back of the other ambulance and went over to one of the Red Cross workers, pleading for a phone. Standing next to the Navigator, Daniel dialed the service that had come with the car for a remote entry and start. It took two minutes and the woman was assuring him they'd get the manufacturer to overnight him new keys by Friday.

He opened the door and turned to Trey with a smug smile. "Don't disparage my car again, man."

"And how are you going to get into the house?" Trey asked, piercing the balloon of satisfaction around Daniel so perfectly he thought he could hear an audible pop.

Trey's lips twitched. "That's what twenty-four-hour locksmiths are for. There's someone the police department uses. I'll call him, have him meet us."

The hint of Trey's smile let Daniel take the first deep breath he'd had since he woke up to the smell of smoke.

"All right."

The locksmith handed Daniel a new set of keys and an extravagant bill. Trey's status as a police detective had spared Daniel a four a.m. call to the legal owner, Mother. She'd hear about the fire at Trey's house eventually, she had her sources, but at least Daniel could put that conversation off for a few days.

Daniel placed the picture on the dining room table, face up. Trey hadn't looked at it or touched it since they rolled out into the snow. He paced around the downstairs as Daniel watched.

Guilt over his father's involvement kept Daniel's stomach churning. Jesus. How could Trey have lived with it all those years? Everyone thinking his father was a killer.

"I'm sorry," he said again as Trey paused in the foyer.

"For what?"

"My dad. Your house."

"Oh that."

"Yes. That."

Trey shook his head like Daniel was apologizing for putting too many sugars in his coffee.

"At least we know we're right, though."

"Oh at least there's that." Trey's sarcasm jarred Daniel into movement.

He stepped in front of Trey, but he just went around to make another circuit of the living room.

"What are you doing?"

"I'm fishing off the coast of Florida. What does it look like I'm doing?"

"Pacing."

"Got to hand it to you, Danny. You're quite an analyst."

"What's wrong?"

Trey looked at him, face still covered in black streaks, an over-large sweatshirt from the Red Cross hanging from his shoulders.

"I mean other than being homeless." Daniel winced as soon as the words left his mouth. He definitely should have tried them out in his head first.

"It's not like it's the first time," Trey said. "But other than being homeless, let me think. Yeah. Someone tried to kill us and you say 'At least now we know we're right'?"

"Well, we do."

"Jesus," Trey muttered, adding a long, drawn-out sigh of disgust.

"So now what?"

"Didn't you hear me last night?" Trey paced toward him from the living room and there was something predatory about his even steps, his big body moving as gracefully as a tiger's.

He was close enough now for Daniel to see the pattern the soot had left, almost black tears under his eyes. Trey stopped a few feet away. "I want you to let this go. Stay here if you have to until the closing, but then I want you to go home to D.C. and never even think about what Howie Irving and Mike Kearney were doing in Vietnam."

"And what are you going to do?"

"I'm going to find someplace else to live. And then I'm going to go back to work."

Daniel swallowed. "He killed your mother."

Trey's hands went around his own throat. Like he was choking himself as a substitute, but whether it was for Daniel or Kearney, Daniel didn't know.

"Don't you think I know that now? But bringing Kearney down isn't going to bring her back." Trey started to turn away.

"We can't let him get away with it. Trey, it's not just your mom and dad. He's the fucking Vice President. How can we let someone who'd kill to cover up their secrets have that much power?"

"Fuck, can you really be that naïve?" Trey shook his head.

"I know he's not the first, but...didn't you swear an oath? Because I did. And I can't unknow this."

Trey grabbed Daniel's shoulders and slammed him back into the wall. Daniel had a moment to be glad his mother had already packed everything but the furniture or he'd have been wearing the imprint of a Hudson River school landscape across his shoulders. And then he looked at Trey's face and stopped thinking about anything but wanting to erase the bleak look in his eyes.

"You think the oath for my badge means more than my

promise to my father? But I still don't care."

"How can you n—"

Trey didn't let him finish. "Because of you, Danny. God, I can't." Trey shut his eyes and swallowed hard but his hands still kept Daniel pinned to the wall. "If you'd been killed..." His grip softened, thumbs rubbing Daniel's collarbone. "You're all I've got."

Daniel brought his arms up and through, knocking Trey's hands away. "I don't want to be."

"What?"

"I'm all you have? So I'm only something you want because you've lost everything else? Fuck that."

Trey grabbed his arm. "That's not what I said."

"Really? Because I think that's what it's always been. I'm just something you do when you don't have anything else." Daniel stepped into Trey until their hips touched. "Isn't that why you used to sneak into my bed?"

Trey took a deep breath, and Daniel could see him work to pin his tongue between his jaw to keep him from saying whatever it was he meant to blurt out. Daniel wished he could force the words out of him.

He dug deeper. "That was why, right? Because I was convenient."

"Christ, Danny, nothing about you has ever been convenient."

"Nice to know I'm a consistent disappointment."

Trey released his arm. "Will you stop and just listen to me?"

Daniel nodded.

"Let's leave this—us—out of it. But, Danny, something like this, it's too big for you and me to work. I couldn't...live with anyone else dying because of this mess."

"Do you really think if you stop looking now he's going to forget about you? Forget that Ron Eriksson's son is onto him? If we don't finish this, someone else is going to die. You. You think I want to live with that?"

"And if your dad goes down with him?"

"Let him. If he had anything to do with..." After Trey had moved in, the drinking had gotten worse. What if the reason Dad couldn't stand the sight of Trey wasn't because Dad missed his friend Ron, but because of the guilt of knowing he was in jail for a murder he didn't commit? Dad *should* have been the one to die. "Fuck him."

"You don't know what it's like. You think you can handle seeing your dad in prison?"

Rage sent Daniel off across the hall, and he barely managed to pull back his fist before it smashed into the plaster. "I am sick of everyone telling me what I can handle. Do you think the FBI just hands you a badge and sends you on your way?"

"Okay."

Trey's sudden agreement left Daniel with a whole lot of angry arguments and no target.

"Okay what?"

"Okay we'll try to finish it. But it's my fight, Danny. The risks are mine. If I say we lay low, we lay low."

Daniel nodded. Trey took a deep breath and turned to go into the dining room.

"More pacing?" Daniel asked lightly.

"I'm calling a cab."

"What for?"

"I need some clothes and then I'm going to a hotel." Trey looked past him, eyes unfocused.

"Without a credit card? I thought you were staying here."

"I don't like being a Gardner charity case any more than you like being convenient."

"So you're leaving? That's fucking original."

"Jesus. Last time, Danny. You were the one who cut me off. Don't tell me you didn't know goddamned well where the fuck I was all this time."

Trey did not get the high ground in this one.

Daniel closed the distance between them. "And why the hell was I supposed to care? How was I supposed to know you wanted me to find you? You didn't exactly give me a lot of reasons then."

The anger seemed to slip away from Trey on a sigh. "I told you. I was a dick. I was scared." He reached out and put his hand on the back of Daniel's neck, but didn't pull him closer, just rubbed his thumb at the base of Daniel's skull. "And you can't let that go. So why do you want me to stay?"

It sounded ridiculous when Trey put it like that. Like Daniel was a petulant child. But it had never been as simple as that. He never hated Trey for leaving, for putting the need to find out what happened to his family first. What he'd hated was that Trey wouldn't acknowledge what was going on between them. Trey had felt more a part of Daniel's life than anyone in his family and when Trey left it made a big empty space. And now, even if Trey wanted to, Daniel wasn't sure he could fit Trey back into it.

"Mother told you this was your home for as long as you needed it. The stores don't open until ten."

Trey's hand slid off his neck.

Daniel wished he had all the answers. Or at least the answer that would get back the Trey he'd had last night.

"I'd feel better if you were here."

Trey ran his hand up behind his head and then nodded. "I'll sleep on the couch in the basement."

After forcing himself to lie in bed until eight, Daniel went into the kitchen to find Trey drinking a mug of coffee. He was still in his hobo clothes, and even washed clean of soot, his face looked like he'd spent the night in hell.

Daniel hadn't been able to face a mirror, but he was sure he didn't look any better. Trying to find his footing, Daniel opened a couple of cabinets, mind racing for something that could break the silence without breaking what felt like an armed truce.

He grabbed at a mug, and then put it back when he remembered the only coffee they had was instant.

"This is shit," Trey said at last.

It was. And it was getting on nerves already worn thin, but Daniel still didn't know what to say. Leaning on the counter for support, he turned to face Trey.

"I hate instant. It's worse than the stuff at the station when Mancini makes it."

The coffee. "Sorry. Dad broke the coffee maker the other night."

"I remember."

Daniel didn't know he still blushed. "I can call the service again, drive you around to get to the bank or the mall."

"One of the guys from the department is coming to do it. He should be here in a few."

Daniel nodded and fished some money out of his mother's petty cash drawer. "Buy him some coffee."

"I don't need it."

Daniel nodded again. "Well, you know where it is if you do." He was a coward, but he couldn't look at Trey. "Are you coming back later?"

"Do you want me to?"

Daniel turned and faced him. "I think it's safer if we're together."

"Okay."

✧

K.A. Mitchell

Trey hadn't been gone for ten minutes when the house phone rang. Daniel didn't need caller ID to recognize his mother's imperious ring.

"Danny, I just heard about the fire. I was so worried. Are you boys both all right?"

"We're fine."

"My goodness. What a terrible thing. Were they able to save the house?"

"No."

"That poor boy. You told him he could stay at the house, of course."

"Yes."

"I could call my lawyer and have the closing moved to the end of the month again. He'll need time to find another place."

"Trey wouldn't want that."

"Of course he wouldn't want to be any trouble but if you think it's necessary I'm sure it can be easily arranged."

And there was a golden opportunity to put things off. He'd have weeks before he'd have to decide anything. By that time maybe he could figure out if there was a way their lives could fit together. But he'd already made the mistake of thinking time could help him decide anything. It hadn't worked with Scott.

But then Scott wasn't Trey.

"No, Mother. I'm sure the tenth will be plenty of time for Trey to find somewhere."

"If you're sure."

"I'm sure."

"Danny, the paper said the firemen have deemed the cause of the blaze suspicious."

"The Harrisburg paper?"

"I read the *Easton Express* online every day, dear, and don't change the subject." His mother could politely make him feel like an idiot with only the slightest change in her tone.

226

"Yes, Mother. They think it was arson."

"Why? How on earth could that poor boy have any enemies?"

"He's a policeman. Sometimes that happens."

"He could have been killed. You both could have been killed."

"We're fine."

"You were treated at the scene. Treated for what?" All that protestation about closing dates had just been her way of softening him up for the interrogation. She should give a course at law enforcement academies.

"We had to go out through a window, and we broke it. There was glass everywhere. A few cuts, that's all."

Daniel was waiting for the bonus round, when his mother would ask what he was doing at Trey's house in the middle of the night.

"Do they have any suspects?"

He thought about asking her about Kearney. She had known him, socially. But Daniel wasn't going to risk involving anyone else and certainly not his mother. "Not yet."

"I hope they do catch someone. After all he's been through, the boy deserves some justice."

That was an odd thing to say. As far as Daniel knew, his mother believed Trey's father was guilty.

"Why did you say that?"

"Why, don't you think it's true?"

"Yes, of course, but..." Why hadn't his mother become a lawyer—or a politician? She certainly had the skills. He couldn't stand waiting for the question any longer. "Aren't you going to ask why I was there last night?"

"No."

"Why not?"

"I've known the answer to that question for years, dear. Please tell Trey I asked about him."

Daniel found himself staring at the phone long after his mother hung up.

Chapter Fifteen

Ginny was next. Daniel wondered if he should get a deli counter so people could take a number. With his name in the *Express*, he wondered who else would call to offer sympathy while looking for the good dirt. He doubted anyone's call would be quite like Ginny's however.

"Get your ass over here. You do not want to know what will happen if you don't."

As Daniel remembered, Ginny was pretty creative. And it beat sitting around the house.

She met him out front, dressed in a green coat, purple scarf and blue hat, and immediately tugged him down the street. "Buy me a cup of coffee." She pointed at the bakery halfway down the block.

Daniel was in no position to turn down potable coffee, in fact it was one of the reasons he'd called the service and driven over, but he looked back over his shoulder at her store. "Isn't that like giving aid and comfort to the enemy?"

"I don't think Jo likes you very much. And I don't want her hearing any of this." They were several buildings past her bookstore when she turned and punched his arm. "Holy fucking shit."

"Ow."

"You guys were almost barbequed."

"That's a bit of an exaggeration, but if you don't mind sharing, I'd like to see the actual paper. Since my computer was barbequed instead I'm feeling information-deprived."

Ginny wiped her nose on her sleeve and pulled a folded paper from inside her coat pocket.

The picture made the front page. It must have been taken near dawn since there was some light revealing the charred skeletal remains. The power lines coated with thick jagged ice crossed the top of the house, almost as if a comic-book villain had used his freeze ray.

Their names weren't mentioned until the front page of the local section. Another picture, smaller, and one of Trey in his uniform inset. "Local Detective's Home Destroyed in Blaze" and under it "Deemed Suspicious." He scanned the article. There was nothing new to someone who'd actually been there. The fire captain's statement about "suspicious origins" was no surprise, nor was that the cause of the fire was under investigation. But "...and his companion, former Easton resident, Daniel Gardner..."

Companion. The paper might as well have put *gay male lover* in bold, all caps. Daniel winced. *Sorry, Trey.* Like he didn't already have enough to deal with, trying to be a cop in the same town as his dad.

"Ouch."

"I didn't even hit you," Ginny protested.

"Not you. This. Trey." He pointed.

She nodded and started walking again. "It is kind of obvious in that quaint terminology way."

"Antediluvian."

She grinned. "You're still pissed I beat your verbal score on the SATs."

"Am not." They crossed the street to the bakery.

She did make him pay. Slurping at his coffee to spare his mouth, he followed Ginny back outside. "Did you notice? They have heat in there."

"Yeah, but I'm stuck inside all day." She led the way farther north on Cattell. "So. What really happened?"

"Just what it says in the paper."

Ginny turned that unnerving stare on him.

"Trey and I think the doors were blocked from the outside before the fire was set."

"Holy motherfucking shit."

"Yeah."

"Thus the 'escaped through a window on the ground floor'?"

Daniel nodded.

"Damn. It's a good thing you guys aren't into kinky bondage stuff."

Heat rose from his neck to his cheeks as Daniel remembered Trey holding him down, telling him he'd cuff him and ride his dick.

Ginny stopped and gaped at him, mouth working like a bass on a hook. "You are."

"No."

"You're blushing."

"It's fifteen degrees. It's incipient frostbite."

"I want details."

"First, no. And second, why would a lesbian want to hear about non-girl-part sex? And third, no."

"Fine. But you have to tell me about the investigation."

Daniel shook his head.

"It's the investigation or the sex."

"Okay. I rammed my dripping cock—"

"C'mon, Danny."

"No. In case you didn't read the paper"—he handed it back—"it's dangerous. You need to keep that cute little nose out of it."

Ginny wiped her cute little nose on her sleeve again. "Just tell me. Is Kearney in it?"

"I don't know."

"Yes, you do. He's got a big bad skeleton in his closet and he killed Trey's parents to hide it and now he tried to kill you."

"Yeah. He took time out of his busy pre-Inaugural schedule to stop in town for a spot of arson."

"You know what I mean. He hired someone."

"Great. All we need now is access to his Rolodex and we're all set."

"Jesus, Danny, don't you care?"

He stopped walking. The oak tree hanging out on the corner of Cattell and Monroe groaned and snapped as the wind ground its bare branches together.

"Yeah, I do. But I am not kidding, Ginny. Don't talk about it, don't even think about this. Whatever is going on, people have died. I don't want you to be one of them."

The ends of Ginny's scarf whipped him in the face as she came closer. "Or him."

A strand of scarf fringe stung the corner of his eye. "Or him."

"Did you tell him?"

"What?" He started back down Cattell, where the buildings were thicker, shielding them from the wind. He wondered if the wind had stirred up the flames again, if the firemen were still aiming their freeze rays on the black timbers of Trey's house.

"That you love him and you're afraid he could die." She had to jog to catch up to him and her voice was a little breathy. "Or are gay guys like straight guys, all 'Me man, no talk feelings'?"

Slowing his pace, he asked, "And what would you know about straight guys?"

"I've got three sisters and two brothers, remember? All avowed heterosexuals. Trust me. You can't swing a cat without hitting a straight guy most days. Even in a bookstore."

Daniel looked straight ahead. "He told me."

"He told you he loved you?" She stopped, grabbing his arm, forcing him to face her.

"Yeah, I think he did."

"You think? Why? Was it one of those I'm coming I love yous?"

"No."

"So what did you say?"

Daniel tried to find a reason to keep holding the coffee cup to his lips, but it was long since empty. He looked for a garbage can. "I told him I knew it was dangerous, but we still needed to nail the bastard."

"Okay, but what did you tell him about the other thing?"

"What other thing?" Daniel sucked in his bottom lip or he would have laughed at her. Ginny and her advice and she couldn't even say the word.

"That you love him."

"No, I—I—Christ, Ginny, I'm still trying to figure it out."

"Don't do this, Danny."

"Do what?"

"Don't hide behind that I'm-too-smart-and-cynical-for-love shit. Trust me." Spinning away, she took off down a side street so fast he had to run to catch up.

"Ginny."

When he touched her arm, she shook him off, stepping away.

"What happened?" he asked.

"Like you care. But you know, it sounds cool like the anti-love-sonnet thing you did in high school, all 'love is so pedestrian', but being world-weary and above it all is a lousy way to go through life." This time she used her scarf to wipe her nose. Her eyes were shining with tears.

All the pieces were there, and they snapped together for him. "She's still in love with you, you know."

"What? Who?"

"Joanna. The woman running your café. The one you're better business than bed partners with? She's in love with you."

"No, she isn't."

"How do you know?"

"We bought the building and started the store. And it worked. It was great." She gave him a watery smile. "So I got scared and I fucked around." Ginny looked at the dirty snow on the sidewalk and then back up at him. "I cheated on her, Danny. She said she'd never forgive me, and I don't blame her. How could she ever trust me again?"

"Because she loves you. You can see it in her face. Even I can."

Ginny lifted her scarf and blew her nose in it.

Daniel rolled his eyes. "God knows why."

"Shut the fuck up." She smacked his chest. "This is where you're supposed to hug me, you asshole."

He put an arm around her shoulders, and she burrowed into his chest, sobbing. Daniel sighed and held her tight, frozen snot and all.

Cold turkey sucked. But Trey had lived through it when he decided to quit smoking, and he could break himself of his Danny Gardner habit that way too. It would be easier if they weren't in the same house, but Danny was right. It was safer. Trey could keep an eye on him this way.

Part of going cold turkey was avoiding triggers, so he shied away from Thai and Valenti's for takeout, bringing home a couple of hoagies from the deli on Tenth Street. He'd thought about replacing the coffee maker, but neither of them were going to be in the house much longer.

They sat across from each other at the dining room table, the gleaming walnut finish protected by plastic plates and paper towels.

"That instructor I told you about called me back," Danny

said, ripping open the bag of chips. "The one with the background in the Southeast Asian drug trade."

So they were only going to talk about the case. Trey could do this. Pretend Danny was just another cop, even if pretending it was just another case was impossible. "And?"

"He gave me a rundown of some of the players at the time."

"Did he mention our mysterious Australian?"

"No. But he had names of some of the local drug lords. The ones with the refining operations. Did you have any luck?"

"Yeah." In between getting clothes, a new cell phone, ID and meeting with the insurance company and investigators, Trey had actually struck gold.

He savored it for a minute, taking another bite of roast beef.

"So?" Danny's eyes were wide and bright with expectation. Stringing him along was like withholding crack from an addict.

"I managed to track down Amy Dawson."

"Who?"

"Howie Irving's niece, recipient of all his worldly goods."

"And?"

"I told her we were putting together an exhibit from his Vietnam unit, and she said we could see if there was anything we wanted."

"Where?" Danny almost choked on his turkey trying to get the question out.

"Charleston."

"South Carolina?"

Trey shook his head. "West Virginia."

Danny's fingers twitched like he was tapping on a keyboard. Trey was surprised he hadn't already gone out and bought another laptop.

Danny finished calculating in his head. "It's almost five hundred miles."

"Eight hours by car."

"Hmm, if we flew—between security and a rental and connections—yeah, we'd be better off by car, especially if we find something we want to take. If we leave around four in the morning..."

"She said she'd be home tomorrow."

"We're taking the Navigator."

Trey laughed. "Okay. The Navigator. But, Danny, it could still be nothing. It's a hell of a long drive for nothing."

"And it could be everything."

Not everything. Not anymore. But if he didn't get to have Danny, at least Trey could keep his promise to his dad. He wrapped up what was left of his sandwich and carried it into the kitchen. "Four, you said, right?"

Danny seemed to be coming off his information high. His voice was a lot flatter as he answered, "Yeah. I'll set an alarm."

"Okay." But Trey was pretty sure he'd be awake.

Daniel couldn't remember the last time anticipation kept him awake like this. Even before a big exam he'd always been able to sleep. The last time he'd been through this must have been a Christmas Eve when he was a kid, but it was so long ago he couldn't remember.

With the trouble Trey usually had sleeping, Daniel knew one of them should be well-rested for the drive, but the logical part of his brain couldn't seem to subdue the part running like a hamster on a wheel. He turned the clock away to avoid the frustration of watching the hours slip by and stared at the ceiling. He still wasn't asleep, almost floating in a trance, when he felt someone watching him. Turning his head on the pillow, he picked out Trey standing at the door.

Daniel's movement must have been what Trey was waiting

for because he came forward, stripping off his clothes.

"Cold turkey sucks," he muttered as he put a knee on the bed.

"Huh?" As Daniel lifted the covers, he felt like he'd jumped in a time machine to the past. Trey's skin was clammy, like he'd been sweating, like it did when he'd had one of those nightmares.

Trey shook his head and pulled Daniel's T-shirt over his head. Daniel reached down to help Trey get his briefs out of the way and then they were pressed together, skin to skin, chest to chest, hip to hip. Trey's dick hardened against Daniel's belly, and he drove his own against Trey's thigh.

"One more for old time's sake?"

"Shut the fuck up." Trey held Daniel's face between two big hands and kissed him.

Daniel opened for him, for Trey's tongue, his body. Hand at the small of Trey's back, Daniel spread his legs and pressed them together, shifting so their cocks lined up in that old familiar rhythm.

Trey on top this time, Daniel pulling him tighter, wanting Trey to sink inside flesh and bone, because it was the only thing to do with this feeling driving them together. Daniel arched up, needing more, more pressure, more friction, more Trey.

When Trey raised his head for a breath, Daniel panted the words into his ear. "Fuck me."

Trey groaned and ground down faster, harder. Daniel slid his hands lower until he could cup Trey's ass, dragging him up until the rough pull of their cocks against each other was almost too much.

Daniel bit Trey's neck, just behind his jaw. "Fuck me, Trey. Please."

"God, I would." Trey's hands slipped through his hair, smoothing it away and letting it spring back. "If I thought it would change anything, I would."

Trey's voice rumbled against Daniel's chest, pushed inside his head. The friction was slicker now, sweat and precome smoothing the way. His balls started to climb, the buzz spreading out from his spine to his dick.

Trey's voice dropped even lower. "I would. Finally. I'd fuck you in this room in this bed, like you wanted before. I'd do you raw, on nothing but spit until I filled you with my come." Trey pushed the words into the skin of Daniel's neck, hot and wet like tears. "If I thought it would change anything I would." First Trey's mouth, then his teeth, tightened on the skin where Daniel's neck and shoulder met, a sweet rush of pain that yanked the orgasm out of Daniel's balls, his cock spitting bitter warmth on their bellies as his hips jerked tight and fast.

"Yeah, Danny." Trey licked at the bite, reaching down to lift Daniel's hips.

Daniel had time for one quick, alarmed breath before Trey's cock slipped along the crack of his ass in a slow swiveling grind along the crease. Daniel tightened on him, and Trey groaned through a few short thrusts before shooting onto Daniel's back.

Daniel's breath had barely stopped making a wind-tunnel effect in his ears when Trey lifted his head, eyes glittering in the dark.

"Why did you always let me, Danny? If you didn't want to be convenient, why did you always let me?"

Great. Instead of afterglow, Trey was opting for nausea-inducing interrogation.

Daniel shoved him off and rolled away. "Asshole. You know why." He pushed off the end of the bed and went to take a shower.

Chapter Sixteen

On his way to the Gulf, Trey had spent twelve hours in a jump seat and harness, packed like clowns in a car on a troop transport plane. That had been a pleasure cruise compared to eight hours in a luxury SUV with Danny. After their first exchange about food and rest stops, it was clear they'd run out of things to say to each other. For the next four hours, Danny kept his satellite radio on some alternative rock station. The bands all sounded the same, whining complaints about women, drugs, their parents and the general state of the world.

Maybe it wasn't that they had run out of things to say, only the things that could make it possible for Trey to keep Danny in his life. Trey would settle for friendship if that's all he could get. He didn't have to have Danny in his bed—ah fuck. Who was he kidding? He wanted it all. But the same fucked-up past that kept throwing them together was exactly what the stubborn asshole sitting in the driver's seat kept using to keep Trey at arm's length.

Danny pulled off the interstate near Morgantown to refuel and switch drivers. He didn't say a word when as soon as Trey buckled his seat belt, he switched the station, searching for a college bowl game.

It carried them almost all the way into Charleston. When Trey had squeezed out the last of the distraction possible from the post-game show, he muted the radio.

"How do you want to handle this?" Trey asked.

Danny was enough of a cop that he understood the question. "I think your cover was good, and it's close enough to the truth that we don't really need to rehearse it."

The GPS led them right to Amy Dawson's big white house with green shutters.

Trey pulled up to the curb two car lengths away. No snow on the ground here, but even at noon there was a low ground fog, a damp chilly mist. A black mountain bike leaned against the front steps, a minivan sat in the driveway.

Trey studied it for a few minutes, points of entry, places of concealment and ambush.

"Do you think it's a trap?" Danny asked after a few minutes.

One corner of Trey's mouth lifted. "I think we've both seen too many cop shows." But he could still feel the low charge running through him, the level of awareness he took into any scene where he might have to draw. His service pistol had been retrieved from the house, but it was too damaged to carry. The only comfort he had was a small pistol in an ankle holster, borrowed from Officer VanAuken who'd chauffeured Trey around yesterday.

"You were right." Danny's words came slowly, like he was measuring them in that head of his.

"What about?"

"Me. I put all the blame for what happened before on you."

"Christ, Danny, you're going to do this here? Now?"

"I just wanted to say something in case—"

"No." Trey popped open the door. "Nothing's going to happen. And even if it were, I don't want to hear your just-in-case speech, okay?" Not waiting for an answer, he stepped down.

"Fine."

Knowing damned well he hadn't heard the end of it from Danny, Trey lengthened his strides so Danny couldn't catch up until Trey was knocking on the door. Howie Irving's niece was about forty, a bit harried looking and stiffly polite until Trey reminded her of their conversation yesterday. Her smile broadened and she welcomed them into hall. In the living room to the left, two teenaged boys played a video game, enthusiasm launching them off the couch at varying intervals, a two-man stadium wave.

"It's up in the attic somewhere, a foot locker. I never had the heart to throw it away, but I didn't know what to do with it. I always liked Uncle Howie. He was funny." She tilted her head. "I'm sorry to hear about your father's passing, Mr. Eriksson. It's good of you to do this to remember them."

Trey could feel Danny's look. "I really appreciate it, ma'am. This is Daniel Gardner. His father also served with your Uncle Howie. Daniel's helping us put together the exhibit."

Her smile included Daniel now. "Is your father still alive, Mr. Gardner?"

"Yes he is, ma'am."

Trey hoped he was the only one who could hear the resignation in Danny's voice at that admission.

"That's good. So many veterans die young. I think Uncle Howie felt forgotten."

Trey supposed it was as good a reason as any for a heroin habit.

"He had several medals, you know." She smiled. "He showed me how to bet at poker with them."

A timer went off and a young girl's voice started squealing about princesses and ponies. The owner of the voice ran into the living room, a messy ponytail and crown on her head.

"Matthew." Amy Dawson's tone grew sharp. "The timer means it's Jennifer's turn." A few grumbles and whines and a very different video game came up on the screen. "I'm afraid the timer also means that my cupcakes are done. There's a church bake sale tomorrow. Matthew, show these gentlemen up to the attic."

Matthew slouched over and stomped up the stairs, the other boy trailing behind.

It was almost creepy how normal the family seemed. Of course, Trey didn't really know what was normal for a family these days. What he saw as a cop didn't exactly showcase normal.

Matthew opened a door in the upstairs hall. "The attic. I've never seen the stuff Mom's talking about, so it's probably in the back." He eyed Trey for a minute and then added, "Sir."

As they climbed the stairs, Trey said, "Do I look like a cop all the time?"

Danny shrugged. "The kids down here are raised to be polite."

They split up. Trey found a lot of dust, some old clothes and a very undusty and prodigious collection of *Penthouse* magazines. He was guessing that if the footlocker were anywhere near the magazines, Matthew would have seen it. He started in another direction. There was quite a lot Amy Dawson couldn't seem to part with. A box of her high school report cards. A box of puzzles. A box of eight-track tapes.

In the end, Trey almost walked by it. He'd definitely been watching too many movies because in his head he saw the trunk standing alone in a soft ray of light, not under a pile of clothes and some empty paint cans.

"Got it," he called.

Danny joined him, pulling away the clothes while Trey shifted the cans.

"So go on, open it."

Trey put a hand on the latch. "It's probably nothing."

"Yeah. I'm sure Kearney protected Howie out of loyalty all those years. He seems like the true-blue type."

Trey flung back the lid. More clothes. A lot of clothes that made him glad he'd been too young to remember the seventies.

Some books. He opened one but when he saw that the only

highlighted sections were fuck scenes, he threw it to the side.

Danny was sifting through the clothes, checking pockets and sleeves and folds.

And then, finally, Trey's hand hit metal. A spark of hope flared up as he took the long rectangular box out of the bottom of the trunk.

"What's that?" Daniel asked.

"It's an ammo case. A lot of vets use them as souvenir boxes. They're pretty airtight."

He opened the case. A skin mag, some dog tags, a deck of cards, a pile of letters. He lifted out a chain and read the tags. "I don't think we'll be getting in touch with Tracy Hunter."

"Why?"

Trey tapped the metal. "Howie scratched K.I.A. on Hunter's dog tag. Killed in Action."

Under the letters were more Polaroids, men in their bunks, more names on the back in the now-familiar scribble, but mostly girls. Vietnamese girls.

"Howie sure liked his camera."

The medals were in a bag and Trey shook them out. Meritorious Service, Good Conduct, Marksmanship, a fucking Bronze Star and a Flying Cross. He squeezed them in his palm for a second. Even having good dirt on your lieutenant wouldn't get you a Flying Cross. Howie must have been a hell of soldier before he got mixed up with Kearney—or heroin, whichever came first.

But that was it. Empty box. End of the road.

He lifted the box to put it back on the trunk and stopped. He'd hoisted enough of the cases, full and empty during six years of service. That wasn't right. And it didn't balance. He looked in, felt along the seams and his finger found a tiny slide.

"Howie was a smart son of a bitch."

Danny looked up from sorting through the clothes. "What?"

"False bottom."

"Holy shit."

Trey found the palm-sized notebook first. Leather bound, pages thick from use. He pulled it out and then grabbed the wooden square underneath. It was a box about half the size of a dictionary and a little thinner. The outside was thick with lacquer and covered with so many small pieces of wood glued on the outside it looked like a mosaic.

"It's a puzzle box." Danny took it from him.

Trey opened the notebook, reading it. "And his logbook. Fucker kept track of all their transactions. Guess he didn't want Kearney stiffing him."

"We got him. Trey, this is it."

Trey thumbed through the pages of dates, and numbers. "No, it's not. Maybe we could convict Howie on it, but there's nothing here."

"No mention of Kearney."

"I assume he's the K, but that's not worth shit."

"But if that's all Howie had on him, why would Kearney get his records sealed and keep him out of jail?"

Trey shrugged. "Anything in the box?"

Danny was sliding the pieces of wood around on the top and sides. "I don't know. There could be, from the weight, or it could just be the wood."

"I'm sure we can go get an ax."

"But if there is something in it, we could destroy it. I can figure this out."

Six hours later, Trey paused halfway through another loop of the limited cable offerings at the Pleasant Valley Best Western off of I-79. He looked over at Danny. "Figure it out yet?"

Danny dropped the pen he'd been scribbling with and

moved another piece of wood on the box. "I will." He'd explained that not only did he have to find the right combination of pieces to push, but first he had to figure out which ones were decorative and which actually worked.

"Anything I can do?"

"You could stop asking me stupid questions."

Trey grunted and turned back to the TV, but found himself sneaking glances back over at Danny. Another dead end and Danny still refused to accept it. He'd sit up with that fucking box until morning—longer if Trey didn't check them out of the hotel.

Danny put the box down and looked at it from the side, tapping his front teeth with the pen. It made Trey want to rip the pen out of his hands and kiss him.

Another loop around eighteen stations. What kind of place didn't carry ESPN? "We don't have to cut it open, I could probably force it with a chisel."

"I'll figure it out," Danny snapped.

Jesus. Same story. Danny couldn't let it go, and Trey kept pushing. Their shit had even less variety than the cable. After all these years of spinning his wheels so hard he actually thought he was going somewhere, now Trey could finally see how ridiculous it looked watching Danny wrapped in the same stupid obsession. He wanted to throw the goddamned box out of the window.

But if he did, there'd be no more reason for Danny to be here. Whether the box held the answer they needed or if it was just another waste of time, Danny had made it clear that he was going back to his life in D.C., leaving Trey alone in their tangled mess of a past.

"Same fucking story."

"What?" Danny looked up again.

"You."

Danny put the box on the table and slouched back in the

chair, arms folded, eyes hard. "I tried to tell you in the car."

"What?"

"That I know it was both of us, back then. It was too much of a mess for either of us to fix."

"Wow." But Trey couldn't muster up much enthusiasm for too little too late.

"That's it, just wow?"

"What do you expect me to say, Danny?"

Danny exploded out of the chair, kicking it back to the wall, movement so sudden and violent and uncharacteristic, Trey's training had his hand reaching down for the pistol on his ankle before he realized what he was doing. A blast of cold hit the room as Danny yanked open the door.

"Where are you going?"

"To get a fucking chisel."

One thing West Virginia wasn't short on was home improvement stores. Two of them faced each other across the highway five miles from the hotel. Arms full of anything Daniel could think of that would help them break into that box and finish this—put an end to any reason to ever have to speak to each other again—he unloaded the pile in front of a clerk who had one eye on the clock.

Half an hour later, Daniel dumped two bags on the bed where Trey was lying. "There you go."

The puzzle box was still on the table, and Trey didn't move.

"What are you waiting for?" Daniel turned back toward the door.

"Where are you going now?"

"To get a soda."

"Not sticking around for the big finish?"

"Nope. You never wanted my help with this anyway."

Trey sprang off the bed and scooped up the box, squeezing it in both hands. "I hope to Christ there is something in here. Then this time you'll be able to take off knowing that you fixed it all."

"That's funny. I thought you wanted to do this for your mom and dad."

Trey smiled. Fucking smiled.

"You know, I feel sorry for that guy, what was his name, Scott? Poor bastard." Trey worked the gum from side to side in his mouth. "Because you don't have commitment issues or any other nice convenient excuses for pushing people out of your life. You just don't fucking want to be happy."

Daniel could actually hear his own anger, hot blood ringing in his ears, slamming like a hammer at the base of his skull.

Trey lowered the box to the table. "Yeah, because then how could you feel sorry for yourself?"

Daniel turned and slammed out of the room. He couldn't take more than a few steps before he had to stop and lean his back against the wall, sucking in air to try to cool his burning lungs and skin.

The arrogant fucking prick was right about one thing. Daniel did push people out of his life, if only to avoid their asinine attempts to tell him what was wrong with him. Ginny calling him cynical. Scott calling him selfish. And what, now he was pathetic?

He drove his skull back against the cold bricks, still so flushed he wanted to strip off his sweater, vault over the fence into the swimming pool full of brackish water. His skin was going to burn off if he didn't cool down.

Pressing his palms flat against the rough wall, he tipped his head to watch the shadows in motion in their room. He sank into a squat against the wall, not wanting Trey to know that he was just on the other side of the door.

Fuck it. He should just go back in and he would, as soon

as everything stopped burning. He couldn't remember when the last time was he'd lost his temper. The last time he'd felt anything that made all his muscles shake. It seemed like it always used to happen when he was a kid, when he'd have to get out of the house before he felt like he'd meltdown from the anger and fear burning inside.

He took another deep breath and pushed away from the wall.

The flash hit first, a blinding burst of white at the window, and for a second Daniel's vision was frozen with light, snow-blind. And then the bang, louder than a pistol fired next to his head.

Daniel's existence stopped between breaths.

Trey.

The box. Booby-trapped? A bomb?

He grabbed for the door, shoving and kicking at it like force would have any effect on steel. He squeezed his right hand with his left to stop the violent spasms of his muscles and then reached into his pocket for the keycard. It took three swipes of the goddamned thing before he could make the door work.

At first there was nothing but smoke, a familiar smell like a chemistry lab. No flames.

Trey was on the bed, shaking his head, the box still in his hands. Daniel knocked it away, hands all over Trey as he looked for any blood, any wound. Trey was breathing, mouth open, but he wouldn't answer Daniel's frantic repetitions of his name. Daniel's own voice was faint, covered by a buzz in ears half-deafened from the sound of the blast.

No burns, no blood. Trey was just unresponsive. Daniel shook him and Trey clutched onto his wrists, fumbled up to touch Daniel's face, at last making sounds Daniel could hear.

"Don't. Danny, I'm okay. Jesus, don't cry."

Surprised, he realized he was. He couldn't remember ever crying. Not when his father hit him. Not when his mother was so fucking drunk he couldn't wake her up. Not even when Trey left without a fucking word.

Because this wasn't about feeling sorry for himself. It was relief. Relief like the sweet flood of air when a chokehold was released. Like a governor's pardon when they were looking for a vein for the last IV.

Trey wasn't dead. So it wasn't too fucked up to fix. It wasn't over.

Daniel took a deep breath of the smoke and he remembered that smell. Riot control. Stun grenades. Like a firecracker at close range, they could blind and deafen a target for a minute, but it was only disorientation, just a flash and a bang. Not the kind of bomb where shrapnel exploded to tear through skin and bones. Howie had set up a bright and loud alarm in case someone tried to break into his puzzle box.

Daniel wrapped his arms around Trey and held on. The tears kept coming, but Daniel didn't care.

Trey reached up, fumbling for his face. "I'm okay. Can even see you now. Stop. I'm sorry."

"God, I was scared."

Trey shook his head. "Still can't hear."

It was okay. Daniel would repeat it later if he had to. "I love you."

Trey smiled.

Daniel was glad he had his badge number memorized. Without their physical badges, it took a while to sort things out with the local sheriff's department, but oddly enough, the same story about a Vietnam vet exhibit worked as soon as they produced the ammo box. The sheriff was happy with an excuse as simple as "old ordinance" for his paperwork and after an admonition to be more careful, the sheriff and the hotel manager left with smiles.

Trey flopped back on the bed. "Still reeks in here. Do you think they'll give us a different room?"

"I think that would be pushing it."

Trey looked at him steadily and Daniel hadn't felt this shy or nervous since he had braces and glasses. He looked down.

"So. I thought I remembered getting the lid off," Trey said at last.

"You did." Daniel went into the bathroom and retrieved the puzzle box from where he'd hidden it in the trash. "But all I saw was Howie's last secret stash before I heard the sirens." He put the blackened box in Trey's hands. "There you go."

Trey's fingers brushed the plastic bag containing a lump of black tar heroin. "Even if there's nothing under this..."

"And even if there is," Daniel said.

Trey smiled again. "Okay." He pulled away the bag and found an envelope. "Christ, another fucking Polaroid." He pulled the picture out of the envelope.

The picture was of a pretty Vietnamese girl in front of a field. But as Daniel stared, he realized that affection for the girl wasn't what made Howie hang onto the snapshot and keep it in his puzzle box. Behind the girl, to the right, there was a man wearing a lieutenant's uniform handing something to a Vietnamese man. Forty years hadn't changed much about the handsome face of the Vice President-elect. Both men were turned slightly toward the camera, though clearly the shot hadn't meant to be of them.

Trey flipped it over. Three names.

"Holy shit," Daniel breathed.

"You know the Vietnamese names?"

"I know one after talking to my professor. We've got the bastard, Trey."

Trey held the picture and stared at it.

The hollowness inside, the tearing split in his chest, he

might as well have woken up halfway through his own autopsy. And maybe he had. Maybe he'd been half dead in that cellar, waiting and looking.

All those fucking years.

He shut his eyes and pictured his father. Not the shrunken man in orange, but his father.

Kearney did it, Dad. He may not have pulled the trigger himself but he did it.

Had his father found out and let something slip? Had Howie threatened Kearney with telling their old buddy Ron Eriksson?

He thought about his mom, seeing the familiar face of a guy who'd been all over TV for the past couple of months grabbing her, holding her for the shot to the back of her head that had ripped off her face.

He threw the picture down and jumped off the bed, barely making it into the bathroom before his stomach turned inside out.

And then Danny was there, arm around Trey's hips, a hand awkwardly rubbing the back of his neck.

When his esophagus stopped trying to slinky itself out of his throat, Trey sat back on his heels and took the wet washcloth Danny had ready. At first it felt clean and cold on the sweat of his face and neck, but then he started shivering.

"C'mon. We both need a shower anyway." Danny reached around him.

There wasn't much room in the tiny bathroom, so they were bumping elbows against the walls and each other, but Danny helped Trey strip off his clothes since he couldn't seem to stop shivering long enough to get his fingers working right.

Danny stepped in behind and helped keep Trey on his feet.

"I'm glad my dad couldn't remember much. I'm glad he didn't have to try to convince people it was Kearney."

Danny didn't say anything, just kept his arms locked

around Trey's waist. He let himself sink back, relax under the heat of the water. "How do you think it happened?"

Danny turned him around. "I think Howie threatened to tell your dad and give him the picture and somehow Kearney found out about it."

"Makes sense." Trey ducked his head under the spray and then shook the water out of his eyes.

Danny gave him a disapproving look, but Trey just smiled. Danny would have to get used to Trey shaking his head in the shower. He'd always done it. His brain made a connection and he laughed.

"What?" Danny asked.

"The fucking picture. My house. Kearney must have thought we had the puzzle box picture."

"We do. Now. And"—Danny turned away and found the soap, but he didn't unwrap it, just held it in front of him—"my dad is the one who told Kearney we had it."

Trey pulled the soap out of Danny's hand. "Christ, Danny, I'm sorry."

"No, I am. Because I'm the one who told him."

"But he might not have known."

"Oh, I'm sure he knew. Fuck him." Danny blinked, lashes spiked with water.

Sliding his arms around Danny's waist, Trey took a deep breath. His chest didn't feel like the Grand Canyon anymore. "So, what now?"

Chapter Seventeen

What came next was bed, even if both of them were too tired to do anything but sleep. Trey woke up feeling way better than a guy who'd had a bomb go off in his face the night before and shared the good tight feeling in his chest with Danny by sucking him to the back of his throat before Danny woke up.

Trey's chest got tighter when Danny blinked and looked down at him, lips slowly curving into that smile. Trey wanted this, wanted so hard it stole his breath and he had to pull off, his hand taking over while he breathed against Danny's hip.

Despite the whole tight-chest, not-breathing feeling, Trey had to know the answer. "Could we do this every morning?"

Danny's smile turned into a laugh. "Are you offering me a lifetime supply of blow jobs?"

Trey ignored the way Danny's hips bucked, trying to speed up the light friction from Trey's hand. He lifted his head. "Depends on where your dick's been the night before."

"Oh."

It wasn't exactly a question, but Trey nodded. Corny as it was, he wanted Danny to say it. Because Danny had always told him the truth, even when Trey didn't want to hear it.

"All right."

"Are you just saying that because you want your dick sucked?"

"Not completely. I'm saying it because I want you to fuck

me too. But not every morning. Tuesdays and Thursdays and every other Sunday."

Trey sat up. "Jesus. Could you take something seriously for a second?"

Danny lunged up and dragged him down on top of him. "I am. I've got no problem with it."

"With what?"

"Not fucking around. Now, could we get off?" Danny wrapped his legs around Trey's hips and rocked up into him.

Maybe it was that simple. Trey kissed Danny's neck and throat, hand sliding down to his ass and— Trey lifted his head. "Shit. I don't have anything."

"I don't care."

Trey was working through the possible interpretations of that when he looked straight at Danny's face and got it.

Danny dragged him down again, words hot and slick in Trey's ear. "You said you would. Fuck me raw. If it would change anything. It would."

Jesus. His bare cock inches away from Danny's ass was not the time to be having this discussion. They should talk about it rationally. Think about it. Talk about it again.

Trey rolled off and onto his feet, slipping free when Danny tried to wrestle him back onto the bed. The Pleasant Valley Best Western was thoughtful enough to provide small bottles of shampoo, conditioner and thank-you-God lotion. Because he wasn't going to fuck this up trying it on just spit.

Danny launched himself at him when he hit the bed again, and Trey had a chance to see that glittering excitement in Danny's eyes, the one that used to be there all the time.

"Have you done this before?"

Danny shook his head. "Never got this far. You?"

Trey wished he hadn't. But those first years away from home, so angry he didn't care what happened, he hadn't always been careful. "A long time ago. But I get tested every year when

I have my physical."

"Me too. Now shut up and fuck me." Danny wasn't laughing or teasing. The want tearing into Trey was reflected in that intent green stare.

He'd forgotten how it felt, the wet heat, the twitch of skin, feeling every wrinkle against the head of his naked dick. But Danny was the one to gasp in surprise.

"I can feel that. Oh God."

"Yeah."

Trey slipped the head in and the slick hot walls clamped and pulled on his skin. "Don't, Danny. Please."

"I'm trying. It's—"

Danny's body opened around him, still hot and tight but a sweet slide on every inch of Trey's dick. He moved his hips, every muscle clamping down to keep the feeling from burning through his cock, spilling into Danny before they'd even started.

Bringing a hand to his dick, Danny nodded and Trey started to move. He was going to lose it, couldn't possibly handle how good it felt to have Danny all around him, nothing but skin. Trey forced his eyes open and looked down. "Danny."

Danny's eyes opened too, his body rolling, pushing himself harder onto Trey's cock. "Fuck me harder."

"Wait. Just a little longer, please." Trey held Danny's hips and worked them slowly. Even fucking into Danny, Trey still felt full inside. "Love you, Danny."

Hands slapping onto Trey's shoulders, Danny said, "I love you too. Now will you fuck me?"

"Always in a hurry." But Trey wasn't going to last, not when he started moving fast, the drag and rub of the slick soft walls sending sparks shooting along his nerves. Not with that naked heat on his cock. And definitely not with Danny gasping and slamming up to meet him, their eyes locked, Danny's hands gripping Trey's wrists. Nothing that good could last.

"Danny." Urgency crept into his voice.

"Fuck." Danny reached for his cock. "Now. Coming right now."

Jesus, Trey was going to die from the tight clamp of Danny's ass around him. As Danny's come splashed warm onto their bellies, Trey held on so tight his muscles cramped. "I can pull out," he gasped. *And please tell me no.*

"Don't." Danny locked his legs around Trey's hips. "Do it. Want to feel it."

And Trey wanted to watch, to see it on Danny's face, but Trey couldn't keep his eyes open another second when his orgasm hit, sharp and sweet and long, balls emptying into Danny as his body shuddered underneath.

Danny's ass tightened around him again. "God, I can feel it. Fuck."

Trey dropped on top of him, and Danny held him loosely, wrapped in his arms and legs. Dropping kisses onto Danny's forehead, Trey shifted his hips and Danny pinned him again with his heels.

"Don't."

His dick was still twitching and it was good to just lie there, sticky and sweaty and warm.

"Holy shit." Danny's satisfied sigh brushed against Trey's ear.

"Yeah." Even though he knew he had to be crushing Danny, Trey couldn't seem to stop kissing every bit of salty skin he could reach. He wanted to keep them here, locked away in this room, and let everything else go to hell, but Danny was right. They couldn't let this go. Kearney wouldn't let this go.

"So now what?" Trey lifted his head.

"As soon as I can get it up we're doing that again." Danny's grin was brief. "But then I guess I better make some calls."

By the time the calls became meetings, Trey was really missing that pistol in the anchor holster as they surrendered their weapons before being shown into a conference room with the fucking head of the National Security Agency and the Deputy Director of the FBI. Trey didn't want to sit down, but since the important guys were already seated, they didn't have a choice.

They'd already met with Daniel's instructor and his immediate supervisor, who had been only too glad to kick the matter up a level.

From the pile of papers in front of the NSA guy, it was clear that decisions had already been made and Trey and Danny were about to be given their orders.

"Gentlemen." That was NSA guy, white hair, smooth and polished and tan, like he'd just stepped in after a round of golf. Hell, he probably had.

The guy from the FBI seemed more nervous, fiddling with his pen.

"Let me explain what will happen." NSA guy again, without so much as a *thank you for bringing this to our attention.* "The country needs stability and the people are better served by making sure that this matter"—he opened his hands wide, like he was describing the one that got away—"not become public knowledge."

Trey followed Danny's lead and kept his mouth shut.

"So. Vice President-Elect will enter the hospital and be diagnosed with a fatiguing condition necessitating his resignation. You will sign these nondisclosure agreements and none of this will have ever happened."

"And what about Detective Eriksson's father?" Danny sat up a little straighter.

"What about him?"

"He went to prison for a crime he didn't commit."

The director made brief eye contact with Trey. "No offense, but the man is deceased."

"He should be exonerated," Danny insisted.

"I'm afraid that's not possible." The look in the NSA Director's eyes scared Trey.

"Then I'm afraid we can't sign," Danny said.

"I don't think that's wise. The Deputy Director has worked with your supervisor and come up with some specific violations of your code of conduct, including misuse of government property."

"Fine. I resign," Danny said without any hesitation.

Trey cleared his throat. "Excuse me, could we have a moment to discuss this?"

Those dark eyes flicked back over Trey's face. "Certainly."

Trey urged Danny to his feet and back out into the hall.

"Don't do this for me," he said as soon as they were alone— or as alone as they could be in a building where probably every inch was monitored.

"It's for your dad."

"Or for him. He wouldn't want that."

"Maybe I don't want to work for them anymore." Danny held his gaze.

Trey tried not to think of the director's creepy eyes. "What happens if we don't agree?"

"I guess we'd have to go to the press."

"And it could drag on for months. Longer."

"But—"

"Danny, I spent most of my life getting here. Now I just want to get to enjoy the rest of it. With you."

Danny looked a little stunned. What the hell had he thought I love you meant? "Where?"

"Wherever you want."

"You'd quit the force?"

"You just did."

Danny's eyes were still wide, his breath coming fast, and

then he smiled. Slowly, but it spread to his eyes. "Yeah, I did, didn't I?"

A fucking magnet. Trey could feel that grin pulling him forward just like it had the first time he saw it.

"I almost feel sorry for them." Danny tipped his head toward the door.

"Why?"

"Nobody in Washington can keep a secret. Let's sign their fucking papers and get out of here."

"What's the rush?"

"I thought you wanted to learn how to fish."

A little boat on the bright green water in the Gulf of Mexico. "And?"

"My stepfather had a cabin up in the Poconos. As far as I know, Mother still owns it."

Or freezing in a cabin in Pennsylvania. It really didn't matter. Not when Danny kept grinning like that.

"It's a little cold for fishing. Besides, the Poconos are really close to this shithole of a town on the Delaware River," Trey said.

"I know. But somehow, that town's not quite as shitty as I remembered."

"Really?" Trey let that grin pull him in.

"Yeah. It has some things there you can't find anywhere else."

"Like metallic water?"

"Exactly. And I even know where we can find a book on how to fish." Danny turned like he was going back into the conference room.

"Hey, Danny, just make sure it's a short book. I don't want to waste a lot of time."

"Reading?"

"Or fishing."

About the Author

K.A. Mitchell discovered the magic of writing at an early age when she learned that a carefully crayoned note of apology sent to the kitchen in a toy truck would earn her a reprieve from banishment to her room. Her career as a spin control artist was cut short when her family moved to a two-story house, and her trucks would not roll safely down the stairs. Around the same time, she decided that Chip and Ken made a much cuter couple than Ken and Barbie and was perplexed when invitations to play Barbie dropped off. An unnamed number of years later, she's happy to find other readers and writers who like to play in her world.

To learn more about K.A. Mitchell, please visit www.kamitchell.com. Send an email to K.A. Mitchell at authorKAMitchell@gmail.com.

A passion hot enough to melt a glacier.
A love that shakes them to the core...

Polar Reaction
© 2009 Claire Thompson

The savage Antarctic winter is closing in, and three research scientists are scheduled for the last flight out—until an unexpected blizzard traps all three of them in the compound. There's Tuck, who only joined the project to be close to sexy-but-straight Brendan, the man of his dreams. And Jamie, who has always admired the other two from afar.

Thrown into a dangerous situation, the three of them turn to each other for survival, solace...and more. As Brendan overcomes his confusion over his impulses, the trio begin a sexual exploration that explodes into passion and unbridled lust.

Yet once the rescue helicopter airlifts them to safety, Brendan comes to his senses, returning home to his carefully constructed, closeted life. But there's a Brendan-shaped hole left behind in Tuck's and Jamie's hearts. There's only one way to fill it—by breaking through Brendan's reserve to reclaim the man they both love.

Warning: Dangerously hot m/m/m ménage sex will melt the layers of ice and snow keeping three sexy scientist prisoners on the edge of the world. Peek through your fingers at scorching sex between three men—the possibilities are endless!

Available now in ebook and print from Samhain Publishing.

Music. Sex. Fame. What's missing? Surely not the "L" word...

Adder
© 2009 Ally Blue

Adder has a plan for his life: play his music for millions of adoring fans, who will reward him with money, fame and as much sex as he can handle. It's a goal he's been working toward since his teens and is on the cusp of achieving. The idea of a relationship never entered his mind—until a new drummer joins his band. One taste of Kalil, and all he wants is more.

For Kalil, playing drums for Adder is a dream come true, the creative connection he's always wanted. What he never reckoned on is the deeper connection he finds with Adder. Kalil would rather avoid sexual involvement with a bandmate, but Adder seems just as determined to break through his resistance.

Attraction aside, music and sex are about the only things the hedonistic Adder and the increasingly jealous Kalil can agree on. Still, before they know it they're on the brink of something deeper, something lasting.

And it scares the hell out of both of them.

Warning: This book contains adult language, hot gay sex, weird bands, colorful prophylactics and unforgivable fashion crimes.

Available now in ebook and print from Samhain Publishing.